FLOWERS
FOR DEAD GIRLS

Visit us at www.boldstrokesbooks.com

FLOWERS FOR DEAD GIRLS

by

Abigail Collins

2024

FLOWERS FOR DEAD GIRLS

ISBN 13: 978-1-63679-584-3

THIS TRADE PAPERBACK ORIGINAL IS PUBLISHED BY
BOLD STROKES BOOKS, INC.
P.O. BOX 249
VALLEY FALLS, NY 12185

FIRST EDITION: APRIL 2024

CREDITS
EDITOR: JENNY HARMON
PRODUCTION DESIGN: STACIA SEAMAN
COVER DESIGN BY INKSPIRAL DESIGN

To my mom,
for always believing I could.

FLOWERS
FOR DEAD GIRLS

CHAPTER ONE

There's a ghost in Astra's closet.

It's not an unusual occurrence. But most of the time they at least wait until after she's out of bed before they bother her.

Today, it's the cold that wakes her up, like a sudden burst of autumn wind in the middle of her bedroom. She pulls her comforter up to her chin and rolls over, but it's hard to sleep when she knows she's being watched. The clock above her door reads 6:35 a.m. She sighs and throws off her bedsheets.

She yawns, stretches, and waves at the ghost standing in her closet doorway.

"Morning, George," she says.

He smiles at her, half of his yellowed teeth missing. The wrinkles on his face pull into tight lines around his mouth.

George McCreary looks exactly like the image Astra guesses she would find if she looked up the word *grandpa* in the dictionary. He's old—late eighties at least—with barely any hair on his head, and the hair he *does* have floats around his scalp like cotton, white and wispy. His skin is covered in liver spots and creases, swelling up around the lines like an overinflated balloon, and his entire posture is stooped, from his shoulders all the way to his knees. He probably used a walker or a cane when he was alive, and it's like what's left of him doesn't quite realize that he doesn't need it anymore.

He doesn't even need to *walk* anymore. His feet are a good few inches above the ground, and a clump of cotton-candy hair keeps going through the top of the doorframe.

"Good morning, Miss Astra," he says, slow and sticky like molasses. He looks apologetically at her hitching shoulders. "Sorry about the cold."

Astra shrugs and reaches over to her nightstand to turn off her alarm. She taps on the button one, two, three, four times. Four is a nice, safe number. Five is too sharp. Three is too round. Four is just right.

George watches her, still smiling his wizened grandpa smile.

"How was your night?" she asks him, stepping around him to get into her closet, left foot first. The closer she gets to him, the colder she feels. When he finally floats back toward her window, it's like throwing a warm blanket over her shoulders.

George flickers like television static, like all ghosts do. It's like sometimes they forget how to look human, how to pretend to be the same people they were when they were alive, and they buffer for a second or two before they get it right again. With George, most of it is in his hands. They shake and pull, up and down, and sometimes his fingers look just a little too long or the wrinkles on the backs of his hands disappear. But only for a second or two.

He beams and his entire body phases in and out. "It was great," he says. "They finally found my body. Guess where?"

Astra pauses with her hands up, rifling through a row of sweaters all in shades of blue and gray, and looks over at him. The top of his head is almost through the ceiling.

George McCreary died wearing corduroy pants, a white button-up, and a brown knit vest with tiny white stars stitched into the hem. Dictionary definition of *grandpa*. But if Astra looks past his popped collar and the holes in the knees of his pants, she can also see *how* he died. Or, at least, what his death looked like.

Astra remembers the moment she first met George McCreary, when he floated through her bedroom wall nearly a week ago, looking like a bloated fish. He still looks like that—swollen, blue-green skin, puffy cheeks, eyes bloodshot and bulging. Like he could open his mouth and spit water like a fountain.

Astra turns back to her closet, which is too small to be called a walk-in, and picks out a fuzzy, dark blue sweater. A few threads fall off and float slowly to the floor, and she shakes the rest of them off before tucking the shirt into the crook of her elbow.

"In the river?" she guesses. She has to stoop low to pull a pair of shoes out of the tiny wooden rack on the floor—a pair of beat-up white sneakers with inky stars drawn on the sides in pen.

"In a ravine." George chuckles, and it sounds like wading through maple syrup. "That's why it took so long. I drove right off the edge and sank my car. My wife always said I was a terrible driver."

"Hmm. That makes sense."

Astra doesn't want to know that George had a wife. She doesn't like when they tell her things about their lives. It's easier to just think of them as specters, creatures haunting her and then leaving when they're done. The more they tell her, the harder it is to see them as anything other than *human*.

She cracks her knuckles on the doorframe and leaves her closet to rifle through her dresser for a pair of jeans.

She pulls on the knob with her left hand. She can feel George watching her from the other side of the room.

"I'll be leaving soon, I think," he continues. "I can feel it."

Astra hums, pushing aside a stack of neatly folded pants before slipping out a pair of dark denim jeans and adding them to the sweater on her arm. Most of her wardrobe is blue, dark blue, light blue, or gray. It's all long sleeves to combat the constant cold, fluffy sweatshirts and worn hoodies because they don't make her skin itch. The most colorful thing in her closet is a Christmas sweater—bright red knit with little cotton snowmen on the front and tiny snowflakes embroidered along the hem—that her mother can only hassle her into on Christmas day.

Her mom's wardrobe is the exact opposite. Sometimes Astra wonders if she's overcompensating for her mom's eccentric style by wearing the most muted colors possible, but really it's because bright things give her headaches. And she already gets enough of those from the ghosts that visit her every day.

"Do you…have everything finished? Last request stuff, I mean. Unfinished business."

She looks at George. The clock above her bedroom door ticks loudly behind her.

"I think so. I've just got one more thing to sort out. But I'm ready to go."

Astra nods. She's happy for him—she really is. But she's also maybe a little bit sad, too.

George's blue-purple lips pull into a tight smile and his face flickers in and out of focus like a lightbulb burning out. Astra nods at the clock radio on her nightstand, the neon green numbers flipping over to 6:52 a.m. The clock behind her ticks, and the radio's bright color runs like a flare through her skull. Her head hurts. George floats up until his eyes are hidden above a ceiling panel, and Astra turns away before he can float back down.

"I should probably get ready for school," she tells her bedroom door. "I'll see you later, George."

George hums. "It was nice chatting with you, Miss Astra."

She can feel him leave—flicker out or float back through the wall—because the sudden temperature shift makes her neck sweat. The thermostat isn't even set very high, but it's like diving into a frozen lake and then running full speed into a sauna. Her skin breaks out in goose bumps.

Her mom isn't awake when Astra creeps out of her bedroom and into the tiny bathroom in the hall between their two rooms. She nearly trips over a stack of magazines on the floor that definitely weren't there the night before and steps into the bathroom, left foot first. She locks the door and jiggles the knob four times—two left, two right—just in case the lock didn't click the first time.

It's not even seven a.m. yet, and already Astra is exhausted.

Like everything else in their apartment, the bathroom is tiny. It's barely large enough for one person, let alone two. The sink is as wide as Astra's forearm, a muddy brown and white marble that's supposed to look fancy but really just looks perpetually dirty. Granted, it usually *is*, but the dirt-stain pattern doesn't help.

They've got a shower, small enough that Astra can press her palms flat against the walls on either side if she stretches her arms out. And Astra is *short* compared to her mom. Compared to almost anybody, really. She's short, a little pudgy, nothing all that spectacular to look at. But at least she can fly under the radar most of the time, which is something her mother has never been able to do.

She tries not to look in the mirror, streaky and dotted with toothpaste splatters, while she gets ready for school. She shuffles around quietly, careful not to wake her mom, and only pauses in front of the sink long enough to brush her teeth and run a hand through her hair.

Astra inherited almost everything from her mom. She has her mom's dark skin, her wide brown eyes, and her unruly black hair—

which Astra wears clipper-style, fluffed on the top and buzzed on the sides. *Like a boy*, her grandma used to say. She doesn't like the feeling of hair on the back of her neck—it tickles and makes her feel sweaty. But she's seen her mother's unkempt, uncombed mop, so maybe she's overcompensating for that, too.

There's one more thing that Astra and her mother have in common, though. But Astra has no plans of telling her mom what it is.

She's better off not knowing that her daughter is just as haunted as she is.

Her mom still isn't awake when Astra creeps down the hall and into the kitchen. She has to be at work by ten, but Astra knows that she'll probably sleep until at least nine thirty and then scramble out the door.

Scramble. That's a good word to describe Maria Vaughn. Scrambled, like eggs. Her brain is like a snow globe tipped upside down; the pieces are all there, but sometimes they land in the wrong spots when they come back down.

Their apartment is a good example of Astra's mother's mind. It's impossibly tiny, even for just the two of them—a narrow hallway with two bedrooms and their shared bathroom in between. A living room with a squished beige couch, a low wooden coffee table that's got a stack of papers under one leg to keep it level, and a television mounted to the wall just a little too close to the window. And a kitchen that's cluttered and messy and so cramped that Astra could cook something on the stove and reach behind her into the fridge at the same time.

Every room is painted a different color. That's the first thing her mom did when they moved in. The hallway is egg-yolk yellow, the living room is the kind of red that makes Astra think of children's finger paint, and the kitchen is blue. But not a soft, sky blue. It's sharp and noisy, the sort of blue that people spray on park benches to make it easier to spot them from a distance.

The colors are too bright, and sometimes Astra has to wear sunglasses inside to keep the noise out, even though their apartment is usually pretty quiet.

The only piece of chaos that Astra actually likes is the doors. They're all painted different colors, too, and none of the knobs match. Astra's door is the same soft purple as the walls of her bedroom, and her knob is a pretty glass sphere with tiny bubbles inside it.

Her mom's door is green, somehow bright and dark at the same time, with a golden knob carved into the shape of a lumpy-looking flower.

It takes Astra exactly ten steps to get from the bathroom to the kitchen. She counts them, stepping over the pile of magazines and a couple of stacked boxes filled with cans and bottles that were supposed to be taken out to the recycling bin two days ago. Her headphones are sitting on the counter—the obnoxiously large kind that cover her ears entirely—next to a note from her mom. Astra slips the headphones on, and the buzzing in her brain dims.

> *Honey,*
> > *There's cereal on the counter and milk in the fridge.*
> > *I'm working late tonight, so you're on your own for dinner. You know where to find me if you need anything.*
> > *Good luck today!*
> > *Mom*

There's a heart at the end by the word *mom*, drawn in pen. Astra folds up the note and tucks it into her pocket.

There *is* milk in the fridge, but it's sour. Astra dumps it down the drain, adds the empty container to the recycling pile in the hallway, and throws two pieces of bread in the toaster instead. The lever jams on the way down, and she wiggles it one, two, three, four times before pushing it hard enough to stick.

There's barely enough space on the kitchen counter to sit, so Astra eats over the sink. It smells like sour milk.

❖

Astra wears headphones to school most days.

Not *in* school, but the whole way there—down the stairs from her apartment to the alley outside, one block over and into the public parking lot, and the entire drive until she pulls up in the student lot outside the school.

She wears them at home a lot, too, because they block out the noises that most ghosts make whether they're aware of it or not. Like high-pitched static, like nails on a chalkboard. Especially the ones outside her window.

But she's never needed to wear her headphones in the school hallways, because what kind of ghost haunts a school? She's never encountered one there. It's so peacefully quiet, even with the tornado of loud voices in the crowded halls, the banging of locker doors closing, and bells ringing through the overhead speakers. She feels the least anxious when she's in a crowd of people. *Living* people.

But today, something feels different. Off. It takes her a minute to realize what it is, but then she pulls up her sleeve and sees goose bumps rising on her arm and it all clicks.

She spins around at her locker, but there's nothing there—not even a noise, static or otherwise. Just normal high-school chatter, with enough voices mixing together that she can't make out any individual words. Just the way she likes it.

Maybe the school's heater is broken. But it's nearly April, so it's probably not even turned on anymore.

She sighs and turns back to her locker. She opens it with one, two, three, four spins of the dial lock. Left, right, left, right.

Astra pulls the textbooks for her first two classes out of her locker and shoves them into her backpack. She slides her headphones off her neck and almost throws them into her locker on top of her other books, but at the last second drops them into her backpack too. Just in case.

The cold starts to ease and she takes a deep breath. It was probably nothing. She didn't get much sleep last night, and her exhaustion has her on edge.

And then someone throws an arm around her shoulders and she spins around so violently that she hits her elbow on her locker door and accidentally slams it shut.

"Oh, jeez—are you okay?"

Astra blinks back moisture and stares up at the tree trunk that is Oliver Wiley.

She has no idea why he keeps trying to talk to her. He's a track star with a huge personality; he could be friends with literally anybody he wants to. But there's something a little awkward about him, a little mismatched, that kind of reminds her of her mom, or maybe even herself. So maybe that's why.

He's tall—he's got enough height to play basketball—but instead he uses his long, long legs for running. He always wears the same brown jacket, faded and at least two sizes too big for him, with tiny patches ironed up and down both sleeves. They have PE together, and the only time Astra has ever seen him without his signature jacket is when he's in his gym uniform. She's not sure how he does so well in track, because he's gangly enough that a decent burst of wind should blow him right over.

Astra rubs at her elbow and feels a small bump already forming. She nods and clicks the lock on her locker closed. She spins the dial four times in one direction until the arrow is pointed to zero.

Oliver takes just a moment to make sure she's okay before he loops his arm around hers and tugs her down the hall. They also have English together. Astra is just thankful that they don't share any other classes.

Oliver is nice, but he's also more than a little distracting.

"So," he says when they reach the stairs, not turning around to look at her. From this angle, she can just barely see the shiny gold hoop in the left side of his nose. "I'll bet you ten bucks Pierce brings coffee from the shop by the mall this morning."

Astra frowns, watching her feet and making sure her left foot is on the first step. "That's not fair. He brings coffee *every* morning."

"Not from that place. The one on Twelfth. With those biodegradable cups that smell like dirt."

She wants to ask him how he knows what the cups smell like, but she's already starting to get a little winded. Oliver's legs are *long*, and hers are *not*, and she's also not a track star, so it's really not fair. He's got a loose grip on her arm that she could easily slip out of, but she doesn't. Even if she never invites him over to her house, it's nice to pretend that she has a friend. Even if it's only during school hours.

"Why would he go there? It's on the other side of town."

Oliver stops on the top step and turns around to grin at her. His smile is a little crooked, pulling up on one side of his mouth more than the other. His long black hair nearly whips her in the face when he crouches down closer to her. Someone pushes into her backpack, and a freshman girl mutters something rude as she elbows past the space on the stairs that they're blocking.

"Because I saw him yesterday. You know those apartments by

the mall? The ones with the umbrella tables outside?" Astra nods. Someone's backpack knocks into Oliver's shoulder and he turns around just enough to scale the last two steps and move out of the way. "I think he was on a date."

Astra wrinkles her nose. "Ew. But what's that got to do with coffee?"

Oliver just shrugs, his lopsided grin still firmly in place. It takes her a second to process.

"Oh...*ew*."

He chuckles and throws out his hand, pulling her the rest of the way up the stairs and down the hall to their English classroom.

The Languages section of the school is a long hallway with lockers lined up on one side and classrooms on the other. Mr. Pierce's room is at the very end, right next to a large window. The door is always propped open with a stopper because the handle sticks. It's also positioned directly above the science wing, so most of the time it smells like burnt hair and chemicals, and Mr. Pierce refuses to keep the windows open, even in the summer.

Usually, the humidity mixed with the long-sleeved shirts she wears makes Astra sweaty. It doesn't help that her desk is right underneath a heat vent in the ceiling, and the hot air hits her on the top of the head and makes her scalp itch.

But today, she feels cold. She tries not to shiver. Oliver sits down next to her—courtesy of the classroom's mandatory alphabetical seating arrangements—and she can feel him watching her.

She arranges her things on the top of her desk and squares them off—two books, one notebook, and a mechanical pencil loaded and clicked. Four things. She keeps her head down and lines her pencil up with the edge of her notebook until it's just right.

The desks around them start to fill. Out of the corner of her eye, Astra sees Oliver tuck a pencil behind his ear, push his hair back around it, and then eventually remove the pencil and start rolling it across his desk instead. One of his legs is jiggling, his foot tapping on the floor just loudly enough for Astra to hear, and she feels dizzy just watching, so she quickly turns away.

Mr. Pierce walks in a minute after the bell rings, holding a stack of papers in one hand and a paper coffee cup in the other. Oliver bumps Astra's arm with his elbow and grins.

"Told you so."

She tries not to smile, but Oliver's lopsided smirk makes it hard not to. Mr. Pierce shoots them a warning look that she's pretty sure is aimed mostly at Oliver before setting his things down and turning toward the chalkboard. His salt-and-pepper mustache looks extra curly today, for some reason.

Astra tries to pay attention. She even takes notes, but her hands are cold and a little shaky, so half of her letters look like tiny lightning bolts instead.

Oliver nudges her again twenty minutes into class.

"Are you okay?" he asks, leaning down in his chair. His legs are so long he could probably tap the seat of the desk in front of him with his foot if he tried, but instead he folds himself in like a pretzel and looks distinctly uncomfortable.

She nods quickly. "Yeah. I'm fine. I just—"

A voice stops her. It's right in her ear, too close to be coming from any of the desks around hers, and it hits like a gust of arctic wind.

"Hi," the ghost says. "Am I interrupting something?"

Chapter Two

Astra whips around in her seat so fast she knocks all of her things off her desk. Her books hit the ground with a booming thud, and her pencil rolls along the floor and stops right in front of Mr. Pierce's desk.

Everyone turns to look at her, and suddenly Astra feels like she's on fire. It's like there's a spotlight on her, and the eyes of her classmates are burning holes into her skin. She must have been imagining the cold, because right now she's sweating buckets.

Mr. Pierce is exuding grumpy-old-man energy when he sweeps around and fixes her with a firm look—thin lips, narrow eyes, arms crossed, and the piece of chalk still in his hand rubbing white dust on his shirt. Astra is ready to send *herself* to the principal's office.

She looks down at her books, too stunned to reach for them. Mr. Pierce bends down and retrieves her stray pencil from the front of his desk, and Astra knows it's over for her. She's never going to be able to come back here. She might as well give up and become a hermit in the woods somewhere, because that's where she's going to end up anyway. A hermit all alone, with only dead people to keep her company.

That's not so different from her life now, actually.

Mr. Pierce opens his mouth to say something, probably to condemn Astra to a life of solitude in a cave on a mountain with no cell service, when someone beats him to it.

"Oh my gosh, Astra, I'm so sorry."

Astra manages to unstick her frozen limbs just enough to turn in her seat. Oliver is standing at his desk, hands up, holding something small between his fingers. He looks sheepish. The expression is almost perfect, and could probably fool anyone else, but Astra has been sitting next to him for months. Plus, one corner of his mouth keeps twitching.

"Mr. Wiley." Is Mr. Pierce's mustache getting even curlier, or is that just a product of Astra's blind panic?

"Sir," Oliver continues, laying it on thick. "I wasn't thinking. It was just a stupid prank, you know? From that joke shop in the mall. I'm so sorry, Astra, I really didn't think it would hurt that much."

Astra blinks up at him, confused. Then she sees what's in his hand, and she starts to catch on.

It's a small pack of gum with a piece sticking out, like the ones people pull pranks with. You try to pull out the gum, and you get shocked. Astra has seen them on TV before, in the movies her mom watches after work. Never in real life, though.

She realizes another thing at the same time: Oliver is trying to help her. Astra knows what she heard, and what she felt, and Oliver definitely didn't shock her with a fake pack of gum.

Mr. Pierce stares for a minute, his narrow eyes focused on Oliver like he's trying to shoot laser beams out of them. The salt-and-pepper hair on his head is the same color as his mustache, but sparser and thinner, especially in the front. He looks a little bit like a slightly younger, sterner version of George McCreary. But without the bloated fish look.

The teacher sighs and finally moves his eyes away from Oliver, who deflates like a balloon.

"My office, Mr. Wiley. After school. Don't be late."

Oliver nods. "Yes, sir."

He sinks back into his desk, looking slightly put out. His shoulders are slumped and there's a dejected look on his face. Astra is about to apologize, or maybe just melt into a puddle on the floor, when Oliver bends down and grabs her books for her and winks on his way back up.

He slides her books back onto her desk with a lopsided grin, and the second Mr. Pierce turns back to the chalkboard, Oliver pulls the piece of gum out of its wrapper and makes a show of sticking it into his mouth.

Astra tries to rearrange her books, but without her pencil there are only three things on her desk. Three is too round. Five is too sharp. She digs in her backpack until she finds another pencil and she spends nearly five minutes trying to line it up just right before she gives up and knots her shaky hands together in her lap.

Oliver stops tapping his foot on the floor for just long enough to pass her a note. For someone so full of energy, his handwriting is surprisingly contained. Neat, even.

Are you okay? Honest answer.

Underneath are two options, with numbers next to them like she's supposed to choose one.

1. *No.*
2. *No again, but I'm willing to talk to Oliver about it because he's a really good listener.*

Astra smiles, crosses out both answers, and adds a third.

3. *I'm fine. Thank you for covering for me.*

She adds a wobbly checkmark next to it and is about to pass it back to him when someone dumps a bucket full of snow down the back of her shirt. Or, at least, that's what it feels like.

"You don't *seem* fine. You should just tell him the truth."

Astra's hand shoots up before her brain can even catch up enough to tell it to, and she ignores Mr. Pierce's withering glance for just long enough to ask for the bathroom pass.

She leaves all of her things behind—one, two, three, four items on her desk, shoved haphazardly into one corner with Oliver's note right on top. And then she runs out the door, nearly knocking aside the stopper, so quickly she almost forgets to watch her feet.

Thankfully, the nearest bathroom is at the end of the hall, because there's already a stitch in her side when she reaches it. Even more thankfully, it's empty.

A public meltdown would hit a little too close to home right now, especially with how hard Astra is trying to prove that she's *not* like her mother.

The bathroom is quiet, but Astra can feel that she's not alone.

There are four stalls, side by side with their doors half-open, spray-painted the same loud blue that the lockers are. Astra wishes she had grabbed her headphones before she ran out, because the bathroom walls are yellow like bright sunlight, and the floor is marbled white and gray, and the noise is starting to make her head hurt.

Especially the buzzing. Astra sighs and runs a hand through the sweaty hair at the back of her neck.

"You've got my attention," she says to the empty bathroom. "But you need to work on your timing."

Part of her expects nothing to happen. She could have just been imagining things. Maybe she's been imagining things this whole time. There's literally no proof that she hasn't been.

But then a girl floats through the wall of the first bathroom stall, and Astra can't hold back a shiver. But it's not because of the cold this time.

The ghost in front of her is *young*—probably around Astra's age, or maybe even younger. Seventeen at the most. She's a teenager, and she's flickering and floating and undeniably dead. Astra can't help but stare; she's never met a ghost this young before.

The youngest ghost she ever talked to was a man, twenty-three years old according to his obituary, who had died in a car crash and later appeared in her doorway with a gaping hole in his neck and the front of his skull cracked open. He was one of the hardest ghosts to look at, but he didn't stay long. He asked her to check on a few accounts online for him, and then he vanished before she could finish logging out.

The ghost in front of her now smirks, revealing deep dimples in her cheeks. "Take a picture, it'll last longer," she says. There's an odd, almost musical lilt to her voice. "Oh, wait. I probably wouldn't show up on film, huh?"

Astra shakes her head mutely, even though she honestly doesn't know. She's never tried to take a photo of a ghost before.

The ghost girl is pale, with a light dusting of freckles on the bridge of her nose and unnervingly dull green eyes. Her hair is somewhere between blond and brown, like the color of a walnut shell, and it's mostly wavy, but it ends in the middle of her back with a few inches of large, wild curls.

She's tall—maybe even as tall as Oliver—and with her feet above the ground the top of her head nearly brushes the ceiling. Astra feels small. She feels a little unsettled, too, like walking down a flight of stairs and accidentally missing a step. The surprise of seeing a teenage ghost is making her stomach churn.

It doesn't help that the girl doesn't look dead. She obviously *is*, because she's hovering in the air and Astra can see through her to the bright blue stall door behind her back, but she's also wearing a pretty yellow sundress and a red and black flannel jacket, and her hair is bouncy and her skin is pale, sure, but it's clean. Not a single cut or bruise. No bloated fish look, no purple lips or bulging eyes or smashed-in skull. She doesn't *look* like someone who just died.

That makes it worse, somehow.

The girl blows out a breath of frosty air and extends a hand. "I'm Isla, by the way."

Astra just stares. Isla blinks down at her hand for a moment before shrugging and pulling it back to her side.

"Is this your first time seeing a ghost, or…?"

"No." Astra shakes her head so quickly the room spins. "My name's Astra."

The smile on Isla's face makes her look even younger, with her barely-there freckles and deep, deep dimples.

Isla kicks out her legs like she's trying to walk, but only manages to float even higher until the crown of her head is cut off by a ceiling tile. She holds still for a moment, and when she finally comes back down she crosses her legs and hovers over one of the three side-by-side sinks. Astra notices that she doesn't have a reflection.

"Hmm. Pretty name." Isla's feet are in socks. Was she not wearing shoes when she died? "Sorry for interrupting your class, by the way. Just—I've never met anyone who could see me. I got a little excited."

She doesn't look very sorry. She actually looks kind of giddy. It's odd to think of someone as being dead *and* happy, but whatever she died of didn't leave a mark. Maybe she was in a lot of pain. Astra tries not to think about it, but her mind keeps cycling back to it—somewhere between *teenager* and *dead*, like a computer glitching over an unfamiliar string of data. She just can't compute.

"How old are you?" Astra asks before she can stop herself.

Isla hums. "I *was* sixteen. Not sure anymore. Probably still sixteen, I guess."

"You're younger than me."

"How old are you?" Isla asks. Astra notices that Isla flickers the most in her legs. Where George McCreary's hands and arms always hitch and waver, Isla's legs can't seem to stay still. Even with them crossed like a pretzel, her legs shift, stretch, and blur every few seconds. It kind of reminds Astra of how Oliver is always tapping his feet.

"I'm seventeen," she answers. "Can I ask...why are you here? I've never seen a ghost in school before. No offense."

Isla chuckles, and it's light and lilting and sounds like wind chimes. "That explains why you freaked out so bad. And here I thought I was your first." She pauses. One of her knees disappears and then reappears a few seconds later just slightly out of place. She shrugs. "My brother goes here. I was creeping on him and then I saw you, and...like I said. Nobody else can see me."

"Your brother goes here?"

She nods. "Yeah. He's a freshman."

"Do you—did you go here too?"

A shadow passes over Isla's face, and for just a moment her smile slips.

"No," she says, and there's enough finality in her tone that Astra knows not to push.

Astra vowed a long time ago to never pry into a ghost's life—or what *was* their life when they were still alive. That's why she doesn't ask George about his wife—if she's still alive, how long they were married, what she looked like. She doesn't ask about jobs, or kids, or hobbies. These aren't people, after all. They're just the pieces that get left behind when they die.

But Isla looks so real, so alive, so much like a person, that Astra forgets for a moment that she's talking to a creature. To a temporary thing that will leave as soon as it can.

She can't let herself forget that.

Isla unhooks her legs and pushes her arms through the air like she's swimming. Astra wonders if she's doing it on purpose, or if she's just not used to being dead yet. She wonders how long she's been dead for, and what she died of. Not a car crash, not drowning, not a fall from the top of the stairs or a tall building. No broken neck, no open wounds. She wasn't eaten by piranhas or run over by a bulldozer or executed with a guillotine.

Astra shakes her head and tries to think about something else.

There are four stalls in this bathroom, but only three sinks. That's no good. Three is too round a number.

Isla floats around her, legs up and arms out, and circles Astra like she's looking her over. Astra feels oddly exposed, and she picks a few stray threads off the hem of her sweater and flicks them to the ground.

"Are you psychic?" Isla asks from behind her.

Astra spins around, but Isla has already moved. "No, I'm not. It's just—just a ghost thing. I think."

"Have you ever *tried* to be psychic?"

"I don't…" Astra lets out a breathy laugh that's all nerves. "I don't think that's how it works."

"Hmm. Okay."

Isla pokes at Astra's arm, but her finger goes right through and leaves an icy feeling behind. Astra knows that some ghosts can interact with things—like the ghost of a middle-aged woman who had greeted Astra by knocking one of her candles to the floor and accidentally breaking the glass—but it takes a lot of effort. A lot of time and practice, which Isla probably doesn't have, because she's been dead for…how long, exactly?

Isla dives to the floor and floats around Astra's legs. Astra is suddenly very aware of the small hole in the back of her jeans, the pen marks on her shoes, the little zit on the back of her neck that she can't seem to pop.

She holds her breath. She counts the stalls. Debates counting the ceiling tiles. Avoids counting the sinks.

"You're nervous," Isla says from behind her shoulder. "I can feel it."

Astra tries for a laugh. It comes out like a shaky exhale. "What—are *you* psychic now?"

Isla breaths out cold air and wind chimes. "Nope." She pops the *p*. "Just dead."

Astra wants to ask. She's never wanted to ask before. She's never wanted to know. Maybe knowing how she died would make Isla seem a little less…real. A little less human.

When Astra opens her mouth, though, she's interrupted by the school bell. She fumbles for her backpack before remembering that she left it behind. She's going to have to go back and face Mr. Pierce, who probably thinks she's scrambled like her mother. She's going to have to come up with a lie for Oliver and then deal with the rest of her classes while being followed around by a very nosy ghost.

But when she looks back up, one of her problems has solved itself. Because Isla is gone.

Astra stands alone by the sinks, warming the goose bumps off her arms and trying not to think too loudly, until someone opens the bathroom door and the sound jars her awake. She nearly bumps into a baby-faced freshman with pink streaks in her hair in her rush to leave, and then she *does* bump into Oliver outside the door.

"Whoa. Hello." Oliver grabs onto the wall at the last second to keep from falling over, and he drops the backpack in his hands. Astra recognizes the broken zipper and the muted blue and gray pattern. "What's up with you? You look like you've just seen a ghost."

He's not wrong.

Astra swallows down her pounding heartbeat and tries to look casual. She didn't catch a glimpse of her own reflection in the bathroom mirror, but she can guess what she looks like, and she's not nearly as good as Oliver at faking it.

She runs through a quick list of lies in her head, and eventually settles for the truth. Minus the whole *ghost* thing.

"I get...bad headaches. Migraines. They don't usually flare up like that in school, so it caught me by surprise. That's all."

In Astra's defense, she does have a headache right now. The bright blue lockers and the chattering of students in the halls around her certainly don't help. She's tempted to dig in her backpack for her headphones and wear them until she gets to her next class, but then Oliver would probably ask her about them. And she can't tell him that *they block out the noises that ghosts make, but also the noises that colors make, even though colors technically don't make noises.* He wouldn't believe her even if she did.

Oliver shrugs, looking content with her answer. "I get that. Sorry for bugging you about it. You, um...you left your backpack in Pierce's room, and I figured you wouldn't want to go back for it, so..."

"Thanks. And thank you for covering for me. I owe you one."

He smiles, lopsided and toothy, and stoops down to retrieve her backpack. The hallways are starting to clear out, and the noise has gone from jackhammers to bees buzzing inside her ears. Thankfully, her next class is in the first room at the end of the stairs, because the late bell is going to ring any minute.

"Hey, that's what friends do, right?" He holds her backpack out to her with one hand and gives her an awkward shoulder pat with the other. "Just feel better by PE, okay? I can't in good faith kick your ass in dodgeball if I know you're out of commission."

Before she can answer, Oliver backs up down the hall and then turns and jogs the rest of the way and down the diagonal staircase at the end. And for a lightweight, he really can move fast.

Astra barely makes it to her second period math lecture in time, and she spends the entire hour of class pretending to take notes while her brain is somewhere else entirely.

Because she just met a teenage ghost *and* made a friend. All in the span of a few minutes. One of those things has never happened to her before, and the other hasn't happened in many, many years. Not since she was in elementary school. And her brain is stuck on the *how* and the *when*, but most importantly, the *why*. By comparison, quadratic equations just don't seem all that exciting.

And that was just the first hour of the day. The tip of the iceberg. She hopes that at least the rest of the day is less eventful, because she's already exhausted.

CHAPTER THREE

N ice seat covers."

Astra flinches so hard she drops her keys, and she has to reach down by the gas pedal to retrieve them. The ghost girl from earlier hovers over the passenger seat, radiating cold.

"They came with the car," Astra says when she sits back up. The little beige sedan was a gift from her mom for her sixteenth birthday. It's nearly as old as she is, and the paint is peeling over the tires, but it runs well enough. And the heater is really, *really* good, which is probably the most important thing anyway. She turns the key in the ignition and immediately dials the heat up to its maximum.

"Still. It's cool." The hot air blows right through Isla, but she doesn't seem to notice.

Astra sighs and turns toward her. The gaudy fake-leather seat cover squeaks, tiny plastic butterflies and all.

"You can't just…appear like that. I could have been driving. I could have crashed my car."

Isla stretches her legs out, and her feet disappear into the glovebox. "Hey, you've gotta give me more credit than that. I'm not stupid. If I wanted you to crash, I would have waited until you were on the road and then shouted *boo* in your ear or something."

There's something about the way Isla looks—lying straight back with half of her body sunk into the front of the car, and her pale, nearly transparent skin—that gives Astra the chills. More than just the cold, ghostly ones. She reaches out and holds her hands in front of the heaters until her palms are sweaty.

She clears her throat, and Isla blinks and finally bends her legs.

"Okay. If you're not here to wreck my car, then why *are* you here?" Astra wonders if the dull green of Isla's eyes has anything to do with how she died, or if they've always been like that. She doesn't ask.

Isla's shoulders tense up, and she looks almost uncomfortable. Her legs start to flicker again, up and down between the floor and the dashboard, until she makes a grab for one of them and holds it still. Her face scrunches up like it's taking a lot of effort for her to stop moving. One of her arms is shaking.

Then she exhales, rolls her shoulders, and smiles like nothing happened. It's horribly unnerving. She looked almost *human*, just for a moment.

"You're the only one who can see me," she says, like it's that simple.

"And?"

"And"—she stretches out again, and Astra pointedly looks away—"I need a favor."

❖

Astra's apartment is exactly ten blocks away from the school. Back when she still walked to school, before she got her car, she would count the blocks all the way there and back home again. She tried to count her steps, too, but then she lost track and spent the rest of the day agonizing over all of the missed numbers, and rearranging her school supplies on her desk until just the sound of a pencil rolling made her want to tear her hair out.

Now she doesn't count the blocks—because it's *ten*, it's always going to be ten, and she's been in enough near misses to know better than to try to count them while she's driving. So, instead, she listens to the radio and taps her thumbs on the steering wheel.

And today, she thinks about the ghost in the passenger seat. She taps her thumbs, listens to the drone of *American Top 40 Hits* in the back of her mind, and tries not to watch Isla hovering beside her.

But it's hard not to, because she's not really *riding* in the car. She's just sort of…flying around inside it.

Most ghosts can't interact with physical things. So the second Astra threw the car in reverse and started backing up, Isla stayed hovering where she was and ended up floating right through the windshield.

Now she's just flying at the same speed as the car to keep up. She's even doing a superhero pose, with her arms forward inside the dashboard and her legs cut off by the seat behind her. Every time Astra turns the wheel, Isla goes through the window and has to scramble to get back inside, and it's kind of hilarious.

Nine blocks later, Astra parks her car in the public lot down the street and walks the rest of the way to her apartment. One block. Easy to count.

Isla follows along behind her, and they stop outside a red brick building with a rickety metal staircase on one side and a solid wall of shop windows on the other. Home sweet home.

Downtown was maybe a bustling shopping district at one time. Now it's mostly just alleys, run-down shops with their windows boarded up, flat-roofed offices, and dive bars. There's a gym across the alley from Astra's apartment, an ice cream shop two blocks over, and a handful of tiny churches for religions Astra has never even heard of. Everything is brick, metal, and black plastic, and every time it rains the streets flood.

Astra backs up and makes sure she's out of view of the shop windows downstairs. She jerks her thumb in their direction and then looks at Isla pointedly.

"My mom works there. You can't let her see you."

Isla cranes her neck to look. "Your mom is psychic too?"

"Not psychic," Astra repeats. "But she's got the ghost thing. And she doesn't know that I have the ghost thing, so you can't let her see you. Okay?"

Astra emphasizes her words so fiercely she can feel a vein in her neck bulging. Her anxiety is going to give her a heart attack someday, she swears.

Isla seems to get the hint, though, because she floats back toward the stairs without arguing.

Every other step creaks like it's going to give way, but they never do. Fourteen steps. Astra always counts them, like someday the number is going to change without her realizing it. Like maybe one of the steps actually *will* give way, leaving only thirteen, and if she doesn't count them then she'll fall into the empty space and hit the concrete below and break her legs or something.

Isla just floats up along the side of the building and straight through the front door. She's in Astra's living room when she unlocks the front door, and Astra is immediately embarrassed because—this is the first time she's brought someone over. And her apartment is a mess.

The magazines stacked in the hallway are still there, but they must have been knocked over while Astra was in school, because now they're spilled across the linoleum and some of the covers are creased open. The recycling boxes are overflowing, and something murky and yellow is oozing out of the bottom of one of the containers, like mustard. Astra hopes it's mustard.

The living room is a little tidier, but the couch is squished and lumpy and covered in so many throw pillows that it's hard to see the fabric underneath. The coffee table, still being held up on one side by a stack of papers under one leg, is littered with old receipts, open envelopes, and a handful of dishes that need to be washed. Astra steps around Isla and quickly gathers them up, but there's barely enough space in the kitchen sink to put them.

Maria Vaughn isn't just messy—she's chaotic. One living room wall is filled from top to bottom with paintings, but they're not pretty flowers or landscapes or puppies. They're frogs. A whole wall of frogs, in all different shapes and colors and backgrounds. The bookshelf in the corner is crammed full of porcelain teacups and little brass animals, but only a handful of actual books. And the kitchen has more fake food in it than real food, especially on the countertops.

Isla spins around, her yellow dress swirling around her knees.

"Your apartment is very colorful."

Astra cringes. "That's one word for it. My mom is…a little off."

She's crazy, Astra thinks. That's what she's heard, at least. She wasn't there, so she can't say for sure. Her mom seems mostly all right now, but she's still kind of—scrambled. Like eggs.

Astra wonders if she's going to end up like that someday too.

"What about your dad?"

Astra doesn't answer. Isla looks up from intently trying to grab onto a tiny bronze cat with her hand halfway through its head.

"Never mind," she says quickly. She jumps to her feet and her legs flicker through the floor. "That was too personal, I'm an idiot, I didn't—"

"He left," Astra interrupts. She shrugs, trying to look casual, but her shoulders jerk a little too hard. "Four years ago. He calls on holidays sometimes, but…"

"That sucks."

"Yeah."

Astra's head is pounding. The red wall and the green frog paintings make the living room look like Christmas. She counts eight paintings, then nine steps backward to get to her bedroom, and she waits until Isla follows her before closing the door.

If the rest of the apartment is loud, Astra's bedroom is quiet. There's soft purple paint on three walls, and wallpaper with light, leafy vines on it around her closet doorframe. Her room is tiny—there's barely enough space to walk between her desk and her bed—but mostly empty. She sweeps up a loose hoodie from the floor and a stack of papers on her desk, but the rest is tidy. There are a few fake plants and unused candles on the dresser, a tall, thin bookshelf in one corner, and a string of lights behind her headboard that are shaped like tiny stars.

Isla immediately wanders into the closet. She looks disappointed when she tries to pull at a sweater sleeve and it falls right through her open hand.

Astra sits on the bed, and for maybe the first time in her life, she wishes she was alone. Usually, ghosts are a good distraction. She would rather talk to George McCreary about his car and his cat and the time he broke his hip trying to jump his neighbor's fence than sit in her bedroom all alone. But George is old and bloated like a fish. He's dead, and he *looks* dead.

Isla looks like a normal sixteen-year-old girl. Who happens to be floating a foot off the ground right now.

This kind of feels like inviting a friend from school over to her apartment. And there's a reason why Astra does *not* do that.

She clears her throat. Isla pokes her head out of the closet doorway. "I don't see why you need my help with your, um…bucket list?"

"I'm *dead*."

"Okay. Anti-bucket list, then?"

Astra wonders what a sixteen-year-old girl's unfinished business would be. If Astra died right here, in her bedroom on a Friday afternoon, would there be anything holding her back? Keeping her stuck here?

Isla shrugs and disappears back into Astra's closet. "You wear a lot of blue, do you realize that? Like, Evan Hansen levels of blue."

"Who?"

"Never mind. Not important." Astra hears a huff from the closet and then Isla emerges, hovering with her knees bent. She pokes around Astra's bookshelf, floating around it like she did Astra in the bathroom. The poor bookshelf doesn't even realize how much scrutiny it's under right now. "Do you have any books about flowers?"

Astra shakes her head and watches Isla shifting—first sitting, then standing, then lying in the air like she's floating in a pool. "No. Am I supposed to?"

"I like flowers," Isla says simply. "Hey, did you know that there's a flower that smells like chocolate? That's what I've heard, anyway. I've never actually seen one."

Astra blinks. "That's actually kind of interesting."

Isla turns around and smiles. Her dimples look like freckles from across the room, deep shadows in the corners of her mouth. "I know, right? You should get a book about flowers. Let's add that to the list. There's got to be a library around here somewhere."

Something about Isla's tone sticks in Astra's head like a pin.

"You don't know where the library is?"

Isla pauses with her face literally buried in Astra's bookshelf, somewhere between a romance novel she's never read and a historical fiction that she actually has. Most of her books are either classics or nonfiction, but she's got an anthology about ghosts tucked away in the back, behind the rest of them, with the cover facing the wall.

Isla waves her off with one hand. "Nah. I like plants, but books take too much time. I've seen pretty much every movie you could think of, though."

The clock over Astra's bedroom door ticks loudly. It makes even more noise than the color blue, but less than red. Red is loud. Astra doesn't like eating dinner in the living room, because the walls are so noisy, but the kitchen counter is always messy.

Astra doesn't watch a lot of movies. There's only one TV in the apartment, mounted on the living room wall, but they only get cable and half of the channels come through with too much static to be watchable. The noise sounds too much like the buzz that ghosts give off, and Astra really doesn't need to be reminded of that every time she's eating or trying to work on homework.

Isla abandons the shelf in favor of thoroughly inspecting Astra's dresser, looking disappointed when she sees that the only decorations Astra has are a few candles and some fake succulents. Isla huffs and mutters something under her breath that Astra is pretty sure is an insult aimed at her plastic plants. She sniffs at one of the candles and then wrinkles her nose.

"Ew. No wonder you don't light these."

"I don't like strong smells," Astra defends. "Or strong colors. Or loud noises."

Isla nods like that somehow makes sense and doesn't question it. Nobody has ever found out about Astra's weird quirks and not called her out on them. Her interest is piqued. Just a little bit.

"So, what else is on your—anti-bucket list?"

"I like this candle," Isla interrupts, pointing to a dark brown wax in a heavy glass container. Astra is pretty sure it's supposed to smell like cinnamon. "We should go candle shopping, too. Buy more of just *this* one."

"Is that one of your—?"

"Nope." She pops the *p* again. It clicks like the sound of a clock ticking. "But it would be fun. You'll find out the rest when we do them. *If* you agree to help me, that is."

Astra gets the feeling that she doesn't really have a choice. Isla doesn't seem like the kind of person—*ghost*, she reminds herself, *not a person*—who gives up easily.

"You can walk through walls. You don't need my help."

Isla disappears behind Astra, leaving goose bumps on the back of her neck. The only thing on that side of the bed is her desk, and all Isla is going to find is half-finished assignments and a laptop that takes ten minutes to boot up and freezes if there are more than two programs open at the same time.

Astra twists around to look at her.

"Moral support," Isla says. She blows on a piece of paper, and it flutters on top of the desk. "Maybe I'm a coward."

"You don't seem like a coward."

Isla chuckles. "You don't really know me, then."

Astra watches Isla walk across the room—or, more accurately, move her feet like she's walking while still floating a couple of inches above the floor. She keeps her toes pointed like she's trying to touch the ground, but she misses every time. Twice she nearly gets it, but then her feet sink down a little too far and vanish into the carpet. It takes her a painfully long time to reach Astra's bed, and she keeps her eyes down the whole time, looking focused.

Then she sighs a gust of cold air and gives up, flying the rest of the way until she's sitting with her legs crossed at the end of Astra's bed. Her knees jut out, and it's the first time Astra sees her skin with any imperfections, because there's a small, jagged birthmark on the inside of her lower right thigh, dark purple and shaped kind of like a leaf.

The air feels like ice.

She waits for Isla to say something, but she stays quiet. Ghosts don't need to breathe, but every so often she exhales anyway, and the temperature in the room feels like it's dropped a couple of degrees. Astra tries to discreetly pull her comforter over her legs.

And then, "Hey, did you know that broccoli is a flower?"

Astra shifts, and watches the corner of Isla's mouth twitch.

"No way," Astra says quickly. "You looked so serious for a minute there. And then you just drop that *lie* on me?"

"Not a lie." Isla shakes her head. One of her feet keeps twisting around in its pretzel, and without shoes Astra can see the joint in her ankle sticking out. She died wearing pastel blue socks with white polka dots on them. "You can look it up when you take me to the library to find a decent plant book."

Astra gets the feeling that she's going to regret this. But George McCreary is going to move on soon, and she really doesn't mind having someone to talk to in the mornings. It's kind of nice not to wake up alone.

What does it say about Astra, that all of her friends are dead?

She runs a hand through her hair, catching her fingers on a tight coil at the top. Her palms are starting to sweat.

"Fine," she says. "But you owe me one."

Isla shrugs. She looks like she's floating on water, bobbing up and down with the waves. "Sure. First I've gotta figure out how to move stuff. Your little freak-out in school today could have totally been avoided if I could have just written you a note or something."

"Hey, I didn't *freak out*, I was just—"

She's interrupted by the sound of the front door opening. She's thankful for once that it creaks on its hinges so loudly that she can hear it from any room in the apartment.

"You've got to go," she says quickly, waving her arms.

Isla blinks and rights herself until she's standing again. "Go *where*?"

"I don't know! What have you been doing this whole time?"

"Stealing candy from babies and haunting little old ladies, what do you *think* I've been doing?"

Astra's mom's footsteps click on the linoleum in the hallway. She must be wearing her heels—probably the strappy red ones that don't match anything else in her wardrobe. They make her look tall and uncomfortable, and she always points her toes inward when she wears them.

Astra drops her voice down to a whisper. "You can't stay here at night. That's all I'm asking. Okay?"

Isla looks confused. "Why not?"

"I just…can't sleep. With ghosts around. It's nothing personal."

Isla looks like she's taking it *very* personally, but thankfully she doesn't push. She floats out the window and stops when she's on the other side, turning around two stories above the cement sidewalk.

She leans in, and her hair falls into her face. "Try not to miss me too much," she says. "I'll be back in the morning."

Astra rolls her eyes. "Please don't be."

She's only half joking.

Just an hour ago, she wouldn't have been joking at all. Maybe it's because she knows George is going to leave soon. Maybe she's lonely. She wonders if it's better to have friends who are dead, or have no friends at all.

Her bedroom feels quiet when Isla finally disappears. Astra thinks about taking the batteries out of the clock on the wall, but she decides to leave them in.

Chapter Four

"Wakey, wakey! Time to get up! There's a creepy old man here to see you. He smells like dead fish. No offense."

"No, it's true. I do."

Astra groans and pulls her comforter over her head. Her alarm hasn't even gone off yet. There's no reason for her to be awake right now.

"Hey, my name's Isla. Nice to meet you."

"George McCreary. It's a pleasure to meet you, Miss Isla."

"Ooh, a gentleman."

Astra burrows herself in deeper and holds her pillow over her ears. A cold sweat starts breaking out on the back of her neck.

"Tell me, kind sir, do you know how to dance?"

"Indeed I do, Miss Isla."

Cold air swirls around her like a tornado. She can hear humming, but she doesn't recognize the song. After a few minutes of listening to it, she gives up and peeks out from underneath her blanket nest.

It never occurred to her that ghosts could interact with each other, but apparently they can. Because Isla and George McCreary are doing some kind of mock-tango in the middle of Astra's bedroom floor, except it's mostly just Isla swinging poor George around and the two of them periodically phasing in and out of Astra's dresser and closet door.

It's way too early for this.

She pulls the pillow off her head but keeps her comforter up around her neck.

"Don't make me regret showing you where I live," she hisses. Then, "Good morning, George."

"Good morning, Miss Astra," George says.

"Like I couldn't have just followed you home," Isla says at the same time. "Wait, you know him? And here I thought I was your only friend."

Astra throws her pillow. It goes right through Isla's head and lands with a thump on the floor in her closet.

"Watch it. You could *kill* someone if you're not careful."

Astra glances at the clock on her bedside table and sighs. Six fifteen a.m. Even the birds outside aren't awake yet.

Isla pauses mid-spin and looks apologetic. "Sorry. Me and Georgie here don't sleep. We can leave if you want to get a few more winks in."

As much as Astra would love to sleep more, she can't. She's a light sleeper anyway, and once she's awake, she's *awake*. It just doesn't help that she's always surrounded by things that seem to have made it their life's mission to stop her from sleeping. Or their *afterlife's* mission.

She shakes her head and throws back her comforter.

"No, you don't have to leave. But you do have to stay here. I'm gonna take a shower, and if either of you try to perv on me, I'm putting salt on the windows."

❖

Astra can smell something burning when she steps out of the bathroom, left foot first. The pile of magazines has been moved, but in its place is a box that's open on the top and filled with packing peanuts. Astra steps around it and follows the scent of smoke into the kitchen.

Her mom is standing in the middle of the worn linoleum, in her heels that click and make her toes point inward, sorting through an entire supermarket's worth of spice containers. Everything else has been pushed aside, and the counter is packed with small glass jars and even smaller plastic shakers. She's focusing intently on a container of mustard seeds when Astra walks in, and her shoes scratch on the floor when she moves out of the way.

The kitchen is small and blue and *loud*. The cabinets are painted white, but they're scuffed in so many places that the original dark brown wood is showing through. The floor is black and white, but it's stained and scratched, and the black squares are all smearing into the white ones so it looks more like marble than a checkerboard. The countertops are speckled, white with brown dots that look like spills, and more than once Astra has furiously tried to wipe them up without realizing.

"Mom," she says, waving away a cloud of smoke. "Toaster."

Her mom spins around, her heels shrieking, and pulls the plug. The toast that pops up looks less like bread and more like cinder blocks. Crumbs spring out of the toaster and onto the counter, and her mom sweeps them away with her hand.

"Good morning to you, too," her mom says, still holding the mustard seeds. Astra has never seen her cook with them before. Actually, she's never seen her mother *cook*—not anything that requires more than boiling water or heating up a pan in the oven. "At least we still have cereal."

"Milk went bad. I dumped it yesterday."

Her mom shrugs, clanging glass jars together and shuffling them around like she's a juggler in the circus. Astra knows they're all going to end up back in the cabinet again, just in a slightly different order than before. And she's going to be the one who throws them out when they go bad.

"Well, the cereal's still good, right?"

Astra doesn't answer. The cabinet is still open, so she closes it and pushes aside a bowl of fake Styrofoam pears to reach the few inches of bare counter space. She dumps the burnt toast into the garbage, shakes the toaster a few times to empty out the crumbs, and throws two pieces of fresh bread back into it. The handle jams on the way down. She wiggles it four times exactly, because four is a nice, safe number.

While she waits, she watches her mother work—absently sorting through spices, opening and closing drawers, moving things between cabinets, and then changing her mind and putting them back.

If their apartment is colorful and loud, then it's because Astra's mom is, too.

She dresses like a little kid, like a toddler given an hour of unsupervised time in a costume store. Bright, swishy skirts, blouses with poofy sleeves, jackets with sequins and tassels that hang down past her knees. Tall boots, bright red high heels, sweaters in the summer and satin dresses in the winter, and shirts underneath sweatshirts underneath coats. She matches colors like she's colorblind, and no matter what she wears, she always completes her outfit with jewelry—thick layers of necklaces down her throat and so many bracelets that she jangles like a wind chime when she moves her arms.

Sometimes, Astra thinks that her mother knows that she looks like a train wreck, and she wears so many accessories to try and hide the mess underneath. The bright, mismatched colors. The chaos.

Colorful and chaotic. If Astra ever needed just two words to describe her mother, those would be the ones she'd pick.

Today, Maria Vaughn is wearing a mud-brown pencil skirt and a shiny purple blouse. It might actually look nice without the loud, bright red heels and a dozen bangles on each arm. Every time she moves a jar across the counter, her wrists make a sound like bells ringing.

"How did you sleep last night?" her mom asks, abandoning the spices in favor of shifting dishes around in the sink.

The toast pops. Astra jumps and knocks her shoulder on the refrigerator door.

"Fine," she says quickly. "Great, actually. Got my full eight hours in."

Minus the first two and the last one, she thinks, *but close enough.*

The first two weren't really anybody's fault, but she's choosing to blame Isla for waking her up a full hour before her alarm on a Saturday.

She smears peanut butter on her toast and winces at the sound.

"Honey," her mom says. She's using her *mom voice*. It's like a sticky fly trap made out of words. "I heard you last night. Another nightmare?"

Astra shrugs. She can't tell her mom without *telling* her mom. And she doesn't plan on doing that any time soon. Or ever.

Her mom sighs. "I worry about you, you know. You can talk to me about anything. Especially if it's something to do with—"

"Nope," Astra interrupts. "Nuh-uh. Sometimes dreams are just *dreams*, Mom. It's not a big deal."

"So you're really not...?"

Astra shakes her head so quickly the room spins. "No. It was probably just a dream about the biology test I have on Monday. It's worth a quarter of my grade, you know?"

Her mom doesn't look convinced. She stacks a pile of dirty plates up on the counter but doesn't wash them. Astra counts them from where she's standing—one, two, three, four, five.

"Well, if you're sure—"

"I am."

The toast is dry and the peanut butter is oily and has started to separate, and the texture in Astra's mouth feels kind of gross. She hates lying to her mom, but her mother is already one magazine short of a toppled stack, so the less she has to worry about, the better. Especially when it comes to something like this.

Ghosts ruined Maria Vaughn's life. How is she going to react when her own daughter tells her that she can see them too?

"Hey, honey, how about we make today a shopping day? We're out of milk, right? And we could also use some"—she sifts through the jars again and checks a few labels before looking up—"cardamom. We're out. And if you want, we can swing by the mall and check out that new boutique that just opened up—pick you out something with a little more color. You know, I've always thought you'd look beautiful in red."

If Astra had it her way, she would board up the doors and windows and make a nest out of blankets and never, ever leave the comfort of her own bedroom. It's quiet and peaceful, and when she's in bed she doesn't have to worry about watching her feet or counting to four or the colors being too loud. She'd be lonely, maybe, but she would be safe. And George and Isla would still be able to visit her.

But it looks like she's not getting away with that today, and if she has to choose between an itchy red sweater or hanging out with a ghost, then it looks like Isla is getting her flower book after all.

Plus, Astra has no idea what cardamom is. But shopping for it doesn't sound very exciting.

"Sorry, I've got, um…plans. I've got plans."

"Plans." Her mom says it slowly, like it's a word she's never heard before. "You never have plans on Saturdays."

Astra feels a little defensive, a tiny prickle under her skin that's more annoyance than anger. Because, sure, she's never really had friends and she typically spends her weekends shut in her room doing homework and watching videos on her laptop, but her mom doesn't need to point that out.

"Yeah," she says with a little more force than necessary. "Plans. I'm hanging out at the library today. With a friend—from school. A friend from school. We're working on a project. For English."

She pictures Oliver when she's talking, because it's easier to pretend she's meeting one of the few people she might actually consider a friend—maybe—than it would be to fake an excuse for driving to the public library to check out a book for a dead girl she only just met yesterday.

Her mom quirks a perfectly penciled-in eyebrow. Her makeup matches her outfit today, so at least she's not totally colorblind.

"And why have I never met this new *friend* of yours?"

"Mom. It's just homework. I've never even hung out with him outside of school before."

"Him?"

The look on her mom's face tells Astra that she's in the dark about more than just the whole ghost thing. She wouldn't be surprised if her mom put her hands on her hips and gave her *the talk* right here on the scuffed linoleum, but thankfully, her hands are too full of assorted spices to put anywhere.

Astra sighs and picks at the dry edges of her toast. "His name's Oliver."

Sometimes, Astra is thankful for her mother's colorful personality. She gets distracted easily, her mind wanders from one thing to another like opening cabinets and rearranging spice containers, and she never worries about the little things like buying milk or putting out the recycling or making sure she knows who her daughter is hanging out with on a Saturday. If Astra wanted to, she could probably take advantage of her mom's scattered mind and use it to sneak out late or make out with college freshmen.

Instead, she's using it to go to the library, of all places. What a rebel.

"Well," her mom says after a moment, throwing the spice jars back into their original cabinet in no particular order. "You'll have to invite him over for dinner sometime. I'll be sure to cook something special just for the occasion."

"Sure, Mom. I'll do that."

She pictures Oliver with his long, long legs sitting at their squat little coffee table, holding a plate full of burnt toast, and the absurdity of it is almost enough to make up for giving up her quiet Saturday to hang out with a dead girl. Almost.

❖

The library is fifteen minutes away from Astra's apartment by car. She tries to count the blocks, but then Isla stands up in the back seat and sticks her head out like the ceiling is a sunroof, and Astra promptly loses track of her numbers. She makes a mental note to count them on the way back home instead.

The public library is a three-story building made entirely out of tan bricks and surrounded by trees and open fields of grass decorated with benches and fountains and a handful of picnic tables on one side. There's a little garden in the front with half-wilted flowers planted in clusters, and Astra doesn't miss the way Isla pauses for just a moment to look at them before following her through the sliding doors and into the lobby.

Isla bends her knees and her feet flicker out behind her. She does the doggy-paddle in midair while Astra gets her bearings, and clears her throat when Astra takes a step toward the information services desk.

"The nonfiction stuff is on the third floor," she says, nodding at the spiral staircase on her right.

Astra blinks at her. "I thought you said you've never been here before?"

"Well, I've been *here*, obviously. Just not up there."

Astra looks around. The main floor is mostly kids' books, with a small playground on one side and a cluster of beanbag chairs and computer desks on the other. She remembers coming here when she was little and hiding underneath one of the climbing toys, thinking that her parents wouldn't be able to find her and she'd get to stay a little longer and read in peace. The colors didn't bother her as much back then, but the ghosts definitely did.

The headphones at the library computers had given her the idea to ask for her own pair for her tenth birthday, even though she never told her parents what she wanted them for.

The building is old, and even with the handful of updates since the last time she was here, Astra notes that there still isn't an elevator. There are two sets of spiral stairs, winding black metal with wooden slats on the bottoms that creak when she steps down too hard. She counts the steps on the way up both sets of stairs. Sixteen steps each, thirty-two total. Something eases in her mind when she counts the last one and steps onto the dark blue carpet of the third floor. Left foot first, of course.

This floor is a lot quieter than the first, which is a good thing, because Isla is a lot louder.

"Wow. This place is huge. Do you think it would echo if I yelled right now? Can ghosts even echo at all?"

Astra opens her mouth to tell her that she has no idea if ghosts can make an echo, because who even wonders that kind of thing anyway, but Isla beats her to it by shouting *boo* at the top of her nonexistent lungs. And—huh. Ghosts *don't* echo. Isla actually looks kind of disappointed by that.

She gets over it quickly, though, and sets off down the aisles like a bloodhound.

"You look over there," she shouts, waving her hand absently. "And I'll check the back."

"Or we could just look it up on the computer."

"Fine, you do that, then. I'm gonna snoop around."

If anyone could make being in the nonfiction section of a library look fun, apparently Isla can. She floats around the room like she's flying, arms stretched out in front of her, feet pointed behind, and every time she spots something interesting she swoops down and pauses for just long enough to inspect it before she flies back up again. She's got a wide, dimpled smile on her face, and she looks so free and happy that it's hard to believe that she's dead. She's only sixteen, and she *died*. Shouldn't she be crying, or bargaining, or shouting up at the heavens or something? Going through grief, feeling cheated out of a long life, missing what she used to have?

Right now, she looks more alive than any dead person Astra has ever met. More than most of the living ones, too.

Astra watches her for too long before she remembers that she's supposed to be doing something. She tears her eyes away and walks to the computer, but before she can finish typing *flowers* into the search bar, Isla is waving her down excitedly.

"Hey. *Hey*, over here! I found some!"

Apparently, there's an entire shelf dedicated to books on plants and gardening along the back wall, squeezed between a tall window and a section on hunting and wild animals. Isla sinks down, legs crossed, and hovers an inch or so above the carpeted ground. Astra watches her eyes flicker as she reads the titles on the spines, looking unexpectedly serious for once.

Isla reaches for a book with a purple cover and curly white letters along the side, but her hand sinks right through it. She pulls it back and tries again, then closes her eyes, and stretches out her fingertips and waits for just a moment before pushing forward. Her hand disappears into the shelf and she yanks it back with a frustrated sigh.

"Can you just…?"

"Oh. Yeah, sure."

Astra sits next to her on the carpet, legs bent to one side. Isla floats down to her level, sinking a couple of inches into the floor until they're nearly the same height.

"This one?"

Isla nods. "And the one next to it. With the gold letters. Not that one, on the other side. Yeah. And—maybe this one too? Can you flip through it real quick? I wanna check for pictures."

Astra does as she's told, feeling a little rush when she chooses a book and Isla approves, her dimples poking deep divots into her cheeks. She watches Isla lean forward until her nose is nearly touching the bookshelf, and her hair falls over her shoulders in bouncy waves. There are tiny flowers on her earrings—light pink with little green leaves on the sides. She's so excited that Astra can hear it—like the static on the TV when the cable goes out. Her green eyes look a little less dull than they did yesterday.

"Hey, check this out," Isla says, shifting until she's lying flat, nearly touching the ground. The book with the purple cover is open to a page near the beginning—a section about shrubs with a full-color photo of a bush with fluffy, dark green leaves. She takes in a deep breath that she doesn't have the lungs for and then blows out a rush of ice-cold air that makes Astra shiver. The pages turn like a flip book and land on a sprawling image of vines with pale blue flowers along the sides.

"That's really cool. Um—literally. It's really cold in here."

Isla rubs the back of her neck, looking sheepish. "Sorry. Forgot about that. I wish I could just turn the pages myself." She frowns, staring down at the tiny blue flowers. "But that's impossible, right?"

Astra hums and turns the page. This time she actually recognizes the flowers—bright red roses. Isla is watching her, but Astra keeps her eyes on the book.

"Not impossible," she says. "A ghost knocked a candle off my dresser once. I think it was an accident, but that still counts."

"Maybe I can learn, then."

Astra shrugs. "Maybe. But it'll probably take a while."

Isla smiles, small enough to hide her dimples. "I've got time." She reaches down for the book and runs her finger over the glossy photo of the rose bush. For a second, it almost looks like she's touching it, but then she sighs and the pad of her finger slips right through it. "Hey, what's your favorite flower?"

"I don't..." Astra pauses, thinking. "Maybe tulips? Before we moved, we lived in a house with a really big porch in the front. And my mom planted a bunch of tulips the first year—like, *way* too many, and they were all different colors, and when they bloomed it was like a rainbow around the front of the house. Just—*every* color, and she always let me pick as many as I wanted because you couldn't even tell. But they only opened up for a couple of weeks. And then they—"

She stops, the words halfway out of her mouth. There are goose bumps on her arms, but her face feels hot. She ducks her head and fumbles to close the book, setting it aside and pulling another one off the pile.

"That sounds nice," Isla says. "Why did you move?"

Astra feels hot and cold at the same time. She wants to stop talking, but it's also nice to be able to talk to someone. Especially someone who couldn't spill her secrets to anyone, even if she wanted to.

"My parents got a divorce. My dad got the house."

Isla huffs out a cold breath, but thankfully she aims it away from Astra this time. "That's not fair. He kicked you guys out?"

"No." Astra shakes her head. "My mom wanted to leave."

"Did *you*?"

The second book has fewer pictures, and the pages aren't as glossy. Turning them feels like sifting through cardboard, and it makes Astra's hands feel itchy. She slides it back onto the shelf and picks out a different one.

She chews on her words, taking her time paging through the glossary. "I don't know," she settles on. "I miss the house. But I don't miss the way things were when we left. And my mom is more important than a house."

Isla doesn't say anything for a minute. The silence sounds like tiny bees buzzing all around the room. There are two other people on this floor with them—a librarian sitting behind a computer desk, typing slowly, and a patron on the other end of the room, reading in a cushy gray armchair. Astra wonders if either of them can hear her talking to herself.

"Still," Isla finally says. "That's not fair. Especially if you don't get to see your tulips anymore."

Astra smiles. "What do you think about this book?"

Isla hovers closer and looks down. "Turn the page. A few more. Okay, stop." Astra pulls her hands back when she reaches a picture of a cluster of large yellow flowers with their petals fluffed out. They look like puffs of cotton, like dandelions when they're all dried up. "Did you know that chrysanthemums are supposed to symbolize stuff like happiness and long life?"

Astra shakes her head and looks at the picture. She's seen these flowers before. They look like tiny suns. It makes sense that they represent happy things.

"But! In some places they mean death instead. Like, some people think they represent good things, but other people think the exact opposite. Isn't that weird?"

"What do *you* think?"

"Hmm. I think they're just pretty. I don't think flowers are supposed to do anything but just…look nice."

Astra closes the last book and adds it to the one with the purple cover. She stacks them up—one, two, three. She picks a fourth one at random and adds it to the pile.

"What's your favorite flower, then?" she asks as she squares the books off.

Isla smiles and floats up, her feet going through the top of the bookshelf. She hovers for a moment just above Astra's head.

"I'll tell you next time," she says.

And Astra finds herself actually looking forward to it.

CHAPTER FIVE

A stra wakes up to ice water being dumped on her neck.
Or—that's what it *feels* like. She bolts upright and coughs, almost expecting to spit out cold water, and the blurry green numbers by her bed read 1:18 a.m. The string of lights behind her headboard makes everything around her look hazy and yellow, and she reaches out in the dark to turn on her lamp.

Her palms are sweaty, so it takes three tries to pull the lamp cord down all the way. She wiggles it a fourth time, just in case.

Her heart is beating wildly, and even with the ice-cold feeling in her chest, the rest of her is soaked in sweat. Her pillow is damp, and the top of her short mess of curls is sticking to her forehead. She blinks quickly, and as her eyes adjust to the bright lamplight, she immediately sees what woke her up. And she's not sure whether to be relieved or upset.

Astra opens her mouth to say something, but Isla cuts her off quickly. Her hands are up, palms out, and she's hovering in a crouched position next to Astra's bed.

"I'm sorry," she says. She's whispering. "I didn't want to wake you up, but you sounded awful, and I just…I was gonna leave. I should leave, right?"

Astra frowns. "You're not supposed to be here at night."

"I know. I was in your kitchen, and I know that's no excuse, but I heard you, and—"

"Why were you in my kitchen? It's early. It's one in the morning."

Isla smiles, but it's small. No dimples. "Ghosts don't sleep, remember? I was practicing. Your kitchen has lots of small things on the counters. I thought maybe I could try to move something."

"In my kitchen," Astra repeats. Her brain feels like it's full of cotton. "At one in the morning. In my *kitchen*."

"Yes."

Astra throws herself back onto her pillow, feeling sticky with cold sweat and foggy from sleep. She stares up at her ceiling, the light from the lamp cutting long, white lines into the purple paint.

"Don't you have anywhere better to be?" she asks. Then, "Sorry, that sounded rude. It wasn't supposed to."

"No."

"No?"

"Nope." She pops the *p*. Even in the low light, Isla doesn't cast a shadow.

She's quiet for a minute. Astra would almost think she'd disappeared again, but the room is still cold. Astra can tell exactly where she is without looking, because it feels like a fan is blowing from that direction. The cold shifts, and Astra knows that Isla has moved to the end of the bed.

Astra doesn't like being bothered at night, but she was probably having a nightmare. No—she was *definitely* having a nightmare. A pretty bad one, if her sweaty sheets are any indication. Part of her wishes she could remember what it was about, but she's pretty sure she's better off not knowing.

She glances out the window quickly, but there's nothing there. She sighs and pushes a few stray curls off her forehead.

"Did you do it?" she asks. Her throat feels dry.

"Do what?"

"Make something move."

Isla hums. Astra can feel the cold seeping through the comforter and onto her feet, and she's thankful she chose to wear socks to bed. "Oh." Isla sounds surprised. "No. I did blow a fake pear off the counter, though."

Astra pictures Isla getting frustrated and taking it out on the bowl of poor, innocent Styrofoam pears. She chuckles.

"I don't think that counts."

She scoots back until her feet are warm again and her back is pressed up against her headboard. The wood digs into her shoulders uncomfortably.

Isla is hovering in a sitting position with her knees pulled up to her chest and her feet pointed down. Her polka-dot socks look like they're glowing in the dim light. She's got her dress stretched up around her legs and her jacket pushed back over her shoulders, the tops of her pale, freckly arms poking out. Every inch of skin that Astra can see is clean—no scars, no open wounds, not even any blood or bruises or *dirt*. If she wasn't floating, if Astra couldn't see straight through her head and into the open closet door behind her, she might not even be dead.

With her chin on her knees, Isla looks like a sixteen-year-old girl. A living one. Her knees are knobby, and Astra can just barely see the funny little birthmark on her right thigh.

Isla looks up. "Hey, your lights are little stars."

Astra shrugs. "Yeah. I like stars."

"I noticed. You drew them on your shoes, right?"

Astra blinks and glances into her dark closet, like her favorite pair of beat-up sneakers is going to jump out at her if she's not looking. She's pretty sure that no one has ever paid enough attention to her to notice what she scribbles on her scuffed-up, secondhand shoes. There were stains on the sides when her mom bought them for her, and she remembers debating for hours about what to cover them up with. They're just rough little pen drawings, done underneath her desk during second period Spanish last year, but it feels like it means something that Isla noticed.

Astra has tried for most of her life to blend into the background, to be the exact opposite of someone like her mom. She's not sure how to feel about being *seen*, though. It's a little unnerving. She pulls her comforter a little closer and tries to think of something to say, but her throat feels dry.

Isla smooths down her dress and stretches her legs. "I should probably go," she says quietly. "I shouldn't have bugged you. I don't want to wake your mom up either, so I'll just…go find somewhere else to practice. Or some old ladies to haunt, or something."

She stands up, pulling the cold with her, and Astra reaches out without thinking. Her hand sinks halfway through Isla's wrist.

"Wait," she says, punctuated by a rolling shiver. Her fingers are shaking, but the rest of her is warm.

Isla turns to look at her, and Astra feels like she's been caught. She should have just let her go and tried to get some more sleep. But Astra doesn't like being alone after a nightmare, and...

"I'm wide awake now," she finishes. She bites back a yawn and throws her feet over the side of the bed. "Plus, I know the perfect place for you to practice. Lots of little stuff for you to blow over, and we're guaranteed to have the place to ourselves."

❖

The keys stick in the lock, and Astra jiggles the handle one, two, three, four times before pushing the door open. The little bell above the door chimes softly. Isla floats in through the window, her feet disappearing into a display case by the door, while Astra fumbles for the light switch.

The lights are dim, and one near the back of the store flickers every few seconds. Astra throws her keys onto the counter and watches Isla fly around the room, looking like Peter Pan with her arms out and her legs kicking behind her. She's lucky she can't touch things yet—or maybe it's the *store* that's lucky, because more than once Isla runs straight through a shelf or dives too fast into a table loaded with merchandise. And Astra's mom *definitely* can't afford to pay for any broken goods.

"This place is great," Isla says as she passes over Astra's head. "Does your mom own it?"

Astra shakes her head. "The lady we rent from owns the whole building. But she's, like, ninety years old and lives in a retirement home. So she never comes around. My mom manages the place, though. Most of the weird stuff you see is one hundred percent her idea."

Isla swoops down and pokes at a ceramic chicken statue, but her finger disappears into its beak.

"I don't know. It's kind of cool. Reminds me of your apartment."

That's because it basically *is* their apartment. It's like everything that Astra's mom couldn't make fit into their tiny two-bedroom just ended up *here*.

The store itself is supposed to be some kind of gift shop, complete with a wall of cards for all occasions, a towering display of candles that make Astra's nose itch, and chocolates that range from normal—milk chocolate roses and gift boxes filled with nougats—to bizarre—Astra swears she's seen someone walking out of the store carrying a tin of chocolate-covered grasshoppers. There are socks with funny sayings on them, coffee mugs with inspirational quotes painted on the sides, and even a little jewelry case on the countertop with bangles and earrings inside.

But there's also the kind of stuff that Astra's mom orders at midnight after a long day of seeing ghosts and having her brain shaken up like a snow globe, and that stuff never sells. Ceramic animals, oddly colored shawls, jars of spicy teas and bowls shaped like fish. And because of all of her weird purchases, the store is packed—filled with circular glass-topped tables, tall bookshelves, and layered wooden display cases. There's barely enough room to move around without knocking something over.

Unless you happen to be a ghost, because Isla seems to be having a great time crashing through glass cabinets and into walls.

She stops at one of the tables near the front of the store and points. "Hey, this looks familiar."

Astra shrugs at the bowl of fake fruit propped up next to a stack of ornamental plates. "Well, all of our weird stuff had to come from somewhere."

Isla grins and blows out a gust of icy wind, and a lumpy, pear-shaped piece of Styrofoam tumbles to the ground.

"So," she says after Astra has retrieved the fruit and arranged it neatly back in its bowl. "What are we doing here?"

"Practicing."

"How am I supposed to practice if I have no idea what I'm doing?"

Astra squeezes between tables until she reaches a wooden shelf, painted purple, on the right side of the counter. The shelves are low, and everything on them is tiny. Most of the brass animals she recognizes from her own apartment, but there are a few other knickknacks that she's pretty sure are new.

"I've met two ghosts who could move things," she begins. "One was this young businessman type I saw at the mall when I was, like, ten. He was just pushing things around, you know? But just a little bit, like it took too much energy to move anything more than a few inches. I never figured out how he did it, though. I didn't ask. I only saw him for maybe a few minutes, and I don't think I realized he was dead until after I got home."

Isla hovers quietly, swiping her hands through the sides of the shelf like she hopes she'll catch them on something without thinking.

Astra continues, "The second one was an older lady, and she did it by accident. She showed up in my room, and I had my headphones on, but I still knew she was there because of the cold. But I had homework, or maybe a test the next day or something, and I was busy. So I ignored her. She was talking, and then she was yelling, and I was lucky my mom wasn't home or she definitely would have heard. And then this lady got mad, because I wouldn't look at her, so she threw a punch at my dresser and broke one of my candles against the wall."

Isla lets out a theatrical gasp. "No! It wasn't one of the nice-smelling ones, was it?"

"How am I supposed to know? I don't like any of them."

"Huh. You need to get out and smell some decent smells. Flowers. Did you know there's one called the Corpse Flower because it supposedly smells like a dead body?" Isla hums. "Maybe that's not the best example for why you should go smell some flowers..."

"*Focus*," Astra says, snapping her fingers. "I'm making a point here. I don't know about the first ghost, but the second one definitely used her anger to move things. So, maybe you just need to think about something that makes you mad."

Isla looks around. "Like...how mad?" She jerks her thumb over her shoulder. "That chicken over there is kind of bugging me. One of the eyes is crooked."

Astra rolls her eyes. She shifts things around on the shelf, straightening the tiny figurines and weighing them in her hands until she finds one that feels just a little lighter than the others. She brings the small wooden turtle to the front and squares it off.

"Madder," she says. "Pretend this turtle is someone you *really* hate."

Isla inches closer, her legs bent and her feet flickering behind her. She reaches her hand out and closes her eyes, but her fingers pass through the wood and the shelf underneath. She lets out a cold exhale.

"That's not gonna work," she says, drawing her hand back. Astra notices another small flaw on her skin that she wouldn't have if she wasn't this close: a tiny yellow callus on Isla's palm, right between her index and middle fingers.

"Who were you thinking of?"

"My third grade science teacher, Mrs. Darby. She always wore way too much hairspray, and I was a dumb kid, so I was flunking her class. And every time I failed a test she would lean over my desk and scold me, and all I could smell was that stupid hairspray."

Astra fights back a chuckle because Isla looks so affronted thinking about her old teacher that it feels a little rude to laugh. But she can't stop herself from smiling at the way Isla's eyebrows are furrowed and how she's frowning so deeply that she looks like one of those clowns with the sad face painted on.

"That's not going to do it," Astra tells her. "You're going to need more feeling. Not just, like, irritation. The lady who broke my candle was probably really confused, or frustrated, because she'd just died. And then she found me and I could see her, and she knew I could see her, but I just…ignored her. Can you imagine how that must have felt? *That's* how you need to make yourself feel."

"Yeah. You *were* kind of a jerk. No offense."

"I was *twelve*."

Isla shrugs. "I wasn't a jerk when I was twelve. Just so you know."

"The lady is long gone by now, so it really doesn't matter, does it? Seems a little silly to dwell on it instead of doing what we came here to do." She pauses, then adds under her breath, "Besides, after she broke my stuff I did talk to her. It's not like I just left her like that."

"Aw, I knew you were a big softie."

"*Focus*."

The little wooden turtle stares at Isla. Isla stares right back. The wood is stained dark brown, but the shell and eyes are painted white. It's light enough that Isla could probably move it just by blowing on it. Isla flicks it with her finger but it doesn't budge.

"I don't think I hate anyone," she says. "Maybe that's my problem."

"Nobody? Not even annoying neighbors or bullies from school?"

Isla is silent for a moment. She gnaws at her bottom lip for a second before answering. Astra wonders if she can feel it.

"I'm a—I was a loner, kind of. I mean, I didn't get into trouble or anything. I just…didn't really *do* much, you know? I stayed out of everyone's way. So people just kind of left me alone."

Astra gets the feeling that there's more to it than that, but she doesn't press. Part of her wants to know, because Isla is a mystery and Astra is curious, because who wouldn't be? But a much, *much* larger part of her doesn't want to know. Because knowing about Isla the human is a lot different than knowing about Isla the ghost. Isla the creature. The not-human *thing*.

Astra can't let herself forget that someday—maybe soon—Isla is going to disappear. Just like they all do. And getting attached will only make it worse.

"Okay," Astra says, forcing a smile. "Then let's try some*thing* that makes you angry instead of some*one*. There's got to be something that makes you mad. You're sixteen, right? That's, like, peak angst year."

Isla's grin slots back into place like a flicker, like when her legs shift positions in short, jerking motions.

"Are we talking *my brother leaving his stinky socks on the floor in the hallway* levels of angst?"

She swipes at the turtle quickly. Her hand cuts through it and she spins around, floating up to the top of the shelf and then back down. Her dress billows around her knobby knees, and Astra watches her birthmark phase in and out along with the rest of her legs.

"More than that, probably. Unless you happen to also hate your brother."

"Nope." Isla's smile shows her pointy canines and her deep, deep dimples. She sinks back down until she's the same height as Astra, which means that her feet are completely hidden inside the floorboards. "I love my brother. He's just got really smelly feet. What about the time I broke my wrist the week before summer vacation?"

"Did it make you mad?"

"Hmm. Not really?" Isla's shoulders jerk up and down in a shrug, flickering like television pixels. "It got me out of doing chores for a month, and my brother let me raid his video game collection. I think it was more annoying than anything else."

Astra moves the turtle forward just a little bit more. She takes her time squaring it off and shifting the figures around it as far back as they can go. The shelf is a little dusty, and it makes her nose itch. The flickering light in the back of the room is giving her a headache, and she's trying not to shiver because she doesn't want Isla to feel guilty for making her cold, but the entire building feels like a big icebox. She jiggles her leg behind the shelf and rubs at her arms when Isla isn't looking to try and relieve some of the prickly goose bumps on her skin.

"I don't think annoyed is a strong enough emotion. Isn't there anything else you can try?"

"I, um." Isla's hand is halfway to the shelf, but she doesn't move it. "There's one. But I don't know…"

Astra bites back a yawn and rubs her hands together. "You should try it," she says. "It doesn't hurt to try."

Isla nods and stares at the tiny wooden turtle. Astra kind of wishes she had kept her mouth shut, because now Isla's smile has turned into a thin line and her dimples are gone. And the room feels ten degrees colder, but maybe that's just Astra.

Isla closes her eyes again and pushes her hand forward slowly. Astra doesn't expect anything to happen. After all, she's met more ghosts than she can count, and only two have been able to move things. Most of them probably never even thought to try, but some of them probably did. And she knows for a fact that a few of them got angry enough to do it.

Maybe anger isn't the key. Maybe it's something else. She was ignoring the ghost lady when she knocked down the candle, but Astra wasn't even looking at her face. She could have knocked it over because of something else, something Astra hadn't even been paying any attention to. She wishes she had just listened. Talked to the ghost in the mall that day. Stopped being so scared and selfish for once in her life.

She opens her mouth to tell Isla to stop, maybe try again another day—anything to bring her dimples back and take away some of the itchy-cold feeling spreading over Astra's arms—when Isla's index finger touches the wooden turtle's head. Just a little bit.

It's just a bump, barely even noticeable, but the turtle's head shifts just a fraction of an inch to the right. Astra can tell because she took her time in squaring it off, and made sure it was *perfectly* in line with the front of the shelf. And when Isla pulls her hand back, Astra can see that it's moved. Barely, but it has.

Isla blinks her eyes open, still frowning. She looks over at Astra with her pale green eyes.

"I really thought that was gonna—"

"You did it," Astra interrupts. Her chest feels a little bubbly, but she's not sure why. "You moved it."

Isla shakes her head. "No, I didn't. It's in the exact same spot it was before."

"No. I was watching. It wasn't much, but…maybe half an inch? Look at the head. It's off to the side. Just a bit."

Isla stares at the turtle, and the turtle stares back—just at a little tiny bit of an angle. Her grin pops out like a flicker, like a wire spring, and Astra's chest feels like a shaken bottle of soda. Fizzy. Light.

"That was amazing," Astra tells her. She feels a little giddy. Maybe it's the lack of sleep. That's probably what it is. "What were you thinking about?"

Isla doesn't miss a beat. "The neighbor's dog. Used to bark at three in the morning on school days and keep me awake."

The corners of her mouth flicker, barely enough for Astra to notice. But she does. And it's painfully obvious that Isla is lying, but it's not Astra's place to ask. She decided a long time ago that she wouldn't get involved in the lives—or deaths—of ghosts.

She's glad Isla didn't tell her. She doesn't want to know.

And if she finds herself in her bed at four in the morning, trying to get back to sleep with Isla still practicing in her mom's store, then it's probably just her star lights that are keeping her awake. Nothing else.

CHAPTER SIX

There are twelve steps on each staircase at school, and two sets of stairs at each end of the building. That's forty-eight steps total, but only twenty-four to get from the first floor to the third.

English class is on the third floor. On Monday morning, Astra climbs twenty-four steps, walks into the room left foot first, and somehow finds herself being haunted. In school, of all places.

But, to be honest, being trailed by a ghost isn't the worst thing that has happened to her in this building.

"You should tell him."

Astra arranges her supplies in one corner of her desk, underneath a pen scribble that's been there since the beginning of the year and on the other side of a small chip in the wood. Two books, pencil, notebook.

She's wearing two sweaters today, even though she's sitting underneath a heater, and she's got her headphones at the top of her backpack just in case.

Isla is hovering on one side of Astra's desk, sitting with her legs crossed like she's meditating, and Oliver is in his own desk on the other side. It's a very weird feeling, sitting between the two of them, and even though Astra's arms are covered in goose bumps, her palms are slick with sweat. She keeps dropping her pencil and having to reposition it again.

She opens her notebook, squares it off, and writes *NO* in block letters at the top. Then she underlines them twice and angles the paper in Isla's direction.

"Why not? He seems nice. I like his nose ring. I've always wanted one. Do you think it's too late for me to get one?"

Astra ignores her. On her right, Oliver's tapping his leg like he's in an imaginary race. Maybe that's why he's in track. All of that pent-up energy of his has to go *somewhere*.

He sees her looking and smiles, and a sour feeling settles in her throat.

Mr. Pierce walks in a few minutes later, his bushy mustache bobbing in time with his steps. He throws down a pile of stapled essays, tugs at the graying wisps around his ear, and carefully deposits a paper cup of coffee on the edge of his desk.

Astra turns to Oliver and sees that he's already wearing his trademark lopsided grin, pointy canines and all. She bumps his elbow and returns the expression.

"Aw, you guys are so cute." Isla uncurls her legs—which flicker and twitch until they finally settle themselves back into a slightly too-long leg shape—and floats on her back, kicking her feet like she's swimming. "I'm already bored. Wake me up when it's over."

Astra makes it through the first ten minutes of class without any issues. She takes notes, avoids looking up at the ghost circling the room like it's a swimming pool, and tries not to think about Oliver. If she doesn't think about him, then she won't think about what happened on Friday, and how she still kind of owes him an explanation for her weird behavior and a huge thank-you for getting her out of trouble with Mr. Pierce.

But it's really, *really* hard to not think about him when all she can hear is his foot tapping and his pencil spinning around on his desk. She can see him moving out of the corner of her eye. Always moving. He's almost as bad as Isla, but at least the ghost is keeping mostly out of her field of vision.

Ten minutes into class, though, Oliver slides a rumpled piece of paper onto her desk, right on top of her notes. She sets her pencil down and smooths out the paper.

Are you avoiding me?

1. *Yes*
2. *Also yes, but I have a good reason, and I'm inviting Oliver over to my house so I can explain it to him.*

She shakes her head and smiles, watching Oliver's leg resume its frantic jiggling. Something cold settles on the back of her neck.

"You should check the second one. I think he would like your apartment. How many patches do you think he's got on his jacket?"

Astra glances over at Oliver without thinking, and he sends back a crooked smile that makes Isla chuckle. Astra tries, in the split second before she pulls her eyes away, to count the patches, but there are too many. Definitely more than four. She wonders if the number matters to him, or if he even knows it. Probably not.

She scribbles out an answer on Oliver's paper and hands it back to him. *Not avoiding you. You can't come over. It's my mom. I'm sorry.*

Then she underlines the *NO* on her own notebook sheet a third time and lowers her shoulders so Isla can see.

Isla hums and blows on the paper. It flutters on the desk, and Astra fumbles to slam it back down with her hands before anyone can see.

"You know, human friends can be just as charming as ghosts. Maybe not as fun, sure, but at least they're not—you know. *Dead.*"

You sound like my mom, Astra writes.

"Well, your mom sounds *extremely* cool, then."

Astra bites back a small smile and forces her mouth into the thinnest line possible. Oliver keeps looking over at her, tapping his pencil and his foot at the same time.

They called her crazy where we used to live, so that makes sense.

"Why can't you be both?"

Astra doesn't answer, and Isla goes back to swimming.

Five minutes before the bell rings, Oliver passes his note back one last time.

If you change your mind, let me know.

"Does anyone know the answer to number twelve?"

Astra looks down at the blank sheet of questions in front of her. She recognizes that it's math, but the rest is just squiggles and lines. And numbers—sharp ones and round ones. They all blend together in her mind, into some kind of sharp-and-round thing that makes her head hurt.

Isla floats behind her. Astra can feel her breath on her neck, even though ghosts don't breathe. Sometimes she swears Isla does it just to annoy her.

"It's B," Isla says, right in her ear. The worksheet slides a little to the right and Astra quickly pulls it back and squares it off with the rest of her papers.

No, it's not, she writes on the bottom of the worksheet.

"Yes, it is."

Astra underlines her previous response and holds the paper down so that it doesn't blow away. Isla retaliates by blowing in her *ear* instead, and the sudden icy wind makes Astra flinch. Her elbow knocks into the edge of her desk hard, and she inhales sharply.

"Miss Vaughn?" Ms. Sterling asks from the front of the room. "Do you have the answer for number twelve?"

Astra looks up, feeling like a deer stuck in headlights. She glances down at the question, but it looks just as squiggly as it did a minute ago.

"Um. B?"

"Nice work, Miss Vaughn."

Astra lets out a long breath and glances back at Isla, who has settled in on top of the unoccupied desk to her left. She's got her legs crossed like a pretzel, and she's grinning so broadly that all Astra can see from the side is teeth and a dimple.

"I don't want to say *I told you so*, but..."

You've taken this class before, obviously, Astra writes, even though that doesn't explain anything. Astra is taking this class *right now*, and she still couldn't have figured out the answer without looking up equations in the book and writing out all of the steps. There's no way Isla could do all of that in her head.

Isla shrugs. "Technically, no." She floats up and down, her feet flickering. "Not *this* class. Maybe I'm just super smart. I died at a quiz bowl competition, you know."

You did not.

"Yep. There I was, about to ring in on the last question—you know, the big one, the one worth *just* enough points to win the game—and the buzzer short-circuited right when I slammed my hand down on it. One big zap, and here I am."

Astra truly, honestly believes her. For all of the five seconds it takes for Isla to burst into laughter.

Not funny, Astra writes.

"A little funny. Come on. If I can't laugh about my own death, then the afterlife is a pretty miserable existence, don't you think?"

Astra has never thought about it before. Sure, George McCreary had joked with her about his body being found in a ravine, but he hadn't laughed. She's pretty sure there's a difference between accepting your own death and finding joy in it, but she's not dead. So it's really none of her business.

She tries to ignore Isla's noise and instead looks back at her worksheet. She circles *B* on number twelve. At least she's got one of them right. One out of ten is good enough to pass, right?

Isla lets out one last raspy chuckle and leans over until her knee passes through the empty desk. "You know, I can figure out the rest of those for you. It's the least I can do, since you've agreed to help me with my stuff."

Astra frowns. *I don't cheat.*

"Right. You just suck at math." Isla kicks out her legs and one of them disappears for a few seconds. She shakes it and it flickers back. "I can help you. Totally legit. No answers, just good, solid math. Hard work, and all that. I'm good at science stuff too, if you're awful at that as well."

At the front of the room, the teacher has written out the answers to two other problems. Astra quickly copies them down and promises herself that she'll figure out the steps later. The clock ticks loudly from above the door; Astra can hear it more clearly in this room because her desk is closest to the door, and it doesn't help that Isla is giving off static sounds from just a few inches away.

Astra squares off her notebook again and lines her pencil up along the side.

She could maybe use a little help with her homework. But only a little.

It's not that Astra is dumb. But it's hard to focus when she's only gotten a few hours of not-so-restful sleep, and it's hard to do homework at the desk in her room when the ghosts outside her window won't leave her alone. Headphones can only help with the noise, not the static and the cold. But she can't do her work in the living room, because the walls are red, and red is too loud. Blue is a little better, but the kitchen is messy, and there's never enough free space for her to spread out all of her books and notebooks and worksheets.

Plus, most of the time her mom is home, and Maria Vaughn is just as distracting as any ghost. Astra has to spend half of her time making sure her mom doesn't burn their apartment to the ground—how is she supposed to worry about her math work at the same time?

And now she has a ghost living with her. Her own personal haunting, twenty-four seven. She'll be lucky if she even manages to graduate high school.

Fine, she writes, shoving the note over the side of the desk so Isla can read it. *But you're explaining everything. I need to pass my tests too, you know.*

Isla's dimples deepen and she jumps up into the air, doing loops of the classroom so fast that a stack of papers on the teacher's desk topples over. Ms. Sterling looks around wildly, gathering up a mess of quizzes and piling them up in a crumpled heap.

Astra smiles, but she hides it behind her sweater sleeve.

Spanish and biology pass in much the same way as math. Isla is some kind of genius, which is especially unfair because she's a whole year younger than Astra, which means she probably hasn't even taken most of these classes yet. Unless she went to some kind of elite boarding school. But Astra finds that kind of hard to believe.

Especially when she spends most of the day swimming laps around the room, ducking in and out of windows like she's in an agility competition, and just being generally annoying.

Lunch is fine, though. Mostly because Isla goes off to check on her brother and leaves Astra alone for the first time all day. And Astra absolutely does not try to follow her with her eyes on her way through the cafeteria doors. She has no interest in knowing who Isla's brother is. Or why he goes to this school, but Isla doesn't. Or why Isla chooses to spend her nights in Astra's mom's store instead of with her own family.

Astra doesn't want to know. So she doesn't look. And lunch passes by as normally as it always has.

Phys ed, on the other hand, is a little different.

The trouble comes in three parts, which is especially annoying because three is too round a number. But maybe that's fitting, because Astra dislikes the number three, and she dislikes PE. Especially today.

Part one: dodgeball. Sure, Astra isn't the least athletic person in her class—she's not thin and fast and wiry like Oliver, but she can run just fine, and her coordination is actually pretty good. Maybe it's from navigating her way around her messy, too-small apartment for four years, hopping over cardboard boxes and dodging stacks of magazines in the hallway.

But dodgeball is possibly her *least* favorite thing, and Astra is literally haunted by ghosts every day.

Part two: Isla. She's determined, for some reason, to make Astra crack up today. It's easy enough to ignore her when they're in a classroom and Astra is sitting comfortably with nothing better to do than focus on tuning her out. But when she's trying to dodge dozens of flying rubber balls? Her guard is down, and Isla knows it.

Plus, Astra can't exactly keep her notebook with her in the gym. It's taking everything she has not to verbally respond to Isla's taunting, because if she did, then she would basically be talking to thin air. That's what got her mom branded as a crazy person in their old city, and Astra is trying her very best to prove that she isn't like her mom. Even though, in this case, the problem is that she is.

Part three: Oliver. Three is a tricky number, and Oliver is a tricky factor in this particular scenario. On the one hand, Astra likes having a maybe, possible friend. On the other hand, she really wishes he could be her friend somewhere else—literally anywhere other than in the same gym where she's currently being haunted by an annoyingly cheerful teenage ghost.

Currently, Isla is standing on Astra's right and dodging balls that would just go through her if she stood still. She's actually pretty good at it, but her constant ducking and jumping is making Astra dizzy.

"Hey, check it out," Isla says, swatting at a stray ball with her palm and managing to do…absolutely nothing.

Astra rolls her eyes and bites down on the inside of her cheek to keep from speaking. A ball comes flying at her and she steps to the side just fast enough to avoid being hit—and just happens to accidentally bump into Oliver in the process.

"Hi," he says, grinning down at her with a ball in his hands. She has to crane her neck to look up at him. It's like staring up the trunk of a really tall tree—like those ones, with the national park named after them, but Astra can't remember what they're called. She's pretty sure Isla would know.

"Hi." Astra takes a step back so she's mostly hidden behind one of Oliver's long, gangly arms. It's technically not cheating. "I think I owe you some kind of explanation."

Oliver shrugs and whips his ball across the dividing line, marked in dark blue tape on the gym floor. He looks different when he's in his gym uniform. The shorts make his legs look even longer, his knees knobby and bruised and almost sharp compared to the rest of him. His worn, baggy brown jacket seems to make him look a little more filled-out, because without it, he's just a noodle. A noodle with arms and legs.

The only difference between Astra with her uniform on and Astra without it is that the shirt has short sleeves and the shorts end just above her knees, and all of that exposed skin *plus* a roaming ghost in the room makes her feel even colder than usual. She's pretty sure that if she stopped moving, everyone would be able to see the goose bumps up and down both of her arms. So she makes sure she doesn't stop moving.

Oliver stretches one of his long, noodle arms out to the side and catches a ball midair. Astra ducks down to avoid another one, and out of the corner of her eye she can see Isla doing cartwheels between some of her classmates.

"You don't have to tell me anything you don't want to," Oliver says, and Astra sighs.

"Good. That's good. Because I really don't have a good explanation for my weird behavior. My weirdness. I guess that's just…me."

"I like weirdness," he says. "Obviously."

She blinks up at him. His long, dark hair is sticking to the sides of his neck, and his shiny nose hoop catches the light when he moves. He's wearing earrings today—little silver arrows that she probably wouldn't have noticed had his hair not been pushed back from his ears.

She wonders about him sometimes—wonders if he's like her. Not the ghost thing, obviously, because Isla is doing flips to avoid red rubber balls, and if anyone else could see ghosts besides her, they would *definitely* be distracted right now. But Oliver doesn't turn around once.

Astra shouldn't assume things about people. She should know better. But Astra has a feeling they have something in common besides just English and PE.

Isla floats over, narrowly missing a ball that would otherwise have gone through her stomach. "Who do you think is taller—me or pretty-boy?"

Astra nearly jumps, but she doesn't. She's getting better at that.

"I don't know," she whispers, turning her head so Oliver can't hear. "Why don't you ask him yourself?"

Isla grins. "Hey, Ollie!" she shouts. If ghosts could echo, her voice would be bouncing off the walls right now. "How tall are you?"

Part of Astra actually expects Oliver to react. After all, how could he not? She was so *loud*. It's hard to believe that nobody else could hear her.

"Please keep it down," Astra mutters. Oliver glances back at her, juggling a ball between his hands.

"Did you say something?"

"Nope. Just...talking to myself. Told you I was weird. There's your proof."

She cringes hard when he shrugs and turns away again. That sounded so stupid.

"Just tell him," Isla says. A stray ball shoots through her right shoulder.

"No. I'm not bringing anybody else into my mess."

Isla gasps theatrically. "I'm offended. Ollie would be *lucky* to get to know me."

"You're invisible."

"So?"

"So, I'm talking to myself, and that's *not normal*."

The squeaking of sneakers on the polished wooden floor and the sound of rubber balls bouncing is giving Astra a headache. Plus, the walls of the gym are painted candy-apple red, the same color as her shorts and the shorts all around her. It makes sense that red is the color usually associated with anger, because Astra can feel her pulse rising.

"It doesn't matter if it's normal. It's cool. Doesn't every kid wish they had psychic powers?"

"Not psychic," Astra hisses between her teeth. She jumps behind Oliver to avoid getting hit, and he shoots her an odd backward glance.

Astra's head is throbbing. It feels like every ball she hears thudding on the floor around her is actually smashing right into the middle of her forehead. *Thud*, throb, *thud*, throb.

She rubs at her temple and tries to pay attention to her surroundings. Isla continues. "It's close enough. He probably would think it's cool. Maybe you could—"

"Please stop talking," Astra interrupts, whirling around to look at her, the words tearing out of her throat a little louder than she intends. Loud enough for people to hear. One person in particular.

She shuts her mouth so fast her teeth click together and turns around just in time to get hit solidly in the chest by a hard, dizzyingly loud rubber ball.

She closes her eyes. She braces for the hit, but it doesn't come. When she blinks her eyes open, she sees Oliver, holding his right arm out as far as it can go and gripping a ball in his outstretched hand. His arm is shaking, and when he drops the ball there's a large red welt on his palm.

Nobody else seems to notice, thankfully. But Oliver definitely heard her, because he barely takes his eyes off her the rest of class. Isla floats around the ceiling, looking a little dejected, and Astra can't help but feel guilty.

Oliver stops her on the way to the locker rooms after all of the balls have been put away, his noodle arms blocking her path.

"I think I'll cash in on that explanation you owe me."

Astra can only nod.

CHAPTER SEVEN

Astra sweeps a pile of junk mail off the kitchen counter and into the garbage can, which is already overflowing.

"This isn't going to work," she says. "He's not going to believe me. Why would he? *I* wouldn't even believe me. I could be out of my mind. You might not even be here right now."

Isla yawns even though she doesn't have lungs and flicks her index finger at a small jar of nutmeg on the countertop. The jar teeters on its edge for a moment, but doesn't fall.

"Okay. So, you're talking to yourself. You want me to leave?"

"No!" Astra says quickly. "He *definitely* won't believe me then. Plus, this whole thing was kind of your idea. Not even kind of. It was your idea."

She reaches around Isla and tucks the jar of nutmeg back into the cabinet next to the other spices—which have been rearranged twice by her mom in the last week. Isla jumps up onto the counter and tries to close the cabinet, but it only creaks halfway shut before stopping.

Astra pauses with the bowl of Styrofoam pears in her hands. "Hey. Why are you so set on him knowing, anyway? Why do you care?"

Isla shrugs. "I thought you guys were friends."

"We are—maybe. I don't know." Astra moves the pears to the top of the fridge and shuts the cabinet the rest of the way. "Wait. He's not… your brother, is he?"

"No! No." Isla pulls a face. "I just think…you deserve to have someone believe you."

Astra waits for the punchline. It doesn't come. For once, Isla is eerily serious.

"Well. Um, thanks. If this works out, then I'll owe you one."

"Don't worry about it," Isla says. Her legs are dangling over the edge of the counter, but she's sitting on air. "You've still got to help me out with my bucket list. So we'll call it even."

"Anti-bucket list," Astra corrects. She'd almost forgotten about it. Isla grins. "Right. I've got the first one all figured out. I think you're gonna like it."

The countertop is speckled in just the right way to make it nearly impossible for Astra to tell what's crumbs and what's not, so she scrubs at the whole thing twice with a dish rag just in case.

"It doesn't matter if I like it or not. It's not *my* list."

Isla kicks her feet out. Her polka-dot socks are just as pristine as the rest of her outfit. "I want you to have fun, too," she says.

Astra's chest feels a little tight. It's probably just from scrubbing too hard. She's warm all over, too, which is odd. She's standing a foot away from a ghost, and she's *warm*.

For just a second, something settles in her stomach—something warm and light that makes her feel a little nauseous. But before she can figure out if the burrito she ate for lunch was poisoned, Isla throws out her foot and sinks it toe-deep into Astra's shoulder.

"Want to know a fun fact about flowers?" Isla asks, a lilt in her voice. "Of course you do. Did you know that apples are related to roses?"

"*Why* would I know that?"

"Because it's a fun fact. There are other fruits too, I think, but I can't remember them all. Remind me to look them up once I can figure out how to turn the pages in those flower books."

"Noted."

There's a knock—one, two, three—on the front door. Fast and loud. And *way* too soon.

Astra spins around, and even though she's managed to somehow clear a decent amount of counter space, the kitchen still looks messy. She could probably clean all day and it still wouldn't be enough. Plus, she hasn't even made it into the living room yet. There are throw pillows covering the entire couch, papers and old receipts and dirty cups on the coffee table, and the TV is streaky and hung up at just the wrong angle on the wall, so no matter where Astra is she has to crane her neck to watch it.

She just has to hope that Oliver stays in her room. That's all.

"Go get 'em, tiger," Isla says, pushing at Astra's back with her icy fingers. Astra can feel a tiny amount of pressure, followed quickly by frost under her skin.

When she opens the front door—left hand, left foot, four quick turns—Oliver is standing on the mat with his fist raised halfway. He drops his hand and awkwardly jiggles one leg.

"Hey," he says. Astra counts five patches going down the forearm of his right sleeve. She spots a car, a tiny green cactus, and a little rocket ship with flames coming out of the bottom. Oliver steps inside and closes the door behind him. He doesn't even look at his feet once.

Before she can tell him not to, Oliver walks past her down the hallway and starts looking around. Isla is watching him from the counter, swinging her feet through a chair.

Oliver picks up a throw pillow like he intends to sit on the couch, and Astra quickly rushes to pull him away.

"I should show you my room," she says. "Let's just go to my room."

There's just one fairly huge problem with bringing Oliver to her room: Astra has never had another person in her room before, besides her mom. Another *living* person, that is. A person who could tell other people what a weirdo she is if her plan doesn't work.

This is a bad idea.

Oliver walks around her room with his hands clasped behind his back. He kneels down, hums into her bookcase, and then straightens back up again. Astra shoves a dirty sweater underneath her bed and makes a lumpy pile out of her homework on top of her desk.

When he turns back to her, she immediately wants to defend her room, her apartment, her *mess*, but she bites her tongue. Isla floats through the door and settles on the clean side of her desk.

"Hmm. I like your wallpaper."

Astra blinks. "That's…it?"

"Um, the frog pictures are nice? What am I supposed to say?"

"It's a mess. My mom is—" She cuts herself off. "I'm embarrassed, I guess."

Oliver shrugs one shoulder, and a little palm tree patch waves. "I've got five siblings, so…"

"So."

Isla chuckles. "So eloquent."

Astra ignores her and sits on the edge of her bed. Oliver perches himself on the other end, his legs so long that his feet touch the floor. He scoots back until he can swing them, and starts jiggling one foot like it's fallen asleep.

The silence in the room feels charged, like static. Like if she moves too quickly, Astra will get shocked. She's pretty sure that friends aren't supposed to be this awkward around each other, but she hasn't had a friend in years, so she can't be sure. Her words feel heavy on her tongue, and she waits for Oliver to say something first, but he just sits there wiggling his leg. It's making her anxious.

"Okay," she says, breaking up some of the thick silence with her breath. "I need to tell you something, but you have to promise not to laugh. Or freak out, or do *anything*. I want literally no reaction out of you. All right?"

"That's a tall order," Isla comments, and Astra shoots her a sideways glance that shuts her right up.

Oliver just nods.

"Okay." Astra takes a deep breath. "Okay. So, you've heard of people who can see ghosts, right?"

Oliver blinks, and for just a moment his leg stops moving. "You mean like psychics?"

From behind her, Isla snickers.

"No! Not psychics. Or, ugh, okay. Sure. Call them whatever you want, the point is, they're real. Like, legit. Not just in movies and stuff."

"O-kay?" Oliver asks, drawing the word out like a question. "And…?"

And nothing! Astra wants to say. *This was all just a joke, obviously. I've got a hidden camera and everything. I got you good, though, didn't I?*

"And that's me," she says instead. "I'm like that. There was a ghost in gym class. And English. And right behind me on my desk, right now."

She can't tell what emotion is on Oliver's face right now, but it's not happiness. His leg taps one last time against Astra's mattress before it goes completely still.

Psych! You're on candid camera. Smile!

"You're…serious."

Astra nods. Oliver holds up one hand, palm out.

"You're gonna need to give me a minute. That's, um…a lot."

Isla pushes herself off the desk and walks through the air, stopping at Astra's side. "My turn?"

"No," Astra says. "Give him a little time first."

Oliver looks up. "What?"

"Not you." She points her thumb in Isla's direction. "Ghost. Right there."

Even though his face has gone pale and he looks kind of like he's going through the five stages of grief all at once, Astra is impressed with how well Oliver is taking this. Unless he doesn't believe her. She wouldn't be surprised if he didn't.

But that's why Isla is here.

"Okay, sure. Yep." Oliver nods, and then he looks like he can't *stop* nodding once he's started. "A ghost. Ghosts are real? Sure. Um, is it—I'm not, like, an asshole if I'm a little…*skeptical*, right?"

Oh God, he doesn't believe me, Astra thinks. *Why did I ever let myself think that this would work?*

"My turn?"

Astra shakes her head. "Not yet."

"What?"

"*Ghost.*" Astra is starting to feel clammy and a little sweaty. Her hair is growing too long in the back, and the few stray curls along her neck make her skin feel itchy. If she had a pair of clippers in her hands right now, she would be tempted to just shave the whole thing off. "It's a lot, I know. You're totally right to think I look like a basket case right now. But I have proof."

"Proof?"

"Yeah. I can show you if you want. Same promise as before."

He nods and jiggles his foot against the mattress. "Okay."

"My turn!"

Isla throws herself across the room in one fluid motion and stops, legs curled and palms pressing down on the air, on the other side of the bed next to Oliver. She takes a deep, lung-less breath, and then blows it out at his ear so hard that his hair goes flying around his face.

Oliver *jumps*. He kind of reminds Astra of a cat getting spooked, the way his whole body leaves the mattress for a split second, and she bites back a laugh. Because this is supposed to be a serious moment. Probably.

"What was *that*?" he hisses between his teeth. Like a cat.

Astra shrugs and tries to look calmer than she feels. "A ghost. I thought I already told you that?"

Isla blows on his hair again and then crosses the room to the window. She huffs a cold breath at the curtains and they whirl around. It takes Oliver a minute to notice, and Astra can see on his face the moment he realizes that the window is closed.

"That's, um. Pretty decent proof."

Isla grins and blows the stack of papers on Astra's desk to the ground. Astra rolls her eyes.

"I had those all cleaned up, you know."

"Just one more thing," Isla insists. She tiptoes around the desk, stepping like she's walking on air, and then hovers next to Astra's dresser. She holds up her hand and closes her eyes, and swipes at one of Astra's candles—a dull red one that smells like a cross between cherries and rubbing alcohol. Her hand goes right through it and she curses under her breath.

"It's fine," Astra tells her. "I think he got the picture."

Isla glances over at Oliver, who's now jiggling *both* of his legs against the side of the bed. Astra's just glad he hasn't run out of her apartment screaming by now.

"No, no. I've got this. We need a good grand finale."

"Okay. If you think you can do it."

"Is that a *challenge*?" Isla's dimples pop and she taps her finger on the outside of the candle. It makes a tinny, clinking noise when she makes contact. Oliver spins around in the direction of the sound, and Astra pictures a cat with its tail all bushed out.

It takes a few tries, but eventually Isla manages to move the candle. Just an inch, maybe less, and she's nowhere near knocking it to the floor, but she still smiles broadly like she's just moved the whole dresser. It must be contagious, because even though Astra is still worried about Oliver's reaction, she can't help but smile back at her.

She turns back to Oliver. "Do you believe me now?"

He nods and swallows audibly. "That's pretty solid proof. Is it, um…always here? The ghost?"

Isla sticks her tongue out at him from across the room.

"*She*," Astra corrects. "Her name's Isla. She's sixteen and *annoyingly* clingy sometimes."

"Sixteen," he repeats quietly. "Does it ever get…weird? Having a ghost around you all the time? No offense, um, Isla."

"I'm offended by both of you right now, actually."

Astra ignores her. "Not really. Sometimes it's nice to have the company. And I'm used to it. I've never *not* seen ghosts, you know?"

"That's kind of cool, actually."

Astra's face feels warm. Oliver has finally started to calm down, lazily tapping one foot on the mattress again, and the relief that washes over Astra is like a warm blanket over her shoulders. He didn't freak out. He didn't leave.

Astra finally managed to get just a little bit of this massive weight off her chest, and the world didn't explode.

From across the room, Isla crosses her arms, looking smug. "Told you so."

❖

Astra can smell something burning, and this time it isn't toast.

She sets down her pencil, squares it off quickly, and leaves her room, left foot first. There are twelve steps to the kitchen from her bedroom.

Her mom is wearing a pastel blue dress today, made out of some kind of shiny material with gems around the collar. It's pretty, maybe a little too muted for her style, but the deep purple blazer she's wearing over it makes her look like a child. Her wrists are covered in noisy bangles, her earrings are so large and heavy that they pull down on her ears, and it looks like she tried to pull her hair back out of her face with clips, but at some point they must have come loose because they're all over the place and one of them is hanging limply over her shoulder.

She's got oven mitts on both of her hands—they don't match, because nothing in this apartment matches—and Astra would be willing to bet her life's savings that the smoke alarm is seconds from being set off.

And her mom is just bustling around the kitchen, looking lost, while whatever is in the oven burns to a crisp.

Astra's chest tightens. She breathes around it, takes four long strides into the kitchen, and quickly shuts off the oven. There's no smoke for once, which is good, but the smell of charred meat makes her eyes water.

After a minute, she opens the oven door and waves away a small furl of smoke with her hand. The motion seems to snap her mom out of her trance, because she pushes past Astra and fumbles to pull a pan of something black and crispy off the rack. She throws it onto the counter, and the thud makes Astra flinch.

"I got home from work late," her mom says, like that explains everything. "I was in a hurry. I just wanted to have a nice dinner together, like we used to."

Astra wants to tell her that a nice dinner isn't necessarily a frozen meal eaten on a sunken-in couch surrounded by throw pillows and magazines and old grocery receipts, but she doesn't. Mostly because her mom looks like she's on the verge of crying.

"That's okay. I don't even like, um, lasagna that much anyway."

She's pretty sure that the burnt brick in the pan is lasagna. She hopes it is, anyway.

Her mom gives a watery laugh. The bangles on her wrists jingle like bells.

Astra doesn't like seeing her mom upset. She changes the subject without thinking. "So, I made a friend. I think."

She kind of regrets it the moment the words leave her mouth, because she doesn't even know if Oliver really even *is* her friend. Technically, they did hang out after school, which is something friends do. Just Astra, her new friend, and the ghost that's haunting her.

Perfectly normal seventeen-year-old girl stuff.

Her mom sniffles and slides her oven mitts off. "A friend?"

"Yeah." Astra nods. "He's in my English class. His name is Oliver. He's the one I went to the library with the other day."

Her mom seems to perk up a little bit. "What's he like?"

The kitchen is starting to smell a little less like smoke. It's still warm, though—almost stifling, but the heat is a welcome change from being cold all of the time.

Astra smiles. She reaches past the bowl of Styrofoam pears that have somehow found their way back onto the counter and grabs her mom's phone.

"Tell you what," she says, handing the phone to her mom. "You order pizza, I'll get the living room cleaned up, and when the food gets here I'll tell you all about him."

The excitement on her mom's face makes every bit of anxiety worth it.

Chapter Eight

A stra grips the steering wheel so tightly that the joints in her fingers crack. She's been driving blindly for half an hour already, and she's starting to sweat.

"Can you at least tell me where we're going?"

Isla shakes her head. "Nope. That would ruin the surprise."

"The surprise," Astra repeats slowly. "Your weird, undead bucket list is a surprise."

"Yep."

The car hits a bump in the road and Isla's head goes through the roof. Astra eases on the brakes and tries to keep her eyes on the road.

"You need to sit down, or I'm gonna crash."

"I *can't* sit," Isla says. "I'll just go through the seat like last time."

"Then grab onto the door. Or, I don't know, just—you're distracting. Try to be less distracting. Please."

Out of the corner of her eyes, she can see Isla's eyebrows wiggle. She leans over the center console and grabs onto the edge of the cup holder to keep from slipping out of the window when Astra steers the car around a curve.

"I'm distracting, huh?"

Astra keeps her eyes on the road. Mostly. She looks around for anything that could even *remotely* be on a teenager's bucket list, but all she sees are abandoned barns and the occasional lonely gas station.

"How much farther is it?" she asks. A new speed limit sign appears on her right and she tentatively presses her foot on the gas pedal. "Because I have homework, you know."

Isla rolls her eyes. "My undead bucket list takes precedence over your math problems. Plus, we're here. So you can stop complaining any minute now."

"I was *not* complaining, I was just—"

"*Any minute now*," Isla interrupts. Astra clamps her mouth shut and glances around.

As far as she can tell, they're in the middle of nowhere. They're still in the city, technically, but they passed the last house twenty minutes ago and the last business just before they got on the highway. And now, half an hour later, here they are.

Where are they?

There's a tiny gravel parking lot on the left side of the road, and Astra steers into it slowly. The tires kick up rocks and the noise makes her head pound.

Isla phases through the car door, her legs shifting at odd angles on the other side, and Astra parks the car and follows her, left foot first. She spins the keys around her finger, counts eight steps between the car and the end of the parking lot, and traces Isla's gaze to a lone building, stretched long and curved on top with a roof made of glass, out here in the middle of nowhere.

It's a greenhouse. Of course it is.

Isla's smile couldn't possibly get any wider. Astra has a million questions on the tip of her tongue, but she swallows them down and follows her over a patch of dry grass and down another, smaller gravel walkway. Isla cycles her legs like she's riding a bike, or maybe jogging in place, but every so often one of her feet gets stuck and takes a moment to realign itself. She shakes it out the same way Oliver jiggled his foot on her mattress, and Astra wonders if she can feel it when her body shifts like that. If it hurts.

A bell chimes when she opens the door, lower and softer than the one in her mom's store. Isla floats through the wall and immediately veers off to the right, but Astra takes her time to look around.

The building looks like it's divided into two parts—the front is a small, wooden-walled room filled with planting tools, seeds, garden flags, and fancy gift items that make her mom's shop look like a thrift store. Which, it kind of *is*, honestly.

Astra picks up a trowel painted blue with yellow swirls all around it. There are matching gardening gloves next to it, and on the other side of the table is a cluster of ceramic garden gnomes with glossy hats and decorative flowers in their hands. Astra sees one holding a shiny yellow tulip and she looks around for Isla, but she's in the other room, hovering over a row of potted plants.

The back section of the building is like what Astra always pictures when she hears the word *greenhouse*. The walls and ceiling are all glass, but the walls are more opaque and less glossy than the ceiling tiles. The room is long and low, and seems to stretch on forever in one direction. Astra has never seen this many plants in one place before, not even in the supermarket during peak gardening season.

There are long rows of flowers in every color of the rainbow, tables full of edible plants just starting to bloom, and prickly cacti that remind Astra of the patch on Oliver's jacket. Her eyes pass over miniature herb gardens, decorative clay pots filled with trailing succulents, and hanging baskets dangling down from metal bars overhead.

A middle-aged woman with gray-blond hair tied back in a bun is watering the plants at the far end of the first row. She greets Astra with a wave.

"Need help with anything, my dear?" she says. Her voice is low and scratchy like sandpaper. Astra shakes her head quickly.

"Just looking around, thanks."

"Hi, Mrs. Reeves," Isla says softly, more to herself than anyone else. The woman doesn't even look up, and Isla's smile flickers for just a moment.

Astra worries that she won't be able to talk to Isla with someone else in the room, but Mrs. Reeves hangs up her hose a minute later and walks down the middle aisle and back into the front room that Astra had just been in. Astra notices that she's got a limp in her right leg, and she's wearing an apron with little daisies embroidered into the bottom hem.

Astra joins Isla next to a table filled with colorful flowers, and Isla's smile slots back into place, dimples and all.

She points down at a pot with white flowers in it, their petals open and curling outward delicately. Astra recognizes them, but she doesn't know enough about plants to name them.

"Lilies," Isla says, like she's just read her mind. "I said I would tell you next time, and now it's next time, so there's my answer."

Astra's brain is foggy and filled with static even on a good day, so it takes her a painfully long time to figure out what Isla is talking about—and then she remembers. Isla's favorite flower.

It's lilies.

It makes so much sense, Astra thinks. The pretty little flowers with their dainty curls. They suit Isla like they were made for her.

Isla floats down the row and stops next to another cluster of flowers, one that Astra actually knows the name of.

Isla waves her hand around the table. "Tulips. Your favorite, right?"

Astra nods. She runs her fingers over the pale yellow petals of the nearest flower. They feel like satin and make her the kind of nostalgic that churns in her stomach uncomfortably.

The ceiling tiles seem to magnify the sunlight, and even with a ghost right next to her Astra feels hot.

She clears her throat. "Well, I guess it wouldn't be a proper greenhouse visit if I didn't learn something about the plants, right?"

Isla's smile, it turns out, *can* get bigger. It's all teeth now—shiny, pointy canines and deep, deep dimples. She flies around the table, grazing her feet on one of the support beams in the middle of the room, and drops down on the other side of a tiny herb garden. Astra scrambles to follow her.

"That one's rosemary," Isla says, pointing to a plant that looks a little like the branches of a pine tree, with pointed leaves instead of needles. "Smell it."

Astra raises her eyebrow but does as she's told. This is Isla's bucket list, after all, not hers.

"I'm pretty sure my mom has a jar of this in the kitchen some-where."

Isla shrugs. "Probably. I just like the smell." She continues pointing, floating lazily down the table. "That's mint, obviously. The best kind of ice cream—and don't you dare argue with me on that one. Basil, um…Good in pasta. I don't really know a lot about herbs. They're not really flowers, you know? Oh! But that one's cilantro. It's supposed to taste like citrus to some people, and soap to others."

Astra hums along, only mildly interested in learning about plants. Really, she just likes seeing the face Isla makes when she talks about them. She probably doesn't even realize she's doing it, but her eyes stop being so dull, and her mouth turns up just a little bit more on the right side than the left, and one of her dimples sits *just right* next to a couple of freckles that make it look like a tiny smiley-face on her cheek.

Astra's neck feels unbearably sweaty, and she tugs at the collar of her shirt as she follows Isla down the aisle.

"Daisies, dahlias. Um, gardenias. I think they're supposed to be good luck." She runs her fingers over the plants and every so often manages to actually touch one. The petals bend and spring back up, and Isla's eyes look extra shiny. "Morning glories. They're, like, a symbol of mortality, I think. The flowers only bloom for one day and then they fall off. It's…kind of sad, actually."

Astra picks up a plastic container with purple flowers in it. The petals are long and dense, and the flowers look like puffy cotton balls stuck together. Drops of water fall off them as she turns the container over in her hands, watching the colors shift from dark purple to pink around the edges.

"What about these?"

"Chrysanthemums," Isla says quickly. She doesn't even need time to think about it. "I think I told you about those. They mean—"

"Life and death," Astra finishes. "I remember. I didn't think they would be this pretty."

Isla rolls over onto her back in the air and floats like she's on an inflatable beach raft. She folds her arms up behind her head and crosses her legs, and her hair hangs down loose and wavy, disappearing into the tops of the succulents on the end of the table.

Her pink earrings shine in the sunlight. Astra tries to match them up to one of the flowers nearby, but none of them look quite the same.

"Maybe death isn't always ugly," Isla says to the ceiling.

Astra looks at the girl, floating in an invisible swimming pool with her hair trailing down underneath her, with her pretty yellow sundress, her mismatched red and black flannel jacket, and her polka-dot socks without shoes on top. The little, jagged birthmark on her right leg. She's got her eyes closed. She looks like she could be sleeping.

"Yeah," Astra agrees after a moment. "Maybe you're right."

There's a tiny patch of shade next to the cactus table, created by hanging pots and rolled-up hoses overhead. Astra sits down on the cool concrete, following a trailing succulent's path down the side of its pot with her eyes. She waits patiently for another plant fact, but Isla seems to have run out of them. She's surprisingly quiet for once. Astra can hear the water dripping out of the end of the hose behind her.

Astra wishes she had brought her headphones. Sometimes the quiet is just as bad as the noise.

She counts fourteen drips before she breaks the silence.

"Maybe it's not my place to ask," she says, "but why did you pick a greenhouse for your first bucket list item?"

Isla turns her head and opens one eye. "Anti-bucket list."

"I'm being serious."

"So am I. I'm *dead*." She rolls over onto her stomach. She looks like she could be suntanning if she wasn't wearing a thick flannel jacket and socks. Her shoulders jerk and flicker in a half shrug. "I came here a lot as a kid. Practically every day. Kind of a big part of why I'm such a plant nerd now."

"That's why you knew the lady's name."

Isla nods. "Mrs. Reeves. Her hair wasn't so gray the last time I saw her. She would give me clippings from the flowers she was trimming, and I pressed them and dried them and saved them in this one book I got for my birthday, with clear pockets in the pages so they wouldn't fall out. I would label them and look up facts and write them down next to the names. I've got...I don't know, a photographic memory? Maybe? But I remember all of them. Even if I haven't been back here in a while."

Astra is torn, again, between wanting to ask and not wanting to know. She should be better at this by now. She's met more ghosts than she can count, and she's never had a problem drawing a line between the living and the dead before. Maybe it's because Isla doesn't *look* dead that Astra's brain gets confused, because she's not sure when she gave it permission to start asking questions.

"Why haven't you been back here?" she asks, even though she doesn't want to know.

"Just haven't had time. School, homework, being super popular with lots of awesome friends, going to parties every weekend. Not a lot of free time, you know?"

Astra chuckles and gestures vaguely at herself. "Obviously."

"Nah. Ollie probably goes to parties on weekends. You should ask him to bring you along next time."

"We've got bucket list stuff on the weekends, though," Astra says automatically.

"Oh." Isla pauses. "Yeah, you're right."

Her lilt flattens out, and Astra can feel the words she's not saying bouncing around in the air. *We won't always. Because when we're done, I'll be gone.*

"Daffodil bulbs are poisonous," Isla says suddenly.

Astra looks up, squinting into the sunlight. "What?"

"That's the real reason I haven't been here in so long. Last time I was, I ate a daffodil bulb, and I *died*. Kind of ruins the nostalgia a little bit, don't you think?"

"Oh, you are so *full of shit*."

Isla giggles and makes circles in the air with her arms. "Yeah. I know."

"And you're deflecting."

Her eyes widen comically. "No way, really?"

"And," Astra continues, "you're gonna need to help me pick a plant to buy, because I have no idea what any of these are, and I don't want to accidentally buy a *bad luck* flower or something."

❖

Mrs. Reeves is arranging cut flowers into vases when Astra steps up to the counter with her crinkly plastic container. It feels so small in her hands, and the little red flower inside feels even smaller.

Isla had laughed when she picked out the withered little geranium. Apparently, it's meant to symbolize *good health*. It had taken nearly five minutes to calm Isla down after Astra held up the black plastic pot and asked if it seemed like a good fit.

"For you, yeah. Me? Not so much."

Isla is waiting in the car while Astra pays. Astra's eyes catch on a streak of gray hair that's fallen out of Mrs. Reeves's bun and she's pretty sure she can guess why Isla didn't want to stay.

Astra picks out a pot from a display near the counter. It's nearly the same shade of purple as her bedroom, and the soft color takes away a little bit of the noise coming from the bright red flower. She chooses one that's slightly larger than the crinkly plastic cup, with a plate underneath to catch excess water. And plenty of room to grow.

"Excellent choice, my dear," Mrs. Reeves says when Astra hands her the plant. "Geraniums are good insect repellants, did you know? I always keep a few by my window in the summer. Works like a charm." Astra smiles. Mrs. Reeves reminds her of Isla, and she can't help but picture Isla as a child, running between the long rows of plants and excitedly pointing out the ones she recognizes. The thought nearly makes her laugh, until it settles somewhere between her ribs and makes her heart ache instead.

She shouldn't ask. She knows better.

But her brain forms the question without her permission. "Ma'am, did you ever know a girl named Isla? Tall, blond, maybe a little overenthusiastic about flowers?"

The lines around Mrs. Reeves's eyes soften, and when she smiles she looks ten years younger.

She steps around the counter and reaches for a half-full bag of potting soil on top of a cart nearby. Part of it has spilled out, and she scoops it back in with her hands before grabbing a trowel—the same kind Astra had looked at earlier, but with red swirls of paint instead of yellow.

The black plastic container protests loudly as Mrs. Reeves wiggles the tiny flower's roots and dirt out of it. Astra tries not to flinch.

"I remember Miss Isla, certainly," she begins, so long after the initial question that Astra had started to think that she'd forgotten. "Always moving, that girl. I remember the first time she came here— she accidentally knocked over a tray of petunias and threw a fit because she thought she'd killed them all."

Astra bites her lip and nods. She doesn't trust herself to say anything right now.

Mrs. Reeves gently tucks the geranium's roots into the purple pot and starts filling it with soil. The red flower looks so tiny in such a large pot.

"She didn't, of course," Mrs. Reeves continues. "Just one. She stepped on the poor thing and wailed until I told her she could keep it. Press it in a book, if she'd like. Of course, I never found out if she actually did. But I like to think so."

"She did," Astra blurts out. Mrs. Reeves finally looks up at her. There's dirt under her fingernails and a smudge of it on her cheek.

"Were you friends?"

Astra's chest feels tight. She wishes she had just kept her mouth shut.

"Yeah," she says instead. "She told me about her flower collection. That you would give her clippings. And she remembered everything you told her about them."

Mrs. Reeves chuckles under her breath. "That sounds like her. That girl really loved her flowers."

Astra nods silently. She watches Mrs. Reeves scoop one last trowel-full of soil into the pot, and then press it down lightly with her fingers. Her skin is cracked with dried dirt, and her fingernails are all chipped and cut short.

Astra pays for her plant. She pays for the pot. She shifts from one foot to the other as she waits for her change. She can still hear the dripping of the hose, even though she's an entire room away from it now.

She's almost in the clear when she hears it—like an afterthought, like Mrs. Reeves is talking more to herself than to Astra. Astra has already pocketed her change and grabbed her plant and turned toward the door. She's more than ready to leave.

"You know, I was so sorry to hear about what happened to her. The poor dear."

Astra *wants* to ask. More than anything, she wants to turn back around and ask what happened to Isla, why she stopped coming to the greenhouse, why she didn't go to the same school as her brother, why a *plant store* is at the top of her bucket list.

But she doesn't want to know. Or maybe the problem is that she *does*. Too much. The line between alive and dead is getting too blurry.

So she pretends she doesn't hear Mrs. Reeves's comment, and she hurries out the door so quickly she forgets to watch her feet.

CHAPTER NINE

A stra is at her desk doing homework when someone throws a wooden turtle at her head.

"*Ow*," she hisses between her teeth. She picks up the little piece of carved wood and waits for her brain to catch up with her hands. She spins around in her desk chair. "Wait, you—"

"Are awesome?" Isla finishes for her. "You're right. I am."

"How did you manage that? *And* up the stairs, too?"

Isla grimaces. "That part took a little time. All night, actually. And then it rolled back down once. I'm surprised you didn't hear me yelling."

"I'm a heavy sleeper."

"No, you're not."

Astra taps her pencil on the desk, squares off her papers, and circles an answer on her biology homework that she's not even sure is correct. Isla sits on the edge of her bed, floating on her knees.

"By the way, have you seen George?" Astra asks. She glances up at her closet quickly, like she expects to see him standing there like he usually is in the morning. But the door is closed, tipped unevenly on its hinges, and the only cold Astra feels is coming from her bed.

Isla nods, and Astra catches the motion out of the corner of her eye.

"It's his funeral today."

"Oh."

"Yeah," Isla says. "I think I'm gonna go. Pay my respects, you know?"

Astra doesn't want to go. There's a reason she avoids places like that—funerals and hospitals and nursing homes. Places where people die. Places that people go to *after* they've died. It's just too much cold and static and trying not to act like a deranged person.

But she *knows* George. And if she never sees him again, she's going to feel guilty about missing her last chance to say goodbye.

She fiddles with the wooden turtle, then sets it on the edge of her desk next to the pretty purple pot.

"Okay, I'll go with you. But you can't distract me while we're there." She moves her chair back and rifles through her backpack. "And I'm bringing my headphones, just in case."

❖

Astra ends up standing outside the church, wearing an itchy, dark gray dress that she hasn't put on since her aunt's wedding three years ago, and clutching her headphones awkwardly at her side. Her hands are sweaty, and she feels underdressed with a fluffy black cardigan and her white sneakers covered in pen doodles.

"I can't go in," she whispers. Isla floats at her side with her feet curled up underneath her.

"Yes, you can."

"Okay," she says. She lifts one foot and taps it on the wet concrete. It rained last night, and everything is lush and green and damp. The humidity is making the short curls on the top of her head stick up. "Am I moving?"

"Nope."

"How about now?"

Isla sighs. She's wearing the same clothes she always does, and her sunny yellow dress looks out of place next to all of the black. But Astra is the only person who can see her, so it doesn't really matter.

"You're literally just walking in place. Here, let me help."

Isla puts her hand on the middle of Astra's back and gives her a gentle push. If anyone else had done it, Astra might have stumbled, but Isla only manages just enough pressure for Astra to feel it. And she does, even through her ratty gray dress and fluffy cardigan.

The place where Isla is touching her feels cold and tingly. She wonders if Isla can feel it, too.

Isla pushes her hand forward just a little bit and Astra finds herself walking through the front doors of the church. Isla doesn't move her hand until her fingers start sinking into Astra's skin.

The church is small, and there are fewer people than Astra expected. There are flowers everywhere, set up on wooden tables near the front and folding metal stands in the back. There's a guestbook that Astra doesn't sign, a box of tissues that she eyes warily, and a large poster board collage with George's name on it in puffy black letters. His middle name is Elliot, and his birthday is four days before hers.

More things she wishes she didn't know.

She stops and looks at the photos. She recognizes George as an old man, with his sparse hair and wizened smile. He's alone in some of the pictures, grinning gap-toothed with his glasses tipped, but there's a woman next to him in some of them, too. She's got soft brown eyes and curly black hair that's starting to gray, and she reminds Astra a little bit of her mom.

There are some other people in the photos that Astra doesn't recognize—a few middle-aged men, a young woman with braids in her hair, a teenager holding a video game controller and sticking his tongue out at the camera. There's even a baby, sleeping soundly in a crib with a hat barely covering a mop of unruly black hair. George McCreary's family. He had a family. He had kids, grandkids, a wife.

Astra tears her eyes away and looks down at her shoes. She feels like she shouldn't be here.

"That one is my favorite."

She looks up, and George McCreary is standing next to her, pointing a wrinkly finger at a picture on the board. She follows it to a photo of a young woman, maybe in her thirties, holding a toddler on her hip. Her hair isn't salt-and-pepper yet, but the curls and the soft brown eyes are the same.

Astra glances around. People are starting to pack into the tiny church, clustering around the guestbook and standing between the folding chairs set up around the edge of the room. Isla has her legs crossed, and she unsticks them and floats down to give George a sideways hug. She's probably at least a foot taller than he is.

Astra doesn't say anything. There are too many people there, and she doesn't want any of them to think she's talking to herself.

Fortunately, Isla doesn't have that problem.

"She's pretty. You lucked out, old man."

George grins. "I sure did. I always said it was a miracle that our sons took after my wife instead of me. My nose alone would have ruined them."

"I like your nose. It's squishy."

The chatter in the room starts to die down as people take their seats, but once the noise of talking dims, another noise takes its place—a static sound, like tiny bees buzzing all around. It becomes easy to tell which people are alive and which aren't.

In the back of the room, hovering between an arrangement of delicate white flowers and a bulletin board tacked onto the wall, is a middle-aged woman with short red hair and freckles. Next to the piano in the other room is a man maybe a little younger than George, with a buzz cut and jean overalls on. And in one of the chairs near the door, hovering a few inches in the air, is a young woman, probably in her twenties, twirling a lock of wavy brown hair frantically between her fingers.

The temperature in the room plummets, and Astra shudders.

"Hey." Isla touches her shoulder with an ice-cold hand. "Are you okay?"

Astra nods and bites at the inside of her cheek. Her headphones are starting to slip from her sweaty hand, so she puts them around her neck instead and fiddles with the cord.

The ghost in the chair looks up at her from across the room and waves tentatively. Her eyes are big and blue, her skin is the color of chalk, and she's got a dark purple bruise around her neck that makes Astra's stomach roil.

Thankfully, the other two ghosts don't seem to have noticed her yet. The one with the buzz cut has blood on his temple, and when he turns to the side Astra can see a noticeable dent in the front of his skull. The woman with the red hair doesn't look injured at first, but then she spins around and her cardigan shifts, and there's a dark red stain blooming out from the side of her dress. Her eyes are glossy, and she floats slowly back and forth along the wall. If Astra had to guess, she would say that the red-haired woman has been dead the longest.

Astra picks a spot in the back of the room, throws herself down onto a squeaky metal chair, and stares at her feet. The carpet is blue, but not the kind of blue that makes Astra's skin itch. It's dark, like the sky before a storm, and peppered with little gray squares. Astra counts the ones around her feet, and by the time she's hit twenty, the service has started.

"Hello, Miss Astra," George says, lowering himself down into the seat next to hers. "I'm happy you're here."

A man in robes is talking at the front of the room. Astra assumes he's a preacher, but she hasn't been to church since she was little, so she can't be sure. He's reading from a sheet of paper, and his words sound tinny and loud.

There's a coffin behind him, propped up on a pedestal and—thankfully—closed tightly. Next to her, George gestures around him with a broad sweep of his arm.

"Look at how many people came. My sons flew in last night, did you know that? And my youngest granddaughter." He points to a chair in the first row, where a little girl with unruly brown hair is fidgeting in her seat. "Her birthday was last week. She turned four. I wasn't sure I would be able to stick around for long enough to see it."

Astra glances around without raising her head too high. She can hear someone playing the piano. Isla hasn't joined her yet, but she guesses that any minute now she'll see her, floating around on the ceiling or trying to get her voice to echo through the tiny church. She's waiting for it, headphones at the ready.

George continues when Astra doesn't speak. "There are so many people here," he says softly. "More than enough. Everyone I wanted to see, and now I've seen them."

What he's saying clicks, and Astra whispers, as low as she can, "I can't leave. I promised I would stay."

George nods. "Your friend is lucky to have you."

Any minute, Isla is going to start doing cartwheels down the center aisle, or tell a joke that'll make Astra laugh out loud in the middle of a funeral service and look like a complete asshole. Any minute.

She hums and twirls her headphone cord around her finger.

"And you're lucky to have her, as well." George clears his throat even though he doesn't have lungs and moves his arm. "Miss Astra."

She follows his hand with her eyes, and finally realizes where Isla is. And she's not on the ceiling doing backflips.

She's sitting in a chair—or, more likely, hovering just above it—

right next to the young ghost with wavy brown hair and big blue eyes and bruises all around her neck. And they're just…talking.

Astra can't hear what they're saying, but the young woman looks a lot less jittery than she did a few minutes ago. She even starts to smile, small and tentative, and Astra watches Isla bump shoulders with her and grin until her dimples pop out.

And Astra feels…something. Something warm and fluttery just underneath her rib cage. She watches Isla comfort the ghost of a stranger in the middle of a funeral service, and her heart starts beating so wildly that she can hear it echoing around in her ears.

George sits next to her, radiating cold. Music plays, a few people move to the front of the room to talk, and Isla says something that makes the other ghost laugh.

Astra watches her feet. She counts the same little gray squares a second time, and by the time she gets to fifteen, the music has stopped.

George stands up, his arms flickering at his sides. "Thank you for coming, Miss Astra," he says. "I think I'm ready to go now."

She knows what he means. She nods but stays in her chair.

"Goodbye, George," she says softly.

He gives her a toothless smile and bows low, the wisps of hair at the top of his head floating like clouds. And then he's gone.

There are seventeen steps from the folding metal chair to the door. Astra wiggles the doorknob four times and steps out with her left foot first. She counts eight more steps to the curb. The concrete is starting to dry, but it's still cold and a little damp when she sits on it. The humidity and the sudden warmth feel like walking into a sauna.

She's not sad about George being gone. She's *not*. Ghosts aren't people. Astra knows better than to get attached. She didn't even know his middle name until an hour ago.

She doesn't even know Isla's last name.

A cold breeze blows across the back of her neck, and it feels kind of nice. She leans into it just a little and closes her eyes.

"Hey," Isla says from behind her. "My undead wish list needs finishing. Are you gonna sit there all day, or do you wanna go climb something?"

Astra hums. "What did you have in mind?"

❖

Astra looks up at the rusted metal staircase and frowns. "I'm not climbing that."

"Come on," Isla says from somewhere on her right. "Live a little."

"That's easy for you to say."

Isla bumps into her, shoulder-to-elbow, sending a tingling feeling up her arm. "Rude. I'm offended. I don't think I want you tagging along anymore."

Astra shrugs and takes a step back. "Okay."

"No, wait. I've changed my mind. My bucket list *specifically* says that I can't do it alone. And you wouldn't want to be stuck with me forever, would you?"

Astra pretends to think it over while trying very, *very* hard not to think it over.

"No," she says after a minute. "You're right. Falling to my death from an abandoned water tower is totally worth getting rid of an annoying ghost."

"Ouch. I'm very sensitive about that, you know. I actually *did* die from falling off an abandoned water tower. Not this one, though. Different one. You've probably never even seen it before."

"You *do* look like someone who fell off a building. Especially your face. Very grotesque."

Isla elbows her, and this time there's enough force behind it to make Astra stumble. She catches herself and looks up, and Isla is grinning like a madman.

"Come on," she says, grabbing hold of the ladder with both hands. "I want to climb something, and we're already here. I promise I'll wake you up every morning with a turtle to the head if you don't do this with me. Five a.m. Every morning. Turtle to the head."

Astra sighs and bites back a smile. Who is she to argue with that logic?

The abandoned water tower is located on the edge of a huge field, with football goalposts on one half and a small soccer field on the other. The grass is neatly trimmed and damp, and there's a fence around the whole place that's bent in a few spots and littered with gaps. The tower isn't particularly tall or particularly old, but the ladder going up the side is rusty and creaks when she pulls on it. It's cold and wet, and small pieces of white paint chip off and stick to her palms as she climbs.

She's not sure why Isla picked this place for her bucket list. Her anti-bucket list. It's nothing special. Astra honestly didn't even know it existed until Isla directed her to drive off the road and down a rough gravel side street. But Isla doesn't seem to care about the location. She just wants to climb something.

She's pretty good at it, too, from what Astra can see. She could just float up the ladder without even having to hold on to anything, but instead she takes her time, adjusting her hands and shifting her feet and stopping every few minutes to wait for her legs to recalibrate. It probably takes a lot more focus to climb a ladder than to carry a tiny wooden turtle up the stairs, and by the time they reach the top, Isla looks exhausted.

She throws herself down onto the metal platform and floats on her back, closing her eyes and folding her arms over her stomach. She's not breathing heavily or gasping for air, but her face is pinched like she should be. Her hair is going right through the white spray-painted metal and curling gently underneath.

"I think," Isla begins, her voice sounding a little ragged, "I'm more out of shape than you are."

Astra hauls herself up over the top of the ladder and crawls across the platform to sit with her back against the railing.

"I would say I'm offended, but you're not wrong."

"Do you want to talk about it?"

Astra looks over at her, but Isla is facing the sky. "About…how out of shape I am?"

Dark gray clouds are rolling in slowly, leaving just enough sunlight to make everything feel muggy and humid. For once, the cold Isla is throwing off is welcome.

Isla shakes her head and sits up. "No, the funeral. Your friend just *died.*"

"Well, technically he was already dead, so…" Isla stares at her, and Astra notices that ghosts don't have to blink, apparently. She sighs. "He wasn't my friend. I barely even knew him. He just…hung out in my closet sometimes. Which sounds really weird when I say it out loud."

She expects Isla to make a joke about it, but she doesn't.

"Hanging out is what friends do, Astra."

Something about the way she says it makes Astra's skin feel

itchy—or maybe it's just her ratty old dress. It's a little too tight around her arms, and it's making her sweat. It also doesn't help that Isla hasn't blinked in at least five minutes, and her left leg keeps twitching.

"Living friends," she says after a moment. "It's different with ghosts."

She regrets the words as soon as they leave her mouth, because Isla frowns and her dimples disappear, and the little freckle smiley-face turns back into two moles.

"Why?"

The metal bars of the railing are cold and hard against her back. "You know why," she says.

"Humor me."

Astra's chest feels tight. "Because…" She works around a lump in her throat to get the words out. She doesn't look at Isla and her dull green, unblinking eyes. She can't. "Because they leave. I don't want to get attached if they're just going to leave."

Isla doesn't say anything. She shifts until she's sitting next to Astra on the platform, hovering at her side with her back sticking halfway through the railing. Astra feels hot and cold at the same time. It's disorienting. It's uncomfortable. But she doesn't move away.

"I'm sorry," Astra tells her a few minutes later.

Isla jerks her shoulders and smiles, but it's crooked. "Don't be. You're right."

They don't climb back down until it starts raining. And if a little rain manages to fall on Astra's cheeks, neither of them mentions it.

Chapter Ten

A stra can't sleep. The ghosts outside her window probably have something to do with it.

There are two of them. They probably looked like people once, but now they're just glowing, mostly transparent *things*. They're like clouds hovering just outside her bedroom window. She can see right through them if she tries, but she always knows when they're there.

The cold they bring is harsh. Bitter. It bites into her skin and refuses to let go. And even her headphones can't block out their static. She just has to hold on and ride it out, and wait for them to leave. And they always do.

But they always come back, too.

Astra throws off her comforter and slides out of bed. She avoids looking at the window as she pulls a sweater out of her closet—thick, fuzzy, and a blue so muted it looks almost white. Her skin feels itchy and prickly, like it's covered in cactus spikes.

She nearly trips on something just outside her bedroom door, and she looks down to see that the toaster, for some reason, has been relocated to the hallway floor. She steps over it carefully and makes a mental note to ask her mom about it later.

Two cardboard boxes and a teetering stack of envelopes later, and she's down the hall.

She considers, briefly, trying to sleep on the living room couch. But then she would have to move the throw pillows, and the couch is squishy and lumpy and uncomfortable even just to sit on, and she really doesn't want her mom waking up in the morning and finding Astra out of her bed and asking her *why*. She doesn't really have an answer besides the truth, and her mom doesn't need one more thing to worry about.

The lights are on in the store when she unlocks the door.

Isla leans over and blinks at her from behind a shelf, glancing out the front window at the pitch-black sky and then back to Astra in the doorway.

"You're missing out on some very valuable beauty sleep right now, you know."

"Hmm." Astra hums, stepping onto the gray laminate floor with her left foot and closing the door behind her. "It's a shame that ghosts can't sleep, then, isn't it?"

"Wow. You're even worse when you're sleep deprived. I didn't think that was possible."

Astra bites down on a yawn and settles herself into a chair in the corner of the room, careful not to pull off the *Sale* tag pinned to one arm. It's stiff, and the material is ribbed and thick and the kind of bright orange that makes her eyes hurt. She tucks her pajama pants into her socks and tugs the sleeves of her sweater down her palms so that no part of her skin is touching the chair. She can still feel it, though.

"Hey. Catch."

Astra looks up just in time to see something small flying at her face. She throws her hands up and catches it in between them at the last second before it hits her forehead. She rolls it over in her palms. It's a little heavy, smooth and hollow, and painted glossy white and gray.

"Did you just throw a porcelain *cat* at me?"

Isla grins. "Maybe."

"That could have *hurt*. And you could have broken some of my mom's merchandise if you'd missed."

"Do you think she would have noticed?" Isla gestures broadly with her arms, and Astra is pretty sure that the number of trinkets in the room has doubled since the last time she was here. She's tempted to count them, but she would probably be here all night if she did that, and she has school tomorrow.

"Good catch, by the way."

Astra returns the smile easily. "Good throw."

She turns the little ceramic cat over in her hands. It's shiny, with beady little eyes and gray fur painted around its neck. It's still a little cold from being touched by a ghost, and it makes Astra's fingers tingle.

She sets it down gently on the table to her left, next to a vintage food scale and a stack of painted plates.

Isla steps around the shelf and walks on the air across the room. Her legs go right through a low wooden table, and one of them flickers and bends sideways until she shakes it back into place.

She stops at the table next to Astra's chair and runs her fingers over one of the plates. "Rough night?"

Astra shrugs and tries to look casual, but she's wearing blue flannel pajama pants tucked into her socks and she's sitting as far forward on the chair as she can, so she probably just looks uncomfortable.

"You could say that."

"Want to talk about it?"

She shakes her head and says, "Not really."

Isla tries to pick up a plate and nearly drops it. It clatters on its way back down and Isla pulls her hands back quickly. She turns to the food scale instead, pressing her palm into it until the numbers max out and her hand starts to sink.

"Was it another nightmare?" she asks after a moment.

"Yeah," Astra lies. "Probably. I don't remember."

"That sucks. Is there anything I can do to help?"

The metal scale squeaks when it bounces back up. The walls of the shop are yellow, but not soft, pastel yellow like Isla's dress; they're a harsh yellow, like the sun, and looking at them makes Astra's head pound.

She's feeling jittery and tired, hot and cold at the same time. She closes her eyes. "Can you just…talk? Distract me? You're good at that."

"Sure. Okay. Um, did you know that orchids used to be—"

"Not plants," Astra interrupts her. "Something else. Please."

She knows what her brain is doing. It's trying to ask Isla personal questions *without* actually asking her. Because, for some reason, Astra's brain hasn't quite figured out that she doesn't want to know the answers. She found out George McCreary's middle name, and saw a picture of his wife, and that was enough to make her cry. What does she think is going to happen if she learns more about Isla, and then Isla leaves?

She doesn't want to think about that. She focuses on Isla's voice instead, clear and light like a bell.

"All right. I don't know what you want me to talk about, though.

Plants are pretty much all I *do* know how to talk about." Astra hears rustling, but doesn't open her eyes. "I was trampled to death by a herd of buffalo. Did you know that?"

Astra cracks one eye open. Isla is floating by her chair, her legs crossed. "You're a habitual liar, got it. Anything else I need to know about you?"

"I'm also a vengeful spirit. Just in case you were wondering."

"I figured as much," Astra says. "You have a threatening aura."

"So you *are* psychic." Isla chuckles. Astra leans back a little in the chair and lets out a long exhale. Isla seems to be having trouble sitting still, because she keeps fumbling for items on the table next to her and dropping them.

"Well, I've never *tried* to be, so who knows?"

Isla tips over a glass salt shaker and then thrusts her hand in Astra's direction, palm up. "Here. Read my fortune."

"I don't think that's how it works."

She jiggles her hand until it starts flickering, and when she stops moving it her thumb takes a moment too long to slot back into place. It's like watching a video buffering—pieces of it start to move, but the rest stays still until everything else catches up and the whole video is ready to play.

Isla's hand is milky white and unblemished, except for the small callus on her palm, between her index and middle fingers. There's a freckle on her wrist, and pale blue veins that are just for show. Her fingers are long, and Astra blinks her eyes hard when she realizes she's staring.

"Um, sure. Yeah. I can try."

Isla floats closer and jumps into the air, landing on the arm of the chair and perching like a cat. She stretches her legs out and lays her hand on Astra's thigh. It feels kind of like an ice cube is melting through her flannel pajama pants.

She looks at Isla's hand, at the callus and a little patch of rough skin around it that she hadn't noticed before. She reaches down and touches the skin there, and Isla's hand shimmers like a hologram around her fingers.

It feels…odd. Solid and not solid at the same time. She can feel Isla focusing to keep her hand steady, to stop Astra's fingers from going through it, but when she moves suddenly it's like Isla can't anticipate it fast enough and it takes a few seconds for her to shift her point of concentration. Her skin feels like cotton—soft and smooth, but if Astra presses hard enough, it gives way easily.

"Huh." Isla's eyebrows are bunched together and her mouth is cut across her face in a thin line. "That feels weird."

Astra runs her fingers down Isla's palm. It tingles, and it's cold, but Astra doesn't *feel* cold. Just her fingertips. The rest of her feels warm. Maybe the air conditioning unit in the store is on the fritz again.

"You can feel it?" she asks. Isla glances up quickly and then goes back to staring at her hand.

"No, not really," she says. "Not there. But...up here." She points her free hand at her forehead in a sweeping gesture. "Maybe. I don't know."

Astra nods. She bites down on her cheek to keep from saying something stupid. Isla is sitting so close that she should feel like she's in a walk-in freezer, but all she can focus on is her pulse, which keeps jumping back and forth between her throat and the tips of her fingers.

"So, *Madame Vaughn*. Do you have a fortune for me?"

Isla's lips are pulled up into the smallest of grins, like a secret. Astra finds the longest line on her palm and traces it with her index finger.

"Well, this is your life line, right?"

"You're the psychic, not me."

Astra smiles and swallows a lump in her throat. "Right. That's right. And I know what I'm doing, since I've obviously done this before."

"Obviously," Isla says, wiggling her fingers and turning her hand transparent for a second.

"And your life line says"—Astra narrows her eyes and pretends to focus hard on the crease in the middle of Isla's palm—"that you're gonna live a long life. Super long. You'll probably just die of old age, honestly."

"Hey! How did you know? That's *exactly* how I died."

"You look good for a ninety-year-old," Astra says to Isla's hand.

"Thank you."

"And these other two lines, um. This one's kind of curved." She turns her head a little to the right. "That'll be your love line, probably. It says you'll be a widow by age twenty. That's kind of a bummer. But there are some little lines nearby, so that's probably your children. You're gonna have four, five kids? But by twenty. That's super important."

Isla hums. "Five is a good number."

Astra pulls a face. "No, it's not."

"Okay. Four it is, then."

"And—and this last line looks like a tree, kind of. See that little branch there?"

She points to the top line, right underneath the patch of thickened skin and calluses. Isla's palm is starting to shake and flicker a little bit, and it's getting hard to see which lines she's already pointed out and which ones are new.

"Well, I *do* like trees. It would be better if it was a flower, though. Something pretty. If I'm going to be a single mom to four kids by twenty years old, I think I deserve something pretty to look at."

Astra sighs and spreads her fingers out along Isla's palm. It tickles and thrums and she puts just enough weight down for Isla to keep her hand steady.

It feels nice. Comfortable. She could fall asleep, just like this.

She sits up and moves forward on the stiff, itchy chair. When did she lie back?

"Something pretty," she repeats slowly. Her brain feels foggy, and she tells herself that it's just exhaustion. "Do you want to see my favorite place?"

❖

It takes Astra two tries to climb out of the window without making a sound. Her foot catches on the frame the first time, and she has to remind Isla that her mom can hear ghosts just as well as she can, so *please stop laughing.*

The roof above the back half of her mom's store isn't sloped like the rest of it. It's nearly flat, one long rectangular sheet of metal, and it sits just a little lower than the slanted roofing around it. Astra discovered, just two months after they moved in, that she could wiggle her way through the kitchen window and just barely reach the edge of the rectangle. All she has to do is stand on the counter and pull the window open as far as it'll go, until it sticks on the dried paint and starts to creak.

She's not the most graceful when she does this, unfortunately. Her shirt rides up and for a minute she's just lying there, half outside and half inside, kicking out with her feet blindly until she hits something solid.

Isla floats along in the air next to her, rotating between whispering encouragements and full-on cackling.

"I thought you wanted to climb things," Astra says, holding on to the window frame with both hands while she finds her balance.

Isla shrugs. "I did. And now I'm over it. No sense in checking off the same bucket list thing twice."

"Anti-bucket list," Astra reminds her, panting slightly.

"You know, it would be kind of lame to die from falling off a roof and into a dumpster in the alley. So be careful."

"Aw. That might be the sweetest thing you've ever said to me."

She pushes off the window and steadies herself on the dark sheet of metal. It clangs under her feet and rattles like thunder when she walks on it. She tiptoes to the middle and sits down, feeling cold and leftover moisture from the recent rains soaking into her pajama pants.

She lies back, tucks one arm behind her head, and looks up at the inky-black sky. It's swirled with dark clouds, and the moon is hazy and half-hidden, but that's not why she likes coming up here so much.

Isla doesn't make a single sound as she floats across the metal and settles herself down next to Astra, mirroring her position. She blinks up at the sky, a huge velvet curtain drawn around them, dotted with thousands of bright, shiny diamonds of light.

"Wow," she breathes out. "I didn't know you could see the stars so clearly out here."

"You can't. Not in most places. This is the only one I've found so far."

She glances over at Isla. Her eyes are wide, and she's lying almost perfectly still, just a couple of inches away. Even her legs have stopped moving. It takes Astra a moment to realize that she's actually touching the roof, not hovering above it, and she wonders how much energy it's taking her to stay like that.

"Is this where you come when you can't sleep?"

Astra nods, and then realizes that Isla can't see her. "Yeah. Sometimes I just need to get *out*. Maybe I'm claustrophobic or something."

"Hmm. That makes sense."

The stars look like tiny dots in the sky. When she blinks, Astra can still see them on the insides of her eyelids. Isla is giving off a soft, barely-there glow in the darkness. It kind of reminds Astra of a nightlight.

In the morning, she'll probably blame her loose lips on her exhaustion. But really, she's more tired of keeping secrets than she is physically tired.

"I don't like funerals," she admits, keeping her eyes on the sky. "Or hospitals. Too many ghosts. Just one is okay, but more than one is…too cold. Too much noise."

"Noise?"

"You—you don't hear it?" she asks. Even now, in the near silence, she can hear Isla buzzing like radio static.

"No," Isla says. "I didn't realize. You shouldn't have gone if it was that hard."

Astra shakes her head and the metal creaks underneath her. "No, you were right. George was my friend. I'm glad I went."

Isla is silent for a minute. Astra would think she was sleeping if she wasn't so sure that ghosts don't sleep. But she hasn't left, because Astra can still hear her, and she can still see her hazy glow, like clouds floating in around the moon, out of the corner of her eye.

"It was an infection," Isla finally says, so softly that Astra can barely hear her. It sounds like she's talking more to herself than to Astra.

"What?"

"An infection. That's what the doctors said. I remember passing out, but that's about it."

Astra's mind is reeling. She feels more awake than she did a few minutes ago.

"I'm sorry," she says.

"Don't be. Like I said, I don't remember much of it anyway. And I feel better now, so it's fine."

Part of Astra expects her to take it back—to crack a joke and start laughing like she always does. But she can tell that Isla is telling the truth this time. Something feels different, and it just makes sense. She doesn't have a mark on her—not a scratch, or a bruise, and her skin isn't bloated or discolored like George's was.

But there's a difference between joking about her death and being honest about it. It feels too real. *She* feels too real. Like a human, like a sixteen-year-old girl, like someone Astra could get attached to and miss someday.

Astra swallows around a lump in her throat. She's got one hand at her side and the other behind her head, propping it up, and she tries to shift without making too much noise. She's very aware of Isla next to her, throwing off cold and light, and she knows she should say something, but nothing feels right.

"Don't," Isla says instead, her voice low. "Don't make it weird. You already knew I was dead. Just...go back to pretending I was run over by a tank, or skewered by a harpoon, or something."

Astra finally finds her voice. "A harpoon?"

"Fishing. My dad used to take me and my brother fishing when we were little. He had a harpoon gun on the boat but he never used it."

Used to. Astra notices that Isla talks a lot about her childhood, but the stories are never recent. She doesn't go to the same school as her brother, she doesn't fish with her dad anymore, she doesn't go to the greenhouse like she used to. *Didn't.* She *didn't* do those things. Astra files it away in her mind as something to ask her about later, but she kind of hopes she never gets the chance to.

"I've never been fishing," Astra says, because she feels like she has to say *something*.

Her hand on the roof in between them feels colder than the rest of her body. She glances down and realizes that Isla is lying the exact same way she is, and her own hand is just an inch or so away from Astra's. She wonders if Isla has noticed.

"It's not as fun as it sounds. Worms are gross, fish are gross, and I sunburn really, really easily."

"I'm not outside enough to sunburn, I think." Astra inches her fingers just a little closer. "I would probably just be a hermit if I didn't have to go to school."

"We need to get you out more, then," Isla says. "Know of any good parks in the area? It's not just flowers I'm good with, you know. I also happen to know a *lot* about trees."

Astra lets out a breathy laugh. "I know. That's what the line on your hand said."

"It also said I'm gonna live to be ninety."

Astra swallows. "Yeah. And it's never wrong."

The space between their hands feels smaller, more prickly and cold, but Astra doesn't want to risk looking down again.

"Well, you're the expert."

"I am," Astra agrees, smiling softly. "And *you're* the expert on plants. So, tell me more about why going to the park is better than just sitting inside and doing homework all day. Because I'm not totally convinced."

A small, tentative pressure pushes against the side of her hand. She probably wouldn't even feel it if she wasn't already so focused on it. She glances over at Isla, but she's staring pointedly upward and doesn't move. One of her dimples is back, and Astra feels a swell of fondness in her chest at the sight of it.

She opens up her hand and curls her fingers around Isla's, feather-soft. It's warm and cold at the same time, and the sensation isn't as disorienting as it used to be.

Isla takes a deep, lungless breath and starts rattling off more plant facts than Astra is ever going to be able to remember, but she's barely listening anyway.

She feels hazy and comfortable, even on the hard metal roof with her pajama pants still tucked into her socks. She falls asleep a few minutes later, and she wakes up just before sunrise after the first dreamless sleep she's had in years.

CHAPTER ELEVEN

You fell asleep on the roof. Holding her hand. Am I getting this right?"

"You need to *keep it down*," Astra hisses under her breath, even though they're the only two people in the classroom this early. If it wasn't for the stopper keeping the door from sticking shut, they would've probably been locked out and had to wait for the bell to ring to get in. "It wasn't like that."

"Okay. What *was* it like, then?"

Oliver's oversized brown jacket is looking extra rumpled today, and Astra swears there are at least ten more patches on it than there were last week. He leans forward on his elbows and shifts his legs so that he can tap one foot against the leg of his desk. He's already got a pencil tucked behind one ear, and Astra can see that the earrings he's wearing today are little silver butterflies.

Astra bridges the distance between their desks and drops her voice low, even though they're alone.

"She's dead, Oliver. Even if I *did* like her, it wouldn't matter. It wouldn't change anything."

"That doesn't mean you can't still enjoy spending time with her."

"I do," Astra says quickly. "But she's still going to leave eventually. That's kind of the whole point, you know?"

Astra is thankful that Isla hasn't followed her to school since the dodgeball incident, but even though the room is comfortably warm and she can't hear anything other than the sound of her own breathing and Oliver's frantic foot-tapping, she still feels weird talking to Oliver about Isla like this. Like she could float through the wall at any moment and hear everything.

Not that there's anything for her to hear. Because there isn't. But Astra still can't help but feel like she's being watched.

Oliver nods and his pencil slips backward into his hair. "So there aren't any, um…ghosts who have *stayed*? Like, it's not even an option?"

Astra bites her lip. "No," she says between her teeth, trying not to think about the fuzzy, shapeless lights outside her bedroom window. "If it is, I've never seen it before."

The classroom door creaks open and two classmates enter, taking their seats at the front of the room side by side. One of them is chewing gum, and the popping sound makes Astra's head throb.

She sits back up in her seat and works on squaring off her books, even though she already did five minutes ago. One, two, three, four. Her headphones are in her backpack, right on top, and even though she's only wearing a thin sweater today, she doesn't feel cold.

The kids at the front of the room start talking, but Astra isn't paying any attention to what they're saying. One of them has wild brown and pink hair that's spiked around the sides, and they keep scooting their chair back while the legs screech on the linoleum. Three more kids enter the room, one after the other, and Oliver quietly passes Astra a note while the last one sits down in the seat in front of him.

Maybe she could be the exception to the rule.

Astra would be lying if she said she hadn't thought about it, but that isn't what she wants. She doesn't want Isla to turn into one of those *things* that keep her awake at night.

"Maybe," she whispers instead, handing Oliver his paper back.

The bell rings, the door creaks open one last time, and Mr. Pierce shuffles in and kicks the door stopper back into place. His mustache is looking even bushier, maybe a little curlier too, and it wobbles when he throws down the papers in his arms and slides his coffee cup to the end of his desk.

Oliver's paper finds its way back onto Astra's desk a moment later, neat, loopy handwriting scrawled across the bottom.

Look at his cup.

She frowns down at the paper, then up at the teacher's desk, and then at Oliver. His lopsided, all-teeth grin reminds her of Isla.

He slides the paper over to the edge of Astra's desk when Mr. Pierce turns to the board, and continues writing.

It's the same kind he used to bring. Not the fancy biodegradable stuff. How do you think his weekend went?

Astra blinks and scrambles for her pencil.

I don't want to know, she writes in her messy chicken-scratch. *But thank you for that mental image.*

He chuckles under his breath, just loudly enough for Mr. Pierce to turn around and fix him with a *cranky old man* glare. She swears she sees his mustache frown in solidarity.

Then a burst of cold air comes rushing in through the propped-open door, and Astra sighs. She looks up to see Isla, standing in the gap between the door and its frame and looking slightly nervous. She gives Astra a small wave and waits patiently for Mr. Pierce to stop talking and start writing on the board before she speaks.

"Astra! Hi! I'm definitely interrupting something this time, sorry. I just…have a bit of a problem? And I need your help?"

Astra glances pointedly between Isla and the clock above the door. Isla follows her gaze and nods quickly.

"Got it. I can wait. I'll just go haunt my little brother for a while, that's always fun. Just…meet me in the parking lot after school, okay? And bring Ollie. It'll be a good bonding experience for you guys."

Astra waves her hand in a shooing gesture next to her desk, and Oliver shoots her a questioning look. Isla mock-salutes before floating backward out the door, half of her body going right through it, and taking the cold breeze with her.

What was that about? Oliver writes in the margins of his notebook paper.

The school is haunted, Astra replies. *And I'm supposed to ask you if you want to help a ghost with an errand.*

"Um, *hell yes*," he hisses under his breath. Mr. Pierce's mustache looks like it wants to leap across the room and strangle him. And, honestly, so does Mr. Pierce.

❖

Isla has a lot more trouble doing a superhero pose in the car when Oliver is in the passenger seat. So she settles for hovering in the back, holding on to the door handle to keep from falling out and looking distinctly put out by it.

She points out directions that only Astra can hear, and Astra counts twenty blocks before they reach their destination.

It's a house—a small, single-story building with white siding and sky-blue trim. There's a small hedge around the front, a porch with a bench and a couple of potted plants on top, and a rusty bird bath in the front yard. The grass is a little patchy, and the blue paint is starting to peel around the window frames.

Astra parks the car but doesn't get out. The mailbox next to the front door is packed so full of letters that it can't close all the way. She turns around in her seat to look at Isla, sitting with her legs crossed in the back.

"I'm gonna need an explanation before we break into some random person's house," she tells her.

"It's George's house," Isla says. "He asked me for a favor before he went—wherever he went."

"What's she saying?" Oliver asks, but Astra shushes him and keeps her eyes on Isla.

"That still doesn't explain why we're here."

Isla shifts around until one of her feet is sticking out through the door. "Well," she says slowly, "I wasn't totally sure what he wanted me to do. He wasn't super specific. He just said that he wanted me to grab something before the house got sold. Told me it would be *waiting inside the front door* for me. And, um, I guess he was right?"

"I feel like I'm missing something, guys."

"Oliver, just give me a second. And Isla—that explains literally *nothing*. You can touch things pretty well now. You don't need us here just to help you carry something."

Isla shrugs, but there's a glint in her eyes that makes Astra nervous. She's not sure what to expect, but knowing Isla, it could be anything.

"You might just want to see for yourself."

"That's very ominous, thank you."

"I don't like not being able to hear what she's saying," Oliver chimes in from the passenger seat. "I'm feeling super left out right now."

Astra shifts in her seat and pulls her keys out of the ignition. She jabs her thumb in the direction of the house. "This is a dead guy's house.

His name was George and we hung out sometimes. We're helping with his last request, I guess."

Oliver's eyes widen. "That's so *cool*. This is so much better than track practice."

Astra shrugs and steps out of the car, and Oliver follows her a second later. Isla floats through the door and up to the porch, her legs tucked under her and her feet flickering wildly.

Oliver looks around at the potted plants when they reach the top of the steps—one, two, three. The flowers inside look fake, with glossy leaves and frayed bits of fabric on the end of their petals. Isla touches one and then frowns down at it, like it's offended her somehow.

"Did the guy leave a spare key out here somewhere, or...?" Oliver stands up on his toes to peak at the top of the doorframe, and then lifts a pot to look underneath it.

Isla rolls her eyes and disappears through the front door, which is painted the same soft blue as the trim and is starting to chip around the handle.

A second later the lock clicks and the door swings open with a long creak.

"That works too, I guess."

The inside of George McCreary's house is just as small as the outside. There's a square living room on the left, with a dark brown couch that's significantly less squished than the one in Astra's apartment, a low glass coffee table with two coasters on top, and a small television mounted over a wooden electric fireplace. On the right is the kitchen, which is small and yellow, and the light streaming through the tiny window above the counter illuminates the dust floating through the air. There are still dishes in the sink, and the refrigerator is covered in magnets and sticky notes and crumpled crayon drawings on paper that's started to yellow around the edges.

The carpet is squishy and green, like grass. Astra's shoes sink into it, and when she walks she kicks up dust. The TV is still on, playing a cooking show on a low volume, and there's a mug of coffee sitting out on the kitchen counter that's half-full.

Astra is torn between wanting to explore and feeling the strong need to *leave*, right now, before she can get any more tiny glimpses into the person George McCreary was before he died. She glances around quickly, trying not to notice the framed pictures on the wall in the hallway or the threadbare quilt on one arm of the couch that's obviously homemade. She can't see anything worth making a final request out of, though.

She looks down at the floor near the door and then back up at Isla.

"Are we here to get…an umbrella? Or, um…shoes? I thought you said it would be by the door."

Oliver taps his feet on the carpet and they make a muffled thumping sound.

"Just give it a second," Isla says.

Astra is confused. She knits her eyebrows together and stares at Isla, but she's focused on the hallway that continues down the center of the house, branching off into what Astra assumes are bedrooms and at least one bathroom. One of the doors is open, but Astra can't see inside it from where she's standing.

A minute passes. She opens her mouth to ask what, exactly, she's supposed to be waiting for, when the *what* comes sauntering out of the open door, tail flicking out behind it.

It's a cat. Probably. It also kind of looks a little bit like a piece of cotton that's been run through the dryer, though. Or Mr. Pierce's mustache on a Friday morning.

It's orange and white and impossibly fluffy, but the fluff is stuck up like it's been hit by lightning and there are little mats in the fur around the cat's head and tail. Its face is squished flat, with a wide pink nose and squinty yellow eyes, and it walks with a little limp in its back legs.

The cat takes its time walking down the hallway toward them. It meows a couple of times, but it sounds more like a frog croaking.

"That's a *very* old cat," Oliver says. The cat's tail swishes and throws dust and stray hairs behind it.

"Yes," Isla agrees, nodding.

Astra turns to her. "George didn't *tell* you about this? What did he think you were gonna do with a *cat*?"

Isla holds her hands out, palms up. "Don't ask me. Maybe he figured you would help. All he said was that his sons were coming over tomorrow to go through his stuff. And he seemed to think it was important to get his *last request* out before they got here."

"I can't just take his cat."

"But it's his *last request*."

"Guys," Oliver says. "I feel like you're talking over me again. Translation, please?"

"The family is coming tomorrow to look at the house," Astra tells him. "And the dead guy wanted us to take his cat, apparently. He could have just asked me, though."

The cat squeaks and Isla crouches down in midair and waves at it.

"Would you have said yes?" she asks.

"Probably not," Astra admits. She can't picture her tiny apartment, filled with junk, with a cat right in the middle of it all. Her mom would throw a fit. They aren't *cat people*. They're ghost people. Completely different skill set.

Oliver squints down at the cat, bending over until his dark hair is hiding most of his face. "This cat is *old*. You could probably take it to a shelter, but I think they would just put it down. Maybe that's what your, um, *dead guy* was trying to avoid?"

Isla nods, even though Oliver can't see her. "Probably. I'm guessing his sons knew about the cat, but I caught the neighbor leaving food by the cat door when I stopped by this morning. So I'm gonna assume they don't really care what happens to their dad's pet."

The cat creeps slowly down the rest of the hallway and along one side of the kitchen doorway. And then it walks right up to Isla, looks her in the eyes, and *chirps*.

She reaches out her hand, tentatively, and sets it down on top of the cat's head. It leans into the touch, closing its eyes and flicking its tail lazily behind it.

"Holy crap," Isla whispers. "The cat can *see* me."

Astra can hear, just barely, the raspy sound of the cat purring. She bends down next to Isla and inspects the collar around its neck, which is light gray and has a tiny bell in the front.

She turns the shiny silver tag over in her hand. George's name is etched into one side, along with what she assumes is his phone number. On the other side is a name, in all capital letters, with little gemstones glued in around the edges.

"His name is Leonard," she says. "That's…"

"A horrible name for a cat," Oliver finishes for her.

"Did you know cats can see ghosts?" Isla asks. Her hand is phasing in and out of the cat's thick, wispy fur as she pets him behind the ears.

Astra shakes her head. "No. I've never seen any other animals do it, though. There was a guy who died in his sleep across the street from our old house, and he stuck around for a few days after. And he had a dog, but I don't think it ever noticed him. If it did, it never barked or anything."

"Hmm. That's weird. Maybe it's not cats, then. Maybe *I'm* special. I should test it out. Does anybody want to go to the pet store with me?"

Astra ignores her. "This must have been where George went when he wasn't at my place."

"Great," Oliver says. "So now literally everyone in this room can see ghosts *except* for me. I've never been more disappointed to be normal."

"If it helps," Isla chimes in, "you don't seem all that normal to me, Ollie."

Astra clears her throat. "Isla says you're, um, *not* normal? But in a nice way, I think."

"Oh. Thanks, I guess." Oliver turns and faces Isla's general direction. "Am I looking the right way? Are you tall or short? Wait, I don't even know what you *look* like. Now I'm curious."

"Tell him that I look like a supermodel. Really emphasize my height and my super shiny hair. Don't, uh, mention my hands. And tell him I'm eighteen. Make me sound super sophisticated."

"She's blond," Astra deadpans. "Kinda tall. Green eyes. Looks a little bit like a frog when she laughs."

"Hey!" Isla reaches over and tries to shove her shoulder, but her hand sinks right through.

"A very pretty frog," Astra amends. Isla smirks.

"A frog prince. Like in the fairy tale."

"Exactly."

Oliver rolls his eyes. "If you two aren't going to start including me, I'm leaving."

Astra reaches out to pet Leonard, but his purring stops the second he notices her hand on his back. He flicks his tail and growls, low and raspy, and when she pulls back he immediately wraps himself around Isla's leg and chirps happily. Astra frowns.

"If you're leaving, then take the cat with you."

"I can't," Oliver says quickly. "My sister is allergic. And my mom hates dust."

"Which sister is that? Phoebe?"

"No. Molly. She's eight and she's allergic to pretty much everything that moves. Except for turtles, apparently."

Leonard fixes Astra with a warning glare, and she backs away and stands next to Oliver by the door. Isla's static is louder than the TV, but the living room walls are a sharp green color that's already making her head throb, so she takes five long steps across the room and presses the button on the front of the television to turn it off.

"So, you have a turtle, then?" she says over her shoulder.

Oliver grimaces. "Two, actually."

"You poor thing."

"Guys," Isla calls from the kitchen. Her hands are in front of her, palms up, shedding wispy cat hairs like snow. "I can't lift a cat. My amazing ghost powers have a limit, and that limit is cats. One of you is gonna have to carry him."

What comes next is a battle of wills. It's barely even a contest, though, really.

Astra tells her that she can't take the cat. Her apartment is too small, her mom is too scattered—scrambled, like eggs—and she has literally no experience with owning a pet, anyway. She would probably accidentally feed Leonard something poisonous to cats and kill him, and then she would be a *murderer*, and Astra really doesn't need that on her conscience.

If a cat dies, does it come back as a ghost? Astra has never seen a ghost-cat before. She might have seen a ghost-chicken, once, but she was in the back seat of a car on the highway and it might have just been a normal chicken seen through a rain-smeared window.

Astra makes her case, she really does. Oliver even tries to help a couple of times, defending Astra's messy apartment and how there are *way* too many throw pillows on the couch to possibly fit a cat bed.

But then Isla's eyes do that thing where they stop being quite so dull and sparkle a little instead, all wide and green and *alive*. And Astra's chest does that thing where it gets too tight for her heart to fit, so it jumps up into her throat instead and pounds vigorously against the pulse points in her neck.

She swallows and rolls her eyes and refuses to look at Isla, who's rummaging around in the hall closet and trying in vain to pull out a large bag of dry cat food and a gray plastic pet carrier.

"Fine," she spits out. "But he's your responsibility."

The broad, dimpled grin on Isla's face stays the entire way home and makes Astra's hands so sweaty that she drops the cat carrier. With the cat inside. Twice.

CHAPTER TWELVE

It's a bad day. An *unraveling day*.

That's what Astra calls them—the days when her mom seems to unwind like a spool of thread. Like she's gathered up all of her marbles in a big bowl and then tripped and accidentally knocked them all onto the floor. She tries to pick them up, but it's impossible, and some of them get lost under the couch and in between the stove and the kitchen wall.

She never tells Astra when it's a bad day. But Astra knows how to tell by now.

First: Her mom isn't in the kitchen when Astra wakes up. It's a Saturday, and the air in the apartment is clear of the smell of butter-soaked eggs or burnt toast. The coffee maker isn't even on, and it's Astra's alarm that wakes her rather than the sound of her mom's heels clicking across the linoleum.

Astra listens at her door, but all she hears is a car driving past outside and a loud, hoarse *meow* coming from the end of her bed. She spins around quickly and puts her index finger to her lips.

"Leonard, *shush*," she says quietly. "You know the rules. If you want to stay here, my mom can't find out about you."

The cat blinks up at her with his squinty yellow eyes and growls, kneading his claws into her comforter. He's been hiding out in her room for days, and he still doesn't trust her. He perks up and zooms around the room when Isla shows up, though, and Astra isn't sure whether the feeling she gets when this happens is jealousy or fondness. They're both annoying and slightly painful, so it doesn't really matter.

Second: Her mom isn't at work. She sleeps in late even on her good days, when all of the thread in her brain is wound up nice and neat and her marbles have all been found and relocated back to their bowl, but there aren't a lot of places in the apartment where she could be on a Saturday morning. She's not in the kitchen, because the fire alarm isn't going off. She isn't in the living room, because the throw pillows are still piled up on the couch and her purse and its contents are still scattered across the low, wobbly coffee table.

The bathroom door is open, so there's only one other place her mom could be. And if she's in her bedroom on a Saturday at ten in the morning, then she must be having an unraveling day.

"Mom," Astra says softly, shaking her shoulders. Her mom's pajamas have little yellow ducks on them, like a child's. "You have work today."

Her mom rolls over onto her side but doesn't open her eyes. Astra can tell from her breathing that she's awake, though.

Maria Vaughn's bedroom is a lot like the rest of the house: colorful and chaotic. Just like her wardrobe. Just like her brain. All four walls are painted a different color, and they're all bright and noisy—dark purple, grassy green, a deep ocean blue, and the same shade of red that's in the living room. Astra doesn't like coming in here, because the noises hurt her eyes and her head, but her mom seems to like them. Maybe they calm her down in the same way that they make Astra feel anxious. Maybe they're a good distraction.

Her bedroom is full of distractions—from the bright, Jackson Pollock-esque paintings on the walls to the dresser top piled high with half-used candles and incense burners. Books with faded covers and loose spines. Curtains made of beads that sound like wind chimes when they're pulled back. And, of course, more of the same kind of trinkets that are all over the rest of the house and the store downstairs—bronze animals and ceramic cups and even another bowl of fake fruit. Apples this time.

"Are they bugging you today?" she asks her mom. She nods with her eyes closed tight. "There aren't any *here*, though, right?"

Astra knows that there aren't. Isla hasn't come yet, and George is gone. Even the fuzzy lights outside her window usually leave when the sun comes up.

"Not today," her mom croaks. Her hair is wild and smushed in the back from being slept on. Her comforter is yellow like the ducks on her pajamas, with jagged streaks of sunrise-orange going across it.

"Do you need a day inside? I can watch the store. I don't have any plans."

That's not true. Astra promised Isla that they would check off another item on her anti-bucket list today, like they have every Saturday for the last three weeks. But her mom comes first.

She waits for her mom to say something, but she stays curled up on her side, facing the tomato-red wall. Astra pats her on the shoulder gently and stands up.

"I'll go make some tea."

Isla throws a Styrofoam pear into the air and catches it on its way back down. One of her hands disappears for a second when the fake fruit hits it, and she shakes it until it flickers back onto the end of her wrist.

"This is fun," she says. "Is this an average day? Here?"

Astra shakes her head and drums her fingers on the counter. "Saturdays are slow. So are Mondays. And the rest of the week, really. But my mom gets paid the same whether anybody buys anything or not, so…"

They've had a grand total of two customers in the last three hours. If Astra wasn't on the clock, she would have shut the place down by now.

"So, tell me again why we aren't out scaling the Alps right now?"

"I thought you were done climbing," Astra says. "And *I* don't have a death wish."

"That doesn't answer my question. And I think your roof-climbing thing is just as dangerous as climbing a mountain. And a lot less fun."

Astra shrugs. The light in the back of the store is still flickering, and if she turns her head the wrong way, she can see it out of the corner of her eye. She focuses on the countertop, lined with jewelry displays and a couple of fake plants that Isla flicks with her finger every time she passes by them.

"My mom is having a bad day. I'm just helping her out."

"Your mom has the psychic thing too, right?" Isla asks, grabbing a second pear and rolling them between her hands.

"I guess." Astra sighs. "We don't really talk about it."

"About what?"

The bell above the door chimes softly, and a middle-aged woman with choppy black hair and a fluttery beige dress enters. She's got a huge purse on one arm, and her boots have heels on them that scrape the floor as she walks.

Isla silently floats up to the ceiling with her pears and circles the room until the woman leaves. She walks out without buying anything, and Isla sticks her tongue out at her through the door.

Astra debates telling Isla everything. Literally *everything*. Her mom's past, *her* past, the ghosts outside her window, the literal and figurative ghosts in her closet. The way her heart swells a little bit when Isla smiles so wide that her dimples pop out, and how wonderful and terrifying that feeling is.

She trusts Isla. But that's part of the problem.

She exhales a long breath and runs her hand through the ragged curls at the back of her neck. She needs a haircut. Her skin is starting to itch.

"My mom used to be normal," she says, once the woman has left and the door has closed all the way behind her. "Or as normal as someone who sees ghosts can be. My parents were married, and I'm pretty sure they were happy. They seemed happy. My mom *says* they were happy."

Isla floats back down from the ceiling. If someone was standing outside the store and happened to glance through the front windows, they would see two Styrofoam pears flying around the room.

"What happened?"

Astra shrugs. "My dad didn't know about the ghost thing. The psychic thing, whatever. She kept it from him the whole time. She was probably born with it—I was—but nobody knew. Do—do you remember the thing I told you about funerals? And hospitals, and places like that?"

Isla nods. She's hovering a couple of feet above the floor with her legs bent, holding one pear in each hand but not throwing them anymore.

"Too cold," she says. "Too much noise."

"Right. Yeah. And that's why I don't go to places where I know there's gonna be a lot of ghosts. My mom's the same way, but I think it bothers her even more than it bugs me. She had a home birth when she had me. I honestly can't remember a time she ever went to the hospital for *anything*. But then her brother got sick—like, *really* sick—and she had to go. I don't—you can probably guess what happened. It's not hard."

Astra remembers most of it. It was four years ago, and she remembers getting called out of school by her dad. Being told that her mom was being committed. Being told that her uncle had just died. Wondering if she would end up the same as her mom someday.

"She lost control," Astra continues. She stares at the speckled black and white countertop to avoid seeing the look on Isla's face. "It was a big deal. I don't think stuff like that ever really happened where we used to live, so everyone heard about it pretty quickly. And shouting about seeing dead people gets you dubbed *unstable* right away. And—I don't know. Maybe she is. Maybe I am, too. I don't really have any proof that I'm *not*, do I?"

Isla huffs a cold breath that hits Astra in the forehead. "You're not unstable. I'm just as real as anybody else. Catch."

She tosses a pear at Astra, who tries to catch it but fumbles. It falls over the edge of the countertop and rolls away underneath a table.

"I stole a dead guy's cat and I'm talking to myself," Astra reminds her.

"No, you're talking to *me*. And *offending* me." Isla pauses and swoops down through the table to retrieve the painted chunk of Styrofoam. Astra watches her pop back up with her waist stuck in the middle of the tabletop. "Is that why your dad left? Because he found out about your mom?"

"Yeah. I guess he believed what everyone else was saying."

"Why don't you live with him, then? Or part-time? I—that sounds stupid. My parents are still together. I don't know how divorce works."

Astra's throat feels tight. She swallows. "No—you're right. Um, he didn't want me. He didn't fight the custody thing. He just gave us some money and we...left."

"That's super shitty. I'm sorry."

"It's fine. I'm over it."

Astra is absolutely, definitely *not* over it. Some of her nightmares are about how *not over it* she is. But she *is* tired of talking about it. She's told Isla as much as she can today. She feels like a wrung-out sponge, sucked dry and empty, and if she lets out any more, then she won't be able to make it through the rest of the work day without at least needing a nap.

She almost regrets telling Isla about any of it, but only almost. Mostly she just feels a tiny bit less weighed down.

"Hey," she says suddenly, looking up at Isla's thin-lipped frown and trying to will it back into pointed canines and dimples. "Did you know that bamboo is the fastest growing plant in the world?"

Isla gasps. "You read my book!"

Astra smiles. "I skimmed it. The pictures are nice. I don't know how you can remember all of those random plant facts, though. I've been sitting on the bamboo one for *days*, and every time I think about telling you I immediately forget what I'm supposed to be remembering."

"It helps if you have literally no social life and just sit around reading plant books all day."

"That's—exactly what I've been doing lately."

Isla smiles and tosses one of the pears at Astra again. This time, she catches it easily from behind the counter.

"I guess you've got no excuse, then," Isla says. Her dimples make her cheekbones look higher. She floats closer until her shoulder sinks into an earring display, and the sudden drop in temperature makes Astra's skin prickle.

She doesn't have a single cohesive thought. She can't even remember her plant fact anymore. Was it about eucalyptus or bamboo? Was it the fastest growing plant or the longest living one? She should ask Isla. Isla would know.

She opens her mouth to ask, but Isla's eyes widen and she pushes off from the counter and starts talking again before Astra can get a single word out.

"I need to feed Leonard," she says quickly. The sparkle in her eyes has darkened. Her dimples are smooth again. "He's been alone all day. He's probably freaking out."

Astra blinks, feeling confused. "I fed him this morning."

Isla doesn't answer. She just floats up, up, up until her head goes through the ceiling. Above this section of the store is Astra's living room, and she watches silently as Isla's entire body phases into a light panel. The remaining Styrofoam pear falls to the floor and rolls away.

And then the door opens.

The chime startles Astra, and she jumps so hard she knocks her hip into the counter. She leans across it and bites down on a curse as a customer walks into the shop, holding a stack of papers in one hand.

At least she *thinks* it's a customer. He might just be lost. Most of the people who deliberately walk into Astra's mom's store are in their fifties or older, with box-dyed hair, and knock-off purses in the crooks of their elbows. This kid can't be any older than fifteen.

He's got shaggy brown hair that's covering the top half of his eyes, and the remnants of baby fat around his jaw that make him look somehow skinny and not at the same time. His jeans are baggy but his jacket looks a little tight, and he uses his free hand to sweep the hair away from his face twice before he even says anything to Astra.

"Hi, welcome," Astra stumbles to say. "Can I, um—can I help you find anything?"

In this mess, Astra probably wouldn't be able to find anything for him even if she wanted to. She watches his eyes rove around the room, making two quick passes, before settling on Astra herself behind the counter. His eyes are green, but not like grass. Like a plant. Astra can picture it, but she can't remember its name.

The boy steps up to the counter, tucking his hair behind his ear as he goes. He looks a little familiar, but not just his face. His gait, maybe. The way he holds himself. She feels like she's seen him at school before, but not in any of her classes.

"Do you put up flyers here?" he asks when he's standing directly across from her. "Like, in the windows? For benefits, charities, things like that?"

He talks in a rush, but his voice is slightly unsteady. Every other word comes out like a question.

Astra looks down at his hands. There are probably at least a dozen sheets of paper in them, but all she can see from this angle is the black ink showing through the back of the bottom page.

"Um," she says, as eloquently as usual. Isla would be so proud. "My mom manages this place, so I would have to ask her. But I don't see why not? You can leave one, if you want. If I can't put it up in the window, I can always just keep it here at the counter."

"Oh. Yeah. Okay."

He tugs a piece of paper free from the stack and sets it carefully on the counter. He slides it over to her, and she sees the words *Benefit Fundraiser* printed at the top in thick black letters.

"Thank you," the boy says, his hair falling from behind his ear and landing in front of one of his wide green eyes. Green like a plant. But which one?

Astra blinks up at him, but he's already left. The bell chimes again, the door squeaks shut, and Astra looks back at the flyer. She blinks some more and rubs at her eyes. She turns the flyer over in her hands, and frowns down at the cluster of dark, blocky letters.

And the black-and-white photo, printed right in the middle, showing a teenage girl with wavy hair and a broad, dimpled smile.

She skims through the words, her heart hammering in her throat. Something about a benefit, raising money to cover hospital bills. The name of a church and the date of some kind of prayer service. A drop box for donations. The names of a man and a woman, and phone numbers, and right underneath the photo, another with the same surname. Monroe. *Isla* Monroe.

Astra is running out the door before she even realizes she's left the counter. She doesn't even watch her feet or count her steps. The bell hits the doorframe loudly, like a slap, and Astra stands outside on the pavement, listening to the chime and the squeak and the sound of her own heartbeat.

What does a *benefit fundraiser* mean? How long has Isla been dead for? It's been weeks, at least. Astra has known her for weeks. Why is her family only just now starting to raise money for her hospital bills?

How long was she in the hospital? How much pain was she in? How many times has Astra passed by her brother in the hallways at school and never realized who he was?

She looks around quickly, craning her neck to see over parked cars and between buildings, but the boy with the flyers is gone.

And, when Astra finally calms down enough to go back inside the store, the flyer is gone, too.

❖

The unraveling day is over by the time Astra gets home. She can tell, because she walks in to the smell of garlic and oil, and, for once, it doesn't smell like it's burning.

Maria Vaughn is in the kitchen, chopping vegetables at a half-cleared counter while a pan behind her sizzles on the stove. She's wearing a simple blue dress with a long gray cardigan, but her wrists are covered in a rainbow of glass beads that clink together as she chops, and there's a silk scarf around her neck that keeps dangling onto the cutting board.

"Hi, sweetie," her mom says when Astra walks into the kitchen. There are at least a dozen spice jars out on the counter again, and Astra really hopes her mom doesn't plan on using them all in whatever she's making. Among them, she spots chili powder and cumin, which she thinks would be just fine, but the cinnamon and nutmeg pushed up against them might not work so well. And, right on the end—cardamom.

"Hey, Mom. Are you feeling any better? Do you need any help?"

Her mom sweeps around like a ballet dancer, turning the stove down, moving pots around, and shuffling through drawers looking for something that she never manages to find. She hums low in her throat and starts putting the spice containers back into the cabinet, one at a time.

"No, honey, I've got this. It's the least I can do to thank you for covering my shift. The store wasn't too busy, I hope?"

Astra shakes her head, but her mom's back is turned. She clears her throat. "It wasn't too bad. We sold some jewelry and one of those big ceramic jars you brought in last week."

"That's great, sweetie."

She thinks about bringing up the flyer, but there's no point in mentioning it now that it's gone. She's not even sure that she didn't just imagine the whole thing. She was thinking about Isla, so maybe her mind was just filling in the answers to some of the questions she wants to ask but knows she never will.

She'll ask Isla about it, just to be sure, but her mom doesn't need another thing to stress about right now.

"By the way," her mom continues, while actually wiping vegetable juice off the counter instead of letting it dry into a tacky mess like usual, "thank you for cleaning up the kitchen while I was in bed. And for making more tea. You know that always helps on days like these."

Astra looks around, and the kitchen *does* look a little neater than usual. The fake pears are back on top of the fridge, and just enough stuff has been cleared from the counter to fit a cutting board on one end and the toaster on the other. The dishes are washed, and the top of the stove looks like it's actually been wiped down as well.

And there's a mostly empty cup with a tea bag in it, sitting out next to the sink—a cup that Astra definitely didn't fill.

"Sure, Mom," she says. "I'm just glad you're feeling better. I'm, uh, going to head to my room for a little bit. I've got an essay due next week and I haven't even picked a topic yet."

Astra nearly runs the twelve steps from the kitchen to her bedroom, feeling a little dizzy and more than a little confused.

Obviously, Isla made the tea. Who else could have done it? She's getting a lot better at touching things, and she knew that Astra's mom was having a hard day. It makes sense. But if she was up here making tea, then who took the flyer?

Maybe Astra really *is* unstable. That makes more sense than anything else right now.

She opens her bedroom door and enters with her left foot, wiggles the knob four times, and fumbles for her light switch. Isla beats her to it, though, and Astra blinks in the sudden flood of light.

She has an impossible number of questions on her tongue, but just like her fact about bamboo, none of them are forming well enough for her to get them out. She can't focus on just one when there are so many. She feels like she's missing something, some piece of a massive puzzle that'll somehow bring everything together and make it all fit the way it's supposed to. She searches her brain, but it's just not there.

She knows she should say something. Leonard chirps and curls his body around Isla's leg, her feet firmly rooted halfway in the floor. If Astra could just think of *one* thing to say, one question, maybe she could make sense of some of the noise in her head.

But Isla beats her to that, too.

She smiles, floats closer, and says, "Can I ask you a question?"

"Sure."

"How far away does your dad live?"

Astra blinks, confused. "Hmm. Maybe four hours away? Why?"

Isla's grin stretches, dimples and canines. "I think I've got my next anti-bucket list item all figured out. How do you feel about a road trip?"

CHAPTER THIRTEEN

"Y ou've never been on a road trip before?"

"Maybe when I was little, I don't know. But never in the front seat, so I call shotgun."

Astra gestures to the empty car, rolls her eyes, and turns the key in the ignition. It roars to life under her fingers and she settles into her seat with a sigh.

"You're literally the only other person in the car."

"Well, then, you're lucky," Isla says. "I could be asking you to let me *drive*."

Astra waits for Isla to get comfortable before backing out of her parking space. Isla digs her hands into the sides of the passenger seat and kicks her feet through the glovebox, reclining just a little.

"Actually, I think *you're* the lucky one." Astra taps her fingers on the steering wheel with one hand and fiddles with the radio dial with the other. "You're lucky I agreed to this trip in the first place. You know how I feel about my dad."

"You promised to help me with my list," Isla says, shrugging in a single jerk. "It's not my fault that this is one of the things *on* that list."

Half of the radio stations are playing ads and the other half are running the same news segments they have been all day. The traffic light turns green and Astra settles both hands on the wheel, turning past a bank and two gas stations on her way out of town.

"Um, actually, it *is* your fault. You made the list." She gestures to the center console without taking her eyes off the road. "You can pick the station."

"Can't." Isla shakes her head, and Astra catches the blur of movement out of the corner of her eye. "Kinda trying to focus. Sorry."

Isla's hands are on the edges of her seat, holding on so tightly that they barely stop flickering. She's got her seat belt buckled, but it's going right through her body, so there's really no point. Plus, it's not like she can die twice.

Her face is screwed up in concentration, and if Astra didn't know any better, she would say that Isla actually looks *tired*. But ghosts can't feel things the way humans can. They're not human. Isla isn't human.

Sometimes Astra forgets that.

She picks a generic Top 40 music station and turns the volume down. A pop song she vaguely recognizes hums through the car.

Isla floats up until she's on her back, with her hands underneath her still gripping the seat cushion. The position reminds Astra of those sleepover games she's seen in movies—the whole *light as a feather, stiff as a board* thing. She almost makes a joke about it, but then she notices that Isla's eyes are closed and she looks like she could be sleeping, and she decides not to disturb her.

The highway is mostly empty, which means that Astra doesn't have to stress about passing other cars or getting honked at for going too slow. It also means that there's nothing to look at. The two-lane highway is flat, peppered with cracks and tar-patched holes, and the most interesting thing she's seen since she started driving—at exactly six a.m. on a Sunday, no less—was a huge billboard advertising some kind of antifungal cream. With a startlingly realistic photo printed on the entire right side that nearly made her crash into the pickup truck in front of her.

She's not sure why Isla is so intent on dragging her back to her old house. She's not really sure why she said yes, either. She could have refused. It's not like Isla would have been able to drive there without her.

Astra hasn't brought up the flyer yet, either. She's not sure what to say, because Isla isn't acting any different than usual, and Astra isn't totally convinced that she didn't just hallucinate the entire interaction with Isla's brother. She has a plan to find out for sure, though. She just needs to get through today first.

Exactly two hours and eighteen minutes into the drive—not that

Astra is counting—they pull over at an empty rest station on the right side of the main highway and park. Astra watches Isla while she shifts gears and pulls the keys out of the ignition. Isla is slow to pull her hands off the seat, and when she does, her fingers stick in the same bent position and she has to clap them together to shake them loose. Her hands look a little more transparent than usual, and the breath she lets out when she's finally untangled herself from the seat fills the entire inside of the car with arctic air.

She floats out of the car without even bothering to unbuckle her seat belt or open the door. She makes a motion like she's trying to crack her back, but it doesn't work very well since she doesn't actually have *bones*.

"Are you okay?" Astra asks her, forgetting for a moment that she's supposed to be upset at her. Or at least a little frustrated. Probably.

Isla blinks over at her with her unnervingly green eyes, the same exact shade as her brother's.

"Yeah. I'm fine. Can't feel anything when you're dead, right?"

Astra isn't so sure. "Right."

The rest station is the kind of grimy you'd expect out of a place that's in the middle of nowhere and probably doesn't get cleaned very often. The floors are off-white, but they've been smeared with mud tracks in so many places that they've turned mostly gray, and they're *sticky*. Astra doesn't even want to know why.

There's a small lobby in the front, with a long shelf full of maps and pamphlets about local attractions and restaurants. Astra's stomach growls right on cue when she makes eye contact with a full-color photo of spaghetti from some Italian place a few miles south of the main road, and Isla chuckles.

Isla floats up to the tall, domed ceiling to inspect the crown molding while Astra uses the bathroom—which is no cleaner *or* less sticky than the floor of the lobby. She would have been better off just waiting the extra ten minutes' drive and using the Italian restaurant's bathroom. And grabbing an order of spaghetti to go while she's there.

Instead, she buys her breakfast out of a suspicious looking vending machine that's covered in a thin layer of dust. The machine sucks up her dollar bill and slowly pushes a very stale-looking pastry forward—until it gets stuck between the rusty metal coils and the glass.

"You've got to be kidding me," she hisses under her breath, slapping at the side of the machine with her palm. The pastry doesn't move.

Isla chuckles from behind her. "This is really not your day, is it?"

"Yeah, but it's not gonna be good for you either if I don't get to eat something soon."

"You're grouchy even on your good days." Isla grins, floating to the side of the machine. "I'd hate to see what you're like when you're hangry."

She slides her hand through the side of the vending machine until her arm is inside, all the way up to her shoulder. Her face scrunches up as she concentrates, swatting her hand around until it flickers into something solid enough for her to knock the pastry down.

She ends up smacking two candy bars and a bag of chips down with it and breaking off the end of one of the old, rusted coils inside the machine, but she still looks unbearably smug when she pulls her hand out and gestures emphatically to the opening at the bottom of the machine.

Astra glares at her while she grabs her breakfast. She leaves the rest stop without looking back, with Isla following close behind—with two candy bars and a bag of chips balanced in her semi-solid arms.

Astra wipes her shoes off in the grass outside and peels out of the parking lot before she can convince herself to turn around and go back home.

"That looks disgusting," Isla says, eyeing the goo-covered pastry that cost Astra a dollar more than it's probably worth. And it only cost her a dollar.

"You're disgusting," Astra grumbles. She sniffs at her stale breakfast, glances around the mostly empty highway, and then quickly smears a layer of frosting along the top of Isla's hand.

It sticks. Isla's hand is, at the moment, corporeal. She's been fighting to keep her hands wedged in the seat cushion for the last three hours, and Astra swears she can see a nonexistent vein starting to bulge out of her neck.

Isla shrieks and lifts her hand to shake the goo off, and accidentally lets go of the seat. And promptly flies out of the car window.

Astra has to pull the car over to the side of the road and wait for

Isla to catch up. And then wait another ten minutes for her own laughter to subside.

"Not funny," Isla pants.

"A little bit funny," Astra argues.

Isla rolls her eyes and digs her hands back into the cushion, but her dimples give her away.

Another half hour passes before Astra sees the familiar water tower in the distance, painted with red and white vertical stripes. She hasn't seen it in over four years, but it's not something she would ever forget.

She eases into the exit and is just half a mile away before she rolls to a stop right in the middle of the road. She puts the car in park and turns to Isla, who looks relieved to finally be able to relax again.

"I don't think I can do this," Astra says. She's parked in front of Mr. McCluskey's red and yellow house, with its neatly manicured lawn and assortment of garden gnomes surrounding the front porch. She used to walk his dog for him on Saturdays.

Isla rights herself and moves like she's trying to crack her knuckles, but nothing happens. "You can. Trust me."

"You know I used to live here, right?"

Isla nods. "Obviously. That's why we're here."

"You know why we left, right?"

"I do."

Astra pauses, thinking. A car pulls up behind her and starts honking loudly, and she reluctantly eases her foot off the brake and starts driving again.

She passes the parking lot she learned to ride her bike in. The ice cream shop she frequented in the summer. The house that belonged to a little old lady who gave her butterscotch candies sometimes, who died at home and haunted the neighborhood for six weeks before she passed on.

"My dad lives here. My mom had her nervous breakdown here. I shouldn't have agreed to come back."

She's talking to herself more than Isla. She counts the blocks— one, two, three, four—and she knows there are only two more to go.

"You haven't seen your dad since then, right?" Isla asks. Astra shakes her head slowly, keeping her eyes on the road. "And your parents split because he didn't believe that your mom is psychic. Right?"

"Not psychic. But—yeah."

The car speeds up and Isla sinks her fingers into the seat cushion. "What if you could *make* him believe her? And you?"

Astra doesn't say anything. Her head feels like it's going to burst, and Isla's static is getting louder the more agitated she gets.

Isla continues, "You can turn back now. I won't stop you. I got my road trip. But…just give me five minutes. Just so you can get some closure. I think you deserve that, don't you?"

It's tempting. Astra doesn't hate her dad—she never has, not even when he let her mom get committed and used the time she was away to hire a divorce lawyer. Not even when he rented a moving truck and filled it with boxes and waved them away from the end of the driveway. Not even when he promised to call every single day, and then once a week, and then on the holidays and *Christmas, for sure*, and he only managed to keep his promise for two months and twenty-one days. Astra counted.

She digs her fingers into the steering wheel until her knuckles ache. "Fine."

"Really? Okay—it's, um, a left up ahead I think, and then—"

Astra interrupts her. "I know the way."

❖

The house hasn't changed at all in the last four years. Astra's not sure why she thought that it might, but it looks the same as she remembers it. The same soft white siding, the same navy blue trim around the windows, the same porch with the same wicker chairs and stone-topped circular table in the middle. The same flower bed, right out front, with the same colorful field of tulips, just starting to bloom.

Astra's throat feels like it's going to close up. The last time she was here, she was leaving the house she grew up in and following her half-delirious mother to a brand-new town with just the things they could fit in a moving van.

Now, she's following a literal ghost who may or may not be just a figment of her imagination. So, she's making good progress.

"Did you know that tulips are the national flower of Turkey?" Isla says once the car rolls to a stop in front of the house. "I didn't know that. I looked it up after you told me you liked them. These are really pretty. I can see why they're your favorite."

"If you're trying to distract me, keep going. It's working."

"They, um, symbolize love, I think. But not every color. The purple ones are royalty. And the yellow ones are happiness, which I guess makes sense."

"Uh-huh. Fascinating. Have I left the car yet?"

"Nope," Isla says, popping the *p*. "Here, let me help."

She floats through the window and around the front of the car, coming to a stop just outside Astra's door. She focuses for a second with her hand on the handle, then jerks it open and bows in the doorway.

"After you, milady," she says.

Astra steps out and returns the bow. "What a gentleman," she says. Isla's hands are still adjusting, like television pixels, but her dimples are soft and barely there. Astra's stomach swoops and she forgets for a moment why she's here.

She takes a couple of steps toward the house—one, two, three. Then four, because four is a good number. Isla hovers at her side, and Astra stops at the end of the pavement.

"I think…I should go alone. At first. I just—I don't know what's going to happen, and I don't want you to hear it."

Isla nods, looking uncertain. "Okay, but I'll be by the car. If you need me."

"Okay."

Isla sets her hand on Astra's back, right in the middle, and the sudden cold and pressure is enough to make Astra move. The sidewalk is the same as she remembers, too—right down to the long crack cutting through the middle that weeds sprout through in the summer.

The curtains are down, but there's a small patch of light poking out from between them, and her dad's car is in the driveway—a large, shiny gray hatchback with faded stickers in the back window. There's another car parked right next to it, small and red and slightly muddy around the tires, that Astra has never seen before.

She takes a deep breath and knocks on the door.

There's talking inside. The sound of a television playing loudly. A rustling, scraping noise like a chair being pushed out from behind a table. She pictures the kitchen in her mind, with coffee mugs and newspapers on the little square dining table—no lumpy couch, no throw pillows, no stack of papers underneath a wobbly wooden leg.

From behind her, Isla gives her a thumbs-up and a full-dimpled grin. And then the door opens.

Astra's dad hasn't changed much, either. His wispy black beard is a little longer, maybe. The hair on his head is a little shorter. He might have lost some weight, but he's wearing a sweater over his button-up so it's hard to tell. His jaw seems a little less defined, his forehead creases deeper than she remembers. But she would still recognize him in a lineup—with his crooked front teeth, his turned-up nose, and his skin just a little lighter than hers and peppered with moles.

"Astra," he says when he sees her, not even trying to hide the surprise on his face. "What are you doing here?"

A defensive feeling coils in her stomach, like her nerves have been run through with electricity. She's not afraid. She's angry.

She swallows the feeling down, where it lodges in her throat, tight and hot. "I was…taking a drive. With a friend. And I thought I'd stop in and say hi."

"A friend," he repeats slowly. She can see him craning his neck to look at her car, parked on the street. Isla shoots a crude hand gesture at him and Astra is thankful for once that she's invisible.

Astra nods. Her face feels warm. "Yeah."

"Does your mother know you're here?"

She thinks about lying, but she's been doing too much of that lately already.

"No," she says. "That's part of why I'm here, actually. She…had a bad day, yesterday. And I think you're wrong—about her. I *know* you are."

It's slightly satisfying watching the gobsmacked expression settle on his face. He shifts his feet in the doorway. Astra can see the living room from over his shoulder. The sage green has been painted over with a sunny yellow and the couch has been replaced.

"Astra, sweetheart, your mother is *sick*, and—"

"Can I come in?" she interrupts. She can feel her courage starting to wane, and if she doesn't get it all out now, she knows she never will. She wishes she had asked Isla to stay with her.

Her dad taps his hand on the doorframe and sighs. "Now isn't really a good time."

She blinks at him. "I drove all the way out here to see you."

"You should have called first. Showing up in the middle of the day like this is just—"

He's interrupted again, but not by Astra this time. By a noise. A sound. A high-pitched, shrill, awful cry. A baby.

Astra cranes her neck, but she can't see the source of the noise. It's definitely a baby, though, and after a few seconds of wailing it stops, and a clacking set of footsteps and a woman's voice replace it. Astra can tell that the sounds are coming from the living room, but her dad is blocking the doorway just enough that she can't see.

"You have a baby," she says. It's not a question, but her dad still nods.

"He's two months old. His name's Caleb."

"I have a brother."

"You do."

It feels like cold water has been dumped over her head, but instead of feeling cold and shaky, she feels floaty and numb. Like a balloon filled with helium. Like she could just…float away.

She hates it. And, for the first time, she hates *him*.

"You didn't tell me. You could have called, or sent a letter, or a *text*. Does Mom know? Have you told her?"

The baby starts crying again. Her dad is starting to look frantic.

"Your mother—we don't talk. She's sick, and I don't want to cause her any more stress than she's already been under."

"Because of you." She lifts her hand and brushes a stray curl off her forehead. Her hand comes away slick with sweat. Her voice rises in pitch, the words rushing out of her fast and hard and loud. "And she's *not* sick. She's—I don't know. Psychic, maybe. But it doesn't matter, because she was telling the truth. And I know that, because *so am I*."

The second the words leave her mouth, she regrets them. She stands there, gaping like a fish, like if she keeps her mouth open her words will somehow find their way back in. But they don't. They land like a slap, and her dad swivels his neck around like he's got whiplash.

He glances behind him into the living room, toward the soft cries of a two-month-old baby and the gentle voice of the woman who replaced Astra's mom. And then he looks back at his firstborn, and Astra's resolve crumbles.

"You should go," he tells her, like it's a suggestion. But she knows that it isn't.

She nods. Her mouth is still open, but nothing is coming out. She takes four steps backward, left foot first, and once she's down the porch steps the door squeaks shut.

Isla is waiting for her by the car. Her dimples disappear the second she sees Astra's face, and Astra wishes she could fake a smile just to bring them back.

"What the hell did he say?" Isla demands, untangling her pretzeled legs and floating up, up, up.

"He didn't believe me. Or Mom. He's got a new wife, and a baby. And he didn't believe me."

She expects an angry tirade out of Isla, one of her signature rants, but she doesn't get one. Isla schools her face into what's probably supposed to be a neutral expression, and before Astra can tell her not to, she's in the air—and flying straight toward the house.

Astra stands by the car and listens. She doesn't dare move any closer. For ten whole seconds—and she counts—there's silence.

Then she hears a loud bang. The sound of glass. Something heavy falling onto a tile kitchen floor. A shriek from a woman. A shout from a man. A baby wailing loudly.

The curtains flutter, and from in between them Astra can see the lights flickering. And a hand, pushing through the fabric and waving.

A minute later, her dad throws open the door and runs to his car, a blond woman in a lurid green jumpsuit following with a baby in her arms. Isla doesn't come out of the house until the shiny gray hatchback has peeled out of the driveway and halfway down the block.

She floats out with her arms crossed, stops on the bottom porch step, and in one swift movement uproots a large handful of colorful tulips.

When they're both in the car, buckled and idling, Isla holds the bouquet out to Astra. A couple of the stems still have their roots attached, and dirt is flaking off all over the center console.

"What's this for?" Astra asks. She takes the flowers and sets them gently in the cupholder.

"Maybe you can plant them," Isla says. "Or just keep them in a vase. I just—he doesn't deserve to have them. They're too pretty for someone like him."

Astra stares at her, feeling a swirl of emotions in her stomach. Now that her surge of confidence is wearing off, she's mostly just tired.

And frustrated. And something else, something weird, like riding in an elevator or on a roller coaster. That sudden lurch of weightlessness.

Then Isla smiles, showing the points of her shiny white canines and her deep, deep dimples, and Astra finally gets it.

And it's the worst thing possible.

Chapter Fourteen

You're in love with her," Oliver repeats, pausing his foot-tapping for a second.

"It's not funny."

"I'm not laughing."

They're in the lunch room, but Astra has never been less hungry in her life. Every few seconds Oliver reaches across the table and steals a soggy french fry off her tray, and she wonders how he stays like a noodle when he eats practically his entire body weight in pure junk food every day.

He twirls a carrot stick in his fingers, but she knows he's not going to eat it. "She's not, like…here right now, right?"

Astra shakes her head. "She's at home. Or—wherever she goes when I'm at school."

She tries not to think about Isla, sitting alone in Astra's tiny apartment, just waiting for her to get home from school. That's probably not what's happening, though, because Isla has too much pent-up energy to stay still for that long. Still, maybe Astra shouldn't have gotten so upset with her for the dodgeball incident. It wasn't *all* her fault, after all.

And Astra kind of misses her when she's at school. But only a little bit.

"So," Oliver says. "You're not denying it."

He steals another fry. She shoves her tray in his direction and props her elbows up on the edge of the table.

She frowns, staring down at the chipping, blue plastic. "No, I guess I'm not."

She expects him to make fun of her, even though she knows he's not that mean. Maybe she wants him to, though. Maybe if he tells her how wrong her feelings are, or how she's probably just confused, or how none of it matters anyway because Isla is dead—then maybe she can stop. Or at least pretend. That's all she has to do—just pretend nothing has changed until Isla finishes her bucket list and leaves.

Just thinking about it makes Astra's stomach roil.

"Okay," Oliver says. "So, you think you love her. Have you ever, um, loved a girl before?"

Astra shrugs. Her face feels warm. Isla's cold would be pretty welcome right about now.

"I haven't really loved anybody, I guess. Boys *or* girls. But…it doesn't really matter to me *who* it is, you know?"

Oliver nods. She can see him out of the corner of her eye, holding a fry in one hand and a carrot stick in the other. His eyes are almost the same shade of blue as the table, and his nose stud has a tiny diamond on the end today.

Astra is telling the truth, for once. She's had crushes, sure—she *is* seventeen years old, after all. But it's never really about how someone *looks*. Oliver is objectively handsome, with his long legs and his shiny hair and those piercing blue eyes of his, but she's never felt anything other than friendship with him. But there was a boy in the seventh grade who always carried enough spare pencils to loan her one whenever she forgot hers, and he was kind of plain, with short blond hair and muddy eyes and a round, pimply face—and thirteen-year-old Astra would have sworn at the time that she was in love with him.

In the ninth grade, it was a girl with dreadlocks and combat boots, who ended up being her partner for a science project that lasted nearly a month and was worth a quarter of their grade.

Just last year, it was a boy a couple of inches shorter than her who carried a messenger bag instead of a backpack and always smelled like licorice.

But Isla feels different than all of those other crushes, somehow. More real. Which is ironic, because Isla is the *least* real person Astra has ever had feelings for.

"Hey, can I tell you something?" Oliver asks, leaning forward onto the table. He's so much taller than she is, and his arms are so much longer, that he has to fold them on the table and prop his chin up on them to be at eye-level with her.

Astra nods, watching him push both of their lunch trays aside and lean closer. *He could stretch across the whole table top and still stay seated*, she thinks.

He glances around quickly, but they're the only two people at their table. Sometimes Astra wonders why Oliver doesn't sit with the other track kids. The jocks. Why he chooses to be *her* friend, when he could literally be friends with anyone else in the school.

He lowers his voice.

"I'm gay."

Astra blinks. She's not sure what she expected him to say, but it wasn't that.

She had wondered, a little bit. Wondered if he was like her, in some way that didn't involve talking to dead people. But she didn't want to assume that his earrings and long hair meant anything, because she's seen that same look on so many different people.

His patchy jacket crinkles, with a little cat head on his forearm and a peace sign near the cuff of his sleeve, and he's staring down at his hands. And Astra feels so unbelievably *fond* that she swears he must be able to hear her heartbeat from across the table.

She doesn't know what to say. Oliver's hair has fallen forward like a curtain over his face, and the tips of his ears poking out are bright red. His earrings today are tiny red cherries, and it occurs to Astra that he probably wears such small jewelry because it's easier to hide under his long, dark hair.

She swings her legs over the side of the bench, stands up, and shuffles around the table until she's next to him on the other side. Then she sits down and wraps her arms around him and squeezes tightly.

He lets out a little noise of surprise, and then his hands are on her back and his forehead is pushed up against her shoulder. She can hear him breathing—in, out, in, out.

He sniffs and sits back, but his eyes are dry. His face is beet red. Astra has never seen Oliver Wiley *nervous* before.

"Why didn't you ever say anything?" she asks him, keeping her spot next to him on the bench.

He jerks his shoulders in a half shrug. "It never felt like the right time, I guess. Plus, I'm already on thin ice with the track guys. I don't need to give them another reason to hate me."

"Nobody could hate you, Oliver. You're too awesome."

He looks up at her through his long curtain of hair and smiles.

"Thanks," he says softly. "It feels nice. To talk to someone about it."

Astra nods. It really does.

"That's what friends are for," she tells him, and it occurs to her that this might be the first time she's really acknowledged Oliver as her *friend*—outside of lying to her mom or getting teased by Isla. Astra has a friend. A living, breathing, *human* friend.

"Well," he says, "as your friend, you know I can't let your little love confession go without at least being a *little* annoying about it. So, spill. What's she like—besides tall and blond?"

Astra smiles, the butterflies in her stomach bursting up into her throat.

"She's *amazing*, Oliver, you have no idea. She calls you Ollie, did you know that? And—did I tell you what we did this weekend? She tricked me into going to see my dad, and I thought it was gonna be horrible because he thinks my mom is crazy—which means I am, too—but it wasn't. It was kind of amazing, actually."

Oliver tucks his hair behind his ears, little red cherries on full display, and gives her his full, crooked-grinned attention. And the french fries sit forgotten for the rest of the lunch period.

❖

The day is almost over when Astra sees him.

She doesn't even mean to—she's on her way to her sixth period history class, down the winding second-floor hallway, when she spots a familiar mop of shaggy brown hair. She doesn't even realize *why* it's familiar until her feet carry her down the row of lockers and in the direction of the freshmen science department, where a small group of fourteen-year-olds has clustered by the door.

She's not sure why she ever thought she made him up, because she's definitely seen him before. Isla's little brother has been going to class just across the hallway from her all semester, and she never realized it.

Her footsteps are loud, and when he hears them he looks up. She waves and tries for a smile, but his dull green eyes have her stomach in knots.

He nods to his friends, and they walk through the door without him.

He shakes the loose hair out of his face and returns her wave halfway. "You're the girl from that store downtown. The one with all the...stuff."

Junk, she thinks. At least he's polite.

"And you're the kid with the flyer."

"That's right," he says. He's shorter than Isla, Astra notices, but he's still got just enough baby fat that he's probably not done growing. And he's already taller than Astra. "Did you ever put it up?"

Astra shakes her head. "I misplaced it. I wanted to talk to you about that, actually."

The bell rings, and the hallway empties out quickly. Astra takes a few steps away from the door and leans back against the lockers. Now that she's got him here, she's not sure what to say. Part of her never thought she'd actually get this far. Part of her still believed that she'd imagined their entire interaction.

The boy walks over to her other side and leans next to her, shoving his hands in his pockets. He's got the same nose as Isla. This is going to be hard.

"Um," she begins. *Very eloquent, Astra,* she tells herself. *Good job.* "You're Isla Monroe's brother, aren't you?"

His hair is hiding just enough of his eyes to give her some extra breathing room.

"Yeah," he says. "I'm Ricky. How do you know my sister?"

I'm in love with her. She's a ghost. She's a dead girl who haunts my bedroom sometimes. And I'm in love with her.

"We were friends."

Ricky shifts his head just a little bit to look at her. "Were?"

"It's—it's been a while. Since we talked. But I heard what happened to her, and I didn't realize that the flyer was *hers* until after you left, and I just—I was hoping you could tell me what really happened."

His eyebrows knit together, and he fixes her with a hard stare that reminds her so much of Isla that it's like getting whiplash. The late bell rings, and Astra knows she's not going back to class today. At least she's only missing one period.

Ricky sighs. "I probably don't know any more than you do. Nobody tells me anything."

"Try me."

"Yeah. Okay." He shuffles his feet. The lockers clang against his back. "She, um…she got sick. An infection, the doctor said. Like, no big deal, right? But she didn't tell anybody. It just got worse and, I don't know, maybe I should have noticed. But you know how Isla is."

Astra nods. "Stubborn," she says.

"*Very* stubborn," Ricky agrees. "So she passes out, and it's out of nowhere, and…the doctors say it's a miracle she even survived, but I don't think I'd call a coma a *miracle*."

Astra almost nods again, ready to agree with him on anything just to keep him talking. But then his words sink in, slow and sticky like molasses, and her lungs start to clog up with them until it's hard to even breathe. She runs them over again in her head, but they make even less sense the second time. One in particular.

Survived. That's the word he used, right? That's not a word you use when you're talking about a ghost. A dead girl.

She blinks at him. Her throat works around the words stuck inside it like fly paper, and she manages to cough a few of them out.

"Coma," she says. *So eloquent.* "Survived. You said—she's in a *coma*? Right now?"

Ricky looks confused. Astra *feels* confused.

"Yeah?" he says. "I thought you knew?"

"I—I thought she was dead."

Ricky's face pales, turning a ghostly white. It makes him look even more like his sister. "I don't know who told you that, but no, she's alive. But she won't wake up. I don't know what's wrong, but the doctors aren't optimistic. I've heard them talking about it through the wall."

"Isla's in the hospital," Astra repeats, like a mantra. Like the more times she says it, the truer it'll become.

"That's generally where coma patients end up, yes."

His tone is startlingly familiar. He's Isla's brother, all right.

"She could still wake up, right? That's possible?"

Ricky looks at his shoes. "I guess. It's been, like, a month. Five weeks, I think. That's…a long time."

Astra can hear the chatter coming from the classroom on the other side of the lockers she's leaning up against. Someone's shoes squeak on the other end of the hallway, near the bathrooms. Ricky keeps pushing his hair out of his face, but every time he moves it falls back again. It's not even very long—just shaggy. Limp and stringy like it could use a good washing. His posture and his clothes are slack and wrung out, and he's barely looked at Astra once the whole time they've been talking.

He has his sister's eyes and nose and maybe a little bit of her height, but none of her confidence. Astra wonders if that would be different if she weren't in the hospital right now.

"Look," Ricky says after a long stretch of silence, "I really don't wanna talk about this here, okay? She's my sister. It's…"

"I know," Astra says quickly. "I'm sorry. I shouldn't have just jumped on you like that. Or made you miss class."

Ricky pushes back against the lockers with his shoulders until he's standing mostly straight and turns his head to look at her. She notices that his eyes are the same green as Isla's—*sage*, her mind finally supplies—but there's a tiny splash of brown in his right eye near the middle. It looks a little bit like a coffee stain, a smudge, and Astra finds it a lot easier to maintain eye contact with him if she fixates on it.

He sighs, runs his hand through the hair that's nearly covering his eyes, and says, "You really were friends, huh?"

Astra stares at the smudge. "Yeah. I—I cared about her a lot. I still do."

He looks like he's searching for something in her face. He must find it, because he pushes off from the lockers with his palms and takes a small step forward.

"Well, if we're not going back to class, we might as well go see her."

CHAPTER FIFTEEN

Astra gets why her mom doesn't like hospitals. She figures it out before she even puts one foot inside the building.

The hospital that Isla is staying in is a towering, mud-colored brick building. It's split into at least half a dozen smaller buildings in a semicircle around the lot, but the tallest and longest is the one Ricky leads Astra to once she's parked the car.

There are at least a hundred windows. The roofs are flat and dark, and the parking lot seems to go on forever. The name of the hospital is printed in large, shiny brown letters above the entrance, and when Astra walks up the narrow, winding pavement toward the rotating doors, she's greeted by a ghost sitting on a bench outside.

The ghost looks like a man, but it's kind of hard to tell for sure, because most of his face is covered in large, angry welts. He looks like one big blister about to pop. He's wearing a hospital gown and fuzzy gray socks, and he's got stringy patches of blond hair on just the back of his head.

He looks up at her through puffy eyes and slowly raises his hand in a wave. Astra waits until Ricky has gone through the revolving doors before she waves back.

That wasn't so bad, really. She's seen dead people in much worse shape than the guy on the bench. Maybe her mom was overreacting.

Then she walks through the doors, and a gust of frigid air hits her so hard that she nearly falls over.

She stumbles into the edge of the Plexiglas doorframe and reaches out behind herself to grab onto it. Ricky doesn't seem to notice. He walks across the white and blue tiled floor and straight to the front desk without looking back at her once.

Astra rights herself quickly and jogs to catch up to him.

The place is nearly empty of visitors, which isn't surprising at 2:28 p.m. on a school day. Ricky walks like he's got the layout memorized, like he's been here dozens of times before, and it's a little heartbreaking to think that he probably has.

"Hey." He waves her over from the reception desk, which is white and curved in one long arc. He's leaning up over the counter on his elbows. "What's your name?"

He holds up a rectangular yellow *Visitor* pass with his name and the date printed in pen on the front. The receptionist is a young redhead with the whitest teeth Astra has ever seen. On the far right side of the counter, a dead woman missing the back half of her skull is sitting on the floor in a pretty green dress. She doesn't even look up when Astra approaches the desk, but the static sound she emits hits Astra's ears like nails on a chalkboard.

"Astra Vaughn," she says to the redhead. She spells out her last name and watches the woman write it neatly on a second yellow rectangle.

Ricky hums but doesn't say anything.

The noise gets louder the farther into the hospital they walk. Ricky leads Astra down a long, curved hallway with a path marked out on the floor in dark blue tiles. Astra tries to count her steps, but she nearly runs into an elderly ghost floating down the hall in a spotted blue and gray hospital gown, so she settles on counting rooms instead. Seven rooms to get to the elevators. Two bathrooms across from a padded brown bench with fake, leafy potted plants on either side.

Astra huffs out a soft laugh while they're waiting for the elevator. "Isla would hate those."

She points her thumb in the direction of the waxy leaves and Ricky actually smiles.

"She would. She's got, like, a personal vendetta against every fake plant she sees."

"Yeah, "Astra agrees. "But she could talk for *hours* about the real ones."

Ricky stares at her with that same searching look in his eyes that she saw at school. Astra tries to focus on the coffee stain on his right eye and the chime of the elevator as it reaches their floor.

"I didn't know she had any friends."

It's almost a whisper, and he's got his chin tucked into his neck when he says it, so Astra can barely hear. Something sharp and cold settles in her chest that has nothing to do with the ghosts nearby.

"Yeah," she says, because someone needs to say it. Because Ricky needs to know. "She does."

He doesn't say anything, but she knows he heard her.

There are no ghosts in the elevator. Ricky pushes the button for the fourth floor, and Astra breathes in a tiny pocket of warm air. Her skin feels prickly with goose bumps, and she rubs at her sleeves when Ricky isn't looking.

The ICU, however, is *full* of dead people. It makes sense, really, and Astra should honestly have seen it coming, but the cold and the static hit her with full force the second the elevator doors ding open. They hit her so hard, in fact, that she actually *does* fall down this time— straight into the metal bar around the inside of the elevator, landing hard on her shoulder in the back left corner.

She grabs at the bar with one hand and sticks her foot out, and she feels a bit like a cross between a ballet dancer and a circus clown. The doors slide shut again, and the sudden rush of warmth makes Astra feel dizzy.

Ricky leans down next to her. "Are—are you okay?"

Astra nods. Then keeps nodding. Then forces herself to *stop* nodding.

"I'm fine. Dizzy spells, you know?"

"Being in a hospital probably doesn't help," he says. "I always feel a little nauseous when I come here."

"I'm sorry for making you miss school," she tells him.

He shrugs with one shoulder. "I was gonna come here after, anyway. And it's worth it if I can bring a friend to see her. She hasn't had anyone besides family visit yet."

"She—what?"

No, Astra thinks. *That doesn't make any sense.* Isla is funny, bright, cheerful, and one of the most beautiful people Astra has ever met. She's smart, and thoughtful, and Astra's heart always skips a beat whenever she sees Isla's wavy hair and her impossibly deep dimples.

There's no way that Isla hasn't had any visitors. It's not possible.

"Never mind," Ricky says. "I'm just glad you're here. Are you good to go yet?"

Astra tests out her weight on the metal bar and then pulls herself up and holds on to it for a few extra seconds just in case. She feels okay right now—warm, and steady, and a little bit heartbroken—but she knows that once the elevator doors open again, she'll be hit with the same heavy wave all at once.

She nods.

The second time is a little easier, mostly because Astra knows what to expect. But what she *can't* anticipate are the ghosts she'll see, and it's really hard maintaining her composure when the first guy to greet her by the nurse's station is floating without any legs.

"You can see me," the ghost says. Luckily, his hospital gown is covering what's left of his lower half, but there's blood on the front of it and in the corners of his mouth. He gives her a toothy smile and floats right through the nearest window.

Astra sighs. One down, a million to go.

"Isla is in room 421," Ricky tells her. The hallways on this floor are laid out in one big rectangle, split into smaller squares that each have their own nurse's station and set of single-stall bathrooms. The floor is white and speckled with tiny black spots, the walls are bumpy and gray, and everything smells like bleach and latex.

Astra memorizes the room number and tries to pay attention to the route to get there. Three rooms, nurse's station, bathrooms. Visitor's lounge, bathrooms, four rooms—one with an open door, one with a doctor just stepping inside, and another with two ghosts hovering in front of it. One of them is fuzzy and soft, like the long-dead creatures that haunt the outside of Astra's bedroom, but the other one is flickering rapidly, with patches of blood down the front of his shirt and a large rip in the left leg of his jeans.

"Where am I?" he wails. His voice sounds like static, too—like turning the TV up so high that the speakers can't play the sound right, so they crackle and boom instead. His head keeps jerking from side to side, and he floats up to the ceiling and back down again twice before Astra reaches the end of the hall.

And then he lunges at her.

She steps to the side quickly, knocking her right arm into the bumpy gray wall hard enough to bruise. The ghost keeps going until he runs right through her, and her whole body feels like it's been frozen solid. She shivers and pushes back against the wall. Her teeth are chattering.

Ricky rounds on her immediately, his hands up, palms out. "Is this another dizzy spell? Because if you're gonna have a medical emergency, I guess you're in the right place."

Astra takes deep breaths—in, out, in, out. She counts four sets, because four is a good number, and clenches her jaw tightly.

"You're a lot like your sister," she tells him. Her legs are shaking, so she straightens them out and locks her knees. "You look a little bit alike, but you *sound* a lot alike."

"Hmm. You know, I don't get that very much. I guess I'll take it as a compliment."

"It is." She stands up and breathes a sigh of relief when her legs don't buckle underneath her. "Hey, Ricky. Did I ever tell you that I'm afraid of hospitals?"

It wouldn't have been the truth an hour ago, but it feels pretty true right now. Maybe Astra is more like her mother than she wants to admit.

"Really? I couldn't tell. You hide it really well."

Astra grins. "You could be twins, I swear."

She takes a shaky breath. Ricky scans her face again.

"Are you having a panic attack?" he asks. Astra shakes her head and takes a couple of steps away from the wall.

"Not yet. I'll let you know if I do."

"Good. It would be a shame if you had one now, though."

He jerks his thumb over his shoulder. There's a door behind him—solid, light brown wood like the rest, with a set of numbers glued to the wall next to it: 421. Isla's room.

She made it.

Despite the cold and the pounding in her head, Astra nearly runs to the door and pushes her way through. She doesn't even bother to jiggle the knob—the door opens easily, and she walks in without waiting for Ricky to follow her. All that matters is seeing Isla—making sure she's okay. Seeing her *alive*. Everything else is just background noise.

The first thing Astra notices about Isla's room is that it's sparse. There's a lot of space near the door that could probably fit another bed, but it's been left open—just the same speckled white and black flooring as the hallway, and textured gray walls with a few pictures tacked up around them—a grayscale puppy in a wicker basket, a field of wheat with a red barn in the background, a bird in midflight. A black wheelchair has been pushed into one corner, next to a sink and a covered garbage bin.

There's a curtain attached to the ceiling that's been pulled halfway across the room, and Astra can see an uncomfortable-looking wooden chair and a small folding mattress tucked up against the window on the far wall. The chair has a blanket thrown over the back and there are two throw pillows on top of the mattress. Astra wonders how many nights Isla's parents have spent in that chair and on that mattress, just waiting for their daughter to wake up.

Five weeks. That's what Ricky said. Astra's brain chooses the worst possible moment to remind her of that.

Beyond the curtain, there's one last thing that Astra can see, sitting on the windowsill—the ghost of a young woman, probably only a few years older than Astra, with her long red hair braided behind her back and freckles scattered across her face like stars.

There are thick gashes running up both of her forearms.

She's wearing a fluttery white blouse and dark jeans, but her feet are bare. She's kicking her legs over the side of the windowsill, toes pointed and flickering, and there's blood all over the front of her shirt and even a little bit in her hair.

"You can move the curtain, you know," Ricky says from behind her, and Astra jumps. The ghost in the window smiles and keeps swinging her legs.

"Yeah, okay. Thanks."

Astra pulls back the curtain and immediately wishes she hadn't.

There's only one bed in the room, so there's only one place for Isla to be, but at first Astra doesn't even see her through the cluster of machines and tubes. There's a steady beeping coming from one of them, something dripping down a tube next to it, and in the middle of it all is Isla. Only, she doesn't *look* like the Isla that Astra knows.

Astra steps closer to the body in the bed and blinks down at it. It's got blond hair like Isla, curled at the ends and splayed out all around its face, but the hair is stringy instead of bouncy, dull instead of shiny. The body's face is pale, like a ghost, but more gray than white, and the cheekbones are so sunken that there probably aren't even any dimples to show underneath. The freckles are too dark, there are shadows under the eyes that look like bruises, and the lips are chapped and thin and ashy. And not smiling. If this were Isla, she would be smiling.

There's a tube going into its—*her*—mouth, and another with prongs going into each of her nostrils. An IV in her arm. A monitor on her finger, another on her chest, and another around her bicep. There are bruises on her arms like polka dots from needle marks that never healed. She's got at least half a dozen blankets pulled up over her body, but Astra can still see the outline of her skinny waist underneath, and she feels like she's going to puke.

She pulls the chair up closer to the bed and sinks down into it. Her legs give out easily.

Ricky sits on the mattress and fiddles with the tag on one of the throw pillows. "Maybe I shouldn't have brought you here," he says. "It would have been better if you didn't have to see her like this."

"No. I wanted to see her. I—I'm okay."

Actually, she's *not* okay. She's in love with the ghost of a girl who's probably dying, and there's nothing she can do about it. She feels less okay now than she did when she thought Isla was already dead.

"You're new," the ghost on the windowsill says suddenly. Her cold breath tickles the back of Astra's neck. "You're not a doctor or brother or parents. Sister, maybe? Or something else?"

Astra doesn't say anything. She sets her hands on top of Isla's blankets and listens to the rhythmic beeping of the heart monitor. At least her heart is okay. Astra can't say the same about her own.

"She doesn't move," the ghost continues. "It gets boring sometimes."

"Hey, Ricky?" Astra asks. "Do you mind, um—can I just get, like, ten minutes with her? Alone?"

She waits for Ricky to say no, but he just stands and stretches. "Sure. I should probably call my mom, anyway, let her know where I am. You should talk to her. That's what my mom always says. Just in case she can hear you."

"Yeah. I will."

"She can't hear you," the ghost in the window argues. "She's not really in there."

The door clicks shut again and Astra turns around to face the ghost. "I know," she says.

"She comes in sometimes and listens, though. She looks different when she's awake."

"Yeah, she does. I'm Astra, by the way. Friend of Isla's."

The ghost blinks and her eyes flicker in their sockets. "Robin," she says.

"Nice to meet you, Robin."

Astra turns back to Isla. From this close, her skin looks even duller—a strange purple and gray mixture, like one big bruise. The top of a blue and gray hospital gown is poking out over the pile of blankets, and for some reason that's what startles Astra the most. She's never seen Isla in anything but her sunny yellow dress and polka-dot socks.

"What do the doctors say?" Astra asks, even though she doesn't really want to know the answer.

Robin hums. "I change rooms. This one is nice. Isla is good company when she's here. But I don't stay all the time. And the doctors don't come very often."

"You'd better not be gossiping about me, Robin, or I'll sic Johnny on you."

Astra looks up so quickly that her neck cracks. Isla is standing on the other side of the bed, floating through the curtain, looking *way* more alive than the body on the bed.

Robin narrows her eyes. "You *wouldn't*."

"Try me."

There's a small burst of cold wind behind Astra, and then it's quickly smothered by the feeling of a warm blanket over her shoulders, and she knows that the ghost in the window is gone.

Isla floats closer, crosses her legs, and hovers in the air above her body. It's a very eerie thing to see, and Astra isn't quite sure which one she's supposed to be looking at.

She looks down at her own hands instead. "Why didn't you tell me?"

"Look at me, Astra," Isla says. "Not *that* me, *this* me. Which one do you like better?"

Astra looks up. Isla has a small, sad smile on her face, no dimples, and Astra wishes she had never come here.

She hates how easily the answer to Isla's question comes to her, so she swallows it down and changes the subject quickly.

"Did you take the flyer that your brother left in my mom's store?"

"I did."

"Why?"

Isla crosses her arms. Her feet flicker in their blue and white polka-dot socks. She shrugs and her shoulders shift at odd angles.

"Because it doesn't matter. I figured it would just make you more upset if you got your hopes up than if you just thought I was dead the whole time. I pretty much am, anyway. It's just a matter of time."

"Don't say that."

Isla blinks down at her and floats closer. Astra's skin is prickly with cold, but her face is warm and her heart is beating so fast that it hurts.

Isla stops a couple of inches away from Astra's face. Her breath feels like ice. "Why does it matter so much to you?"

Astra should say it. She *knows* that she should. Isla deserves to know how Astra feels about her, no matter what happens to her. But the body in the bed is so pale, and the heart rate monitor is so loud, and nothing about this place feels right. Not for something like that.

"Because you're my friend," she says instead, and it feels close to the truth. She inches her fingers closer to Isla's hand—her real, living hand—on top of the blankets.

Isla's mouth curls up in one corner. "Friends, huh? Only *you* would have more dead friends than living ones."

Astra returns the smile. It only feels a little out of place. She slides her hand over Isla's slowly, hoping she won't notice. She just wants to know what it feels like. That's all.

And it's *warm*. Ever since she stepped through the front doors of the hospital, Astra has felt frozen—not chilled, not cold, but like *ice*. Now, though, she's *melting*.

Above her, Isla shudders and lets out a little noise like a gasp.

"What are you doing?" she asks, uncrossing her legs and hovering closer. "I can—I can *feel* that."

"You can...really? What does it feel like?"

Isla hums. Her smile looks a lot more genuine now, and her smiley-face dimple is right in front of Astra's eyes. It's very distracting.

"It feels normal," she says. "Um, warm. I don't—I haven't felt anything at all since...you know. Not even when the doctors come in or my mom gets all sappy and won't stop hugging me. I didn't think it was possible."

"Well, you know. Maybe it's my *psychic* thing."

"I know you're being sarcastic right now, but I honestly think you might be onto something. You should go buy a lottery card before your mojo wears off."

"I don't think I'm old enough."

"Buzzkill."

And, just like that, the tightly wound rope in Astra's chest uncoils just a bit, letting her breathe a little easier. For just a moment, she can imagine that she's not in the hospital—she's somewhere else, talking to Isla and holding her hand, without a bunch of tubes and wires between them. It feels so lovely that when the door opens and Ricky walks back in and the spell is broken, Astra's heart actually *aches*.

Isla floats back up until her head touches the ceiling. Ricky glances quickly at Astra's hand on the bed, but he doesn't comment on it.

"Hey," he says. "Sorry if I interrupted something super sentimental. Just...my parents are on their way. They'll be here in, like, ten minutes—fifteen if traffic's bad. I don't know if you're up for meeting the fam, so I figured I'd give you a heads-up."

Astra nods. "Thanks. I should probably go."

"My parents don't usually come until after four, if you ever feel like giving her some company again. I don't know if my mom's right, but if she *is*, then Isla probably appreciates it."

Astra doesn't say anything. She waits until Ricky has settled himself back on top of the mattress by the window before letting go of Isla's hand—but not before leaning forward just slightly and pressing a barely-there kiss to her knuckles.

The sputtering noise Isla makes on their way out the door is enough to get Astra to the elevator without noticing a single ghost.

CHAPTER SIXTEEN

Astra's mom is waiting for her when she gets home. Her mom isn't supposed to be home for another hour.

Astra toes her shoes off slowly. Her mom is wearing a thick brown sweater with a mustard-yellow skirt underneath it, large hoop earrings and shiny gold bangles, and a very stern *mom look* complete with narrowed eyes and sucked-in lips.

"Your school called."

Oh, crap, Astra thinks. Behind her, Isla quickly sinks through the wall and makes her escape. *Lucky.*

"Since when do you skip school?" her mom continues. She's even got one hand on her hip. Astra swallows hard.

Maria Vaughn is usually too scrambled—like eggs—to do much more than go to work and sleep. But on her rare days of total clarity, she's a force to be reckoned with.

Astra slides her shoes into the corner by the door and shifts her backpack to one shoulder. She tries to look casual. The only problem is, she's probably the *least* casual-looking person she knows.

"It was just one class," she says defensively. "And I'm all caught up on the homework anyway. So it's not a big deal."

"Skipping school is a big deal, honey. At least tell me you have a good excuse?"

"I was with my friend. Oliver."

Now her mom and Oliver can never, ever meet. It would be disastrous.

"Should I be worried that this boy is a bad influence on you?"

Astra almost laughs, because Oliver Wiley, human noodle, being a bad influence? If anything, Astra is a bad influence on *him*. She made him come with her when she stole a dead guy's cat, after all. She got him in trouble with Mr. Pierce. And she spilled milk on his homework at lunch one time and he only got out of detention because Astra told his teacher the truth and begged her to give him an extension. Astra is *way* worse than Oliver. She's like a magnet for bad luck.

She's also a very, *very* bad liar.

"No, Mom," she says without thinking. As usual. "We were at the hospital."

The moment of surprise wipes the stern look off her mom's face. Astra realizes what she's said and frantically tries to come up with a way to backpedal, but she's a bad liar, and she's even worse at telling the truth.

There are only four steps from the front door to her bedroom. Astra maps out her escape plan in her mind and wonders if her mom can run in heels.

"The hospital," her mom repeats slowly. "Is he okay?"

"Yeah, no, he's fine. It's his—his sister, she's sick, and we were just…visiting. I didn't want to skip, but he wasn't doing too great, and I didn't want to make him go alone, you know?"

Oh, God, Astra thinks. *She's gonna know. You have a tell. Your one eyebrow twitches. It's probably twitching right now. If you can just make it to your room and lock the door—*

Her mom sighs and drops her hand from her hip.

"That's really nice of you, sweetheart. Is his sister going to be all right? Maybe we should send her some flowers."

Astra thinks about Isla. The flower idea isn't that bad, actually.

"I don't really know, honestly. She was sleeping the whole time we were there. But flowers might be nice. I'll bring some next time I visit."

"*After* school," her mom adds.

"After school," Astra agrees.

A few seconds pass. The bracelets on her mom's wrists jingle softly. Astra is just about to sneak away to her room when her mom speaks again, sounding unsure.

"The hospital," she says. "Did it bother you at all? Being there? Did anything feel…off?"

The goose bumps still haven't completely gone down on Astra's arms, and she's probably going to have to wear an extra pair of socks and her thick flannel pajamas to bed just to sleep tonight, but her mom doesn't need to worry about that. Astra shakes her head and hikes her backpack up on her shoulder.

"No. It smelled like bleach and, I mean, I didn't *like* being there. It was sad. But I didn't feel anything weird."

Her mom doesn't look disappointed, but she doesn't look relieved either.

"That's good, honey. You know I worry about you sometimes." She sighs. Her bright red heels shuffle on the floor. "You should go work on your homework. I'll get dinner started. I hope you're in the mood for pot roast."

Astra finally escapes into her bedroom, trying to ignore the look on her mom's face—the look that says she was just caught in a lie.

❖

Astra wakes up at exactly 3:25 a.m. to the sound of something falling. A dull thud, a mumbled curse, and some shuffling echo up from the floor.

She flicks her lamp on, jiggles the cord four times, and sees Isla crouching an inch above the carpet, fumbling with a book.

Leonard chirps from the end of Astra's bed, and when he sees Isla he flicks his tail and starts purring. Isla tries to pick up the book—which Astra recognizes as the one with the dark green cover and gold lettering on the front from the library—but it only raises an inch or so above the ground before it falls through her hands again. She sighs and reaches up to pet Leonard instead.

"Sorry I woke you up," she mumbles. "I was downstairs and you were snoring so loudly I came up to make sure you weren't being murdered or something. And I was bored."

"I had a nightmare," Astra says, "didn't I?"

Isla shrugs. "It's not a big deal. Your mom could sleep through a tornado, couldn't she?"

"She's just used to it, I think."

There's half-dried sweat at the back of Astra's neck. It's starting to itch. She watches Leonard stand and stretch, pushing his face against Isla's hand until it starts to sink through.

The light from the lamp makes everything look hazy and yellow. Astra turns and glances out of her window, expecting to see the fuzzy shapes that are usually there when she has a nightmare, but all she sees are the damp, dark streets and a blue sports car parked by the curb. It's raining a little bit, and the soft pattering noise sounds a lot like Isla's static.

Astra turns back around to catch Isla watching her, with one hand still scratching behind Leonard's ear.

"They're not coming back," she tells Astra. "I doubt that's what your nightmare was about, but they probably weren't helping."

Astra blinks in the fuzzy light. "They're gone?"

"Well, yeah. They were bugging you, right? You always look at the window after you have a bad dream. And they were annoying me, too. I was trying to read and they wouldn't shut up."

"They can talk?"

"Yeah?" Isla looks confused. She's still leaning over the edge of the bed, with her legs floating up behind her, and one of her feet starts to twitch. "They're just old ghosts. I don't know why they wouldn't leave you alone, but I told them to beat it, so I don't think they'll be coming back any time soon."

Astra wonders what Isla saw when she looked at the hazy blobs of light outside Astra's window. She'd just assumed that they looked the same to everyone. She's assumed a lot of things about her *abilities*, though—and she's been proven wrong more times than she can count since she met Isla.

"My hero," she says, and Isla grins.

"That's right," Isla says. "So, do you wanna talk about whatever had you breathing like an asthmatic at three in the morning?"

Astra shakes her head. "No."

"Okay. How about a bedtime story instead?"

"Hmm. Your voice could probably put me to sleep."

Isla swats at her but misses. Leonard squeaks and flicks his tail. "Rude. Very rude. You can make it up to me by grabbing the book I dropped. It's too heavy, and apparently I lost my super huge bicep muscles when I became a ghost."

Astra gets out of bed to retrieve the book. She's thankful she remembered to wear her warm pajamas.

"I saw you in the hospital," she reminds Isla. "And your arms were just as noodle-y as Oliver's."

"I've been in a coma for *five weeks*. I was totally jacked before that."

"Uh-huh. Okay."

Astra's pulse is picking up speed. On the one hand, it's nice to be able to talk to Isla like this again—to be able to banter like old friends, like Astra didn't just discover a life-changing secret of hers that's been eating away at her brain since she saw Isla lying in that hospital bed. But on the other hand, to hear Isla talking about being in a coma like it's nothing, like she's just talking about the weather or something equally unimportant—it's disconcerting. Unsettling.

And it very much implies that Isla doesn't think she's ever going to *leave* the hospital, and Astra doesn't want to think about that.

She picks the book up and runs her hand over the cover. It's missing its dust jacket, so all that's left is the dark matte green with a bunch of fancy script on the front. It's a book about shrubs and trees, and while it doesn't look particularly interesting to Astra, she knows Isla will love it. She thumbs through a couple of glossy, full-color pages before throwing it down onto the bed and climbing back up herself.

She waits for Isla to join her. She's got her hands in her lap now, and Leonard has curled into a fluffy ball and started snoring like a vacuum cleaner.

"Can I ask you something?" Isla says, and Astra nods even though Isla is looking at the floor.

"Sure."

"Can we just pretend like nothing has changed? I just—I wouldn't have lied to you about it if I'd thought there was a chance. The doctors said ten percent, but that was *weeks* ago. And I don't wanna think about it. I just want to work on my bucket list—anti-bucket list, whatever— and have some fun, you know? I like hanging out with you. I like *you*. I don't want to mess that up."

I like you. Astra is pretty sure her brain is going to short-circuit. *I like hanging out with you. I like you.* She nods, but she isn't even sure if Isla asked her a question.

"Okay."

"I mean it," Isla warns, standing up and brushing out the folds of her dress. The sunny yellow fabric flutters just enough to show off the outline of her birthmark, dark purple in the lamplight. Astra tries not to stare. "I've got my next item all planned out. It requires your participation, though, so I hope you're prepared to have some fun."

"Am I required to leave my apartment?"

"Yep," Isla says, popping the *p*. "Maybe even for *two whole hours*."

"Hmm. That might be tough. Is there any physical activity involved? Because you're better off getting Oliver's help with that one. I'm never climbing anything ever again."

"Does dancing count as a physical activity?"

Astra is thankful that the lightbulb in her lamp is very old and very yellow, because her face suddenly feels very warm and very red. Isla has her knees bent in the air and a dimpled smile on her face, and a strand of wavy blond hair is falling over one of her eyes, and she probably can't even feel it, but Astra has to sit on her hands to stop herself from reaching out and brushing it back. Although, if she tried, her hand would probably go right through Isla's hair and she would look like even more of an idiot than she feels just for thinking about it.

She swallows. "I can't dance."

"I didn't say we were going to dance," Isla says. "I was just asking a question."

"Oh. Well, then, yeah. Dancing probably counts as a physical activity."

"Huh." Isla sets her hands palms down on top of the bed but doesn't climb up. "Well, that sucks for you, then. Because we're *totally* going to a dance."

"Again—I can't dance," Astra repeats. "It's like I've got two left feet. I'm clumsy. The last dance I went to was in the fifth grade, and I fell on the snack table and knocked tiny sandwiches everywhere."

"Tiny sandwiches?"

"It was some rich kid's party. There were a *lot* of sandwiches. I've been traumatized by it. I probably couldn't dance again even if I wanted to."

Isla grins and inches closer. "Well, lucky for you, I happen to be an excellent dancer."

"Wow. I feel *so* lucky."

"You should." Isla pushes her hands down on the mattress and jumps, doing a midair cannonball and startling Astra into banging her already-sore shoulder into her headboard. Isla lands on her knees and somehow manages to make the comforter billow.

Astra shoots her a look, but she knows there's no use arguing. Even if it wasn't on Isla's bucket list, Astra would do whatever she wanted anyway. All Isla has to do is flash her dimples, and Astra's protests dry right up on her tongue.

"That's settled, then. Now scoot over so I can bore you to sleep with some fun facts about evergreens."

❖

The second time Astra invites Oliver to her apartment, she's a little less panicked. But only a little.

He knocks three times—Astra waits for a fourth, but it never comes—and Astra rushes to move things out of the hallway before she answers. The recycling box has been moved, but now there's a mini fridge in the middle of the hall, and what does her mom intend to do with a tiny refrigerator? Astra slides it over with her foot until it's right in front of her mom's bedroom door, and hopes she'll get the hint.

Oliver smiles when she opens the door and shoves his hands in the pockets of his baggy brown jacket. There's a thread hanging off one sleeve. His hair is pushed behind his ears for once, and his earrings today are crescent moons.

"You wanted to talk to me about something?" he asks once he's inside.

"Not me," Astra clarifies. "Isla. Technically."

"Oh. Cool, yeah. I've always wanted to talk to a ghost."

Astra chuckles. "Just don't expect me to get out the Ouija board."

"Why would a psychic have a Ouija board?"

She rolls her eyes and pushes open her bedroom door. A cold breeze flows out, but Oliver doesn't seem to feel it. Leonard looks up from his perch on Astra's pillow, which is already covered in wispy orange and white hairs.

Isla glances over at them from Astra's desk chair. She's floating above the white plastic seat, focusing so hard on the pencil that she's holding that her hand is shaking. One of her feet flickers out, and she kicks it through the wall before pulling it back in and crossing it over the other one.

Oliver blinks at the floating pencil. "I'm never gonna get used to that."

"Hey, Ollie."

"She says hi," Astra translates.

"Hey, Spooks," Oliver says in the direction of the desk. "How's, um, being dead?"

Isla glances over at Astra. "You didn't tell him."

Astra shrugs. "It wasn't my secret to tell."

"If you guys are keeping secrets from me, it's not very fair to be talking about it while I'm *right here*."

Isla turns back to the paper on the desk, holding the pencil in her hand like something foreign. Her grip is all wrong, her fingers are bent at odd angles, and she keeps accidentally ripping the paper. There's a small pile of crumpled notebook pages in the trash can next to the desk, and a row of pencils with broken tips next to Astra's homework.

Astra's sparse bedroom is starting to feel a little more lived-in. The candles on her dresser have doubled to now include black cherry, apple pie, and something called Seaside Escape that mostly just smells like laundry detergent to Astra. She still doesn't light them, but she catches Isla smelling them every day, so it's almost worth the thirty bucks she spent on them in the mall.

The little wooden turtle and her potted geranium are still sitting on her desk, side by side. The flower has grown, and there are a few more tiny sprouts cropping up around it now, too.

"Tell him that being dead is fantastic," Isla says without looking up. "I scared a pigeon the other day. Did you know that pigeons can see ghosts too?"

"She says it's good," Astra tells Oliver. "And birds can see ghosts. Which really isn't what we invited you here to talk about."

"We?"

"*Her*. Not me. None of this was my idea. I want to make that clear."

"Hey," Isla says. "Do you have any tape?"

Astra nods and digs through her desk drawer until she fishes out a roll of clear tape. She tries to hand it to Isla, but it goes right through her hand.

"You do it." Isla holds up the paper she's been writing on—a small square with torn edges and scribbled words on it that look like they were written by a kindergartener. "I'll hold, you tape."

She holds the paper up to, of all things, the plant pot. Astra tapes it down on all sides, then turns it toward herself to read it.

George the Geranium
If lost, return to Astra Vaughn

"You made my plant a nametag?" she asks. Isla shrugs. "And— *George*? Really?"

"It suits him. He likes it."

"Okay. But...you're missing something."

She reaches over and grabs Isla's pencil, tips the pot back, and adds her phone number at the bottom. And then, at the last second, tacks *and Isla* after her own name.

"There," she says, standing back to admire her work. "Now it's Oliver's turn."

Oliver holds his hands up, palms out. "Hold on. If I'd known there'd be tape involved, I wouldn't have agreed to come."

"Relax. No tape. I *could* have just texted you or talked to you at school like a normal person, but Isla likes to be dramatic. And this is *her* bucket list, not mine."

Isla makes a grab for a second piece of paper with writing on it, and it takes her a few tries to get a good grip on it. It keeps falling through her fingers and fluttering back onto the desk.

Oliver watches with a lopsided grin on his face. He nudges Astra with his arm, then stretches it out when she looks over at him. There's a new patch on his faded brown jacket, over the crook of his elbow, just small enough and hidden enough that she wouldn't have noticed it if he hadn't shown her—a little flag with a striped rainbow printed on it.

Astra smiles at him. "I think that's my favorite one so far."

"I don't know," he says. "I've got a dog on a surfboard somewhere around here."

He rotates his arms around to search for it and finds it on the back of his right shoulder. Isla finally manages to keep hold of the paper, and she spins around in the chair without touching it.

"I like the rose," she says, and Astra relays her message to Oliver.

"She's a plant nerd," Astra tells him. "Just in case you couldn't tell."

"I would argue with you, but you're not wrong."

Isla floats closer and holds the sheet of paper up to Oliver, wiggles it back and forth a few times, and then blows on his hair for good measure. He jumps back and Isla chuckles like wind chimes, and Astra feels so smitten that it's a miracle that she hasn't accidentally blurted it out loud yet.

Oliver squints to read the paper once it's stopped moving. The words are squiggly and large, but mostly legible. *Pretty good for a ghost*, Astra thinks.

Ollie, will you go to prom with us?

There are three options underneath, with numbers next to them like Oliver uses when he asks Astra questions in class.

1. Yes
2. Yes but in orange
3. No because I want to hurt Isla's feelings

Oliver chuckles. "Nice handwriting."

Isla takes the note back to the desk and spends a painfully long two minutes adding *thank you* onto the bottom. She hands it to Oliver.

He checkmarks the first option, then crosses it out and checks the second one instead.

"I like orange better," he explains. "And I was hoping for an excuse to go to prom. Senior year and all. But you guys could have just gone without me if you wanted to. I'm, like, the biggest third wheel in this scenario."

Astra shoots him a look that her mom would be proud of. "It's just a dance. With *friends*. Plus," she adds, "I can't dance in public with someone who's invisible. It would be very helpful if you just…make me not look like I'm losing my mind."

"Easier said than done," Isla says. Astra picks the nearest thing—which happens to be a broken pencil—and throws it at Isla's head. It passes through and hits the wall with a thud.

"You guys are so perfect for each other," Oliver says with a laugh. The next pencil hits its mark perfectly.

CHAPTER SEVENTEEN

When is he supposed to be done?"

Astra checks the time on her phone. "Twenty minutes? Unless they do overtime, or whatever. I don't know sports."

"It's track," Isla reminds her. "They don't do overtime in track."

"How am I supposed to know that?"

Astra shifts on the metal bleachers. The rigid benches are uncomfortable, and it's getting cold out, and having Isla right next to her isn't helping. Oliver has only been in the locker room for ten minutes, but it feels like an hour.

"We could have just met him at the mall, you know."

"I'm supporting my friend," Astra says. "Just because I don't like sports doesn't mean I can't, like, cheer him on. Right?"

"Aww," Isla coos. "You have a friend. I'm proud of you, you know that? I'm not even being sarcastic. Who'd have thought you'd be sitting through a painfully long two-hour track meet for some boy you wouldn't even invite over to your house a month ago?"

"He's nice."

"I'm not gonna say I told you so, but I'm kind of the whole reason you're here right now."

Astra's mouth does that wonderful thing it's been doing a lot lately, where it starts moving without consulting with her brain first, and she says, "Yeah, you are." And the worst part is, it's the truth.

If Isla had never shown up in Astra's English class that first day, Astra probably would never have become friends with Oliver. She would have still talked to him in school, but she wouldn't have been able to work up the courage to invite him to her apartment if Isla hadn't annoyed her until she agreed to.

There are a lot of things Astra wouldn't have done without Isla. Going to the greenhouse, the library, George's funeral. Conquering her fear of hospitals, finally getting rid of the ghosts outside her window, coming out to someone who isn't her bedroom mirror. Getting a cat, and a plant, and more candles than she'll ever need. Confronting her dad. Falling in love.

Astra doesn't even mind sitting on a hard, cold metal bench. Isla leans over just a little and rests her forehead against Astra's shoulder with the smallest amount of pressure possible, and it feels like static, like sparks. Hot and cold at the same time.

Astra tries not to shiver.

Another few minutes pass before she sees Oliver walking across the field, and she knows right away that something is wrong.

He's holding his gym bag, even though he usually leaves it in the locker room between practices, and he's still wearing his uniform. He's got his patchy brown jacket slung over his shoulders, his hair blowing around his face in the wind, and he's walking so fast that he's nearly running. And he's alone.

They always come out together—the whole team. They're supposed to be having a meeting or something in the locker room today. They're not supposed to be done for at least another fifteen minutes.

Astra runs down the bleachers, jumping over the last two rows and onto the track. Oliver slows down, and that's when she notices it.

His lip is bloody. It's split on one side, just a small cut, and it's bruised purple and sluggishly bleeding. Astra freezes in her tracks and stares, anxiety coiling in her chest.

Oliver stops walking. He looks at his feet, still in their sneakers.

"Are you guys ready to do some prom shopping?" he asks. "Spooks? You here too?"

"Oliver," Astra says. She sounds like her mom. "What happened?"

"What the hell, Ollie," Isla mutters from behind her.

"It's nothing, it's stupid. Can we just stop by the bathrooms in the mall so I can change? I feel all sweaty and gross."

Astra reaches out to touch his face, realizes what she's doing, and then quickly yanks her hand back.

"It's not as bad as it looks," he tells her.

"Who did this to you?"

Behind her, Isla's static has risen in pitch like a tea kettle. Astra can tell without looking that she's angry. Livid. Goose bumps prickle at Astra's skin and she rubs her arms absently.

"It's stupid," he repeats. "I was grabbing my jacket and one of the guys—they were messing with me, and I should have just left it alone. I don't even know why I stayed on the team for so long. They never really liked me, you know? I didn't fit in there."

Astra blinks. "You...quit the team?"

Oliver nods at his shoes. "It's not a big deal. Please don't make it a big deal. I just—I want to have fun at the mall. Please."

He sounds so *small*. His shoulders are hunched, and for the first time, Astra feels like she's towering over him. And then, because her brain is slow and takes time to buffer like a broken computer, his words finally catch up to her and she realizes what he means—a second after Isla does.

"Those *assholes*," Isla hisses. Astra wasn't even sure that Isla knew Oliver was gay, but she must have seen the patch. Just like the track guys did. And now Isla is throwing off such a bitter cold that Astra worries she's going to become hypothermic.

Before Astra can tell her not to, Isla is flying across the field and into the building on the other side. Astra watches her go, and Oliver follows her eyes with his own.

"Did she just...?"

"Yep," Astra confirms. "If this is anything like what she did to my dad, expect them to run out screaming in, like, a minute. Tops."

Oliver winces. "Great."

Oliver's lip doesn't look *horrible*; it's just a scratch, really. It'll probably bruise a little bit more, scab over, and be good as new in a week or two. But it doesn't matter if it's a bruise or a black eye or a punch to the jaw—someone hurt her friend. The reason *why* they hurt him has Astra's blood boiling, and the only thing stopping her from marching down to the locker rooms and giving the idiots inside a piece of her mind herself is the knowledge that Isla can handle them better than she ever could.

Isla is really good at defending her friends, at protecting them.

She's so wonderful, and amazing, and Astra still doesn't understand why Isla chose *her* to hang out with. Astra doesn't deserve someone like Isla. Or someone like Oliver. How did she ever get so lucky?

"Are you okay?" she asks him. He nods.

"It doesn't really hurt. It just surprised me. I mean, Jake has been an ass to me before, but never for something so specific, you know? But I don't want to be on a team with people like that, anyway. I never really liked track. I just like running."

"You should talk to Isla about that. She's fast. I would bet she used to run a lot too."

Oliver grins, then winces when it pulls on his split lip. "You've got it *so* bad for her, oh my gosh. I'm gonna be such a third wheel at prom."

Astra returns the smile. "We want you there. *I* want you there. So there's no use trying to back out now."

"Wouldn't dream of it." He cranes his neck and looks across the field. "What do you think she's doing in there?"

Astra pauses. Listens. "I don't know."

She expects to hear some kind of noise—something falling, someone screaming, the whole building exploding—but it's eerily silent. Nobody comes out running, the ground doesn't cave in. Astra can't even hear Isla's static anymore. It's just...peaceful. Calm.

Which has Astra feeling the opposite of calm.

She jiggles her leg and waits. Oliver drops his gym bag on the ground and chews on his lip, making a face whenever he accidentally catches the sore part in his teeth. His knees look extra knobby in his uniform, and he looks very out of place without his jacket on. Astra hopes he keeps wearing it. *All* of it.

A minute later, Isla comes floating back across the field with her arms crossed and a sour expression on her face. She comes to a stop in front of them and pretzels her legs.

"You guys ready to go?" she asks.

Astra frowns. "What did you do?"

Isla grins, but her nose is pinched like she's just smelled something bad.

"You don't wanna know."

❖

Oliver's parents are loaded, which is really something he should have told her before Astra suggested they shop for their prom outfits at the outlet store in the mall.

"Why do you wear the same ratty jacket every day if you're rich?" Isla asks. Astra shoots her a look but relays her question anyway.

"It was my grandpa's," Oliver says, shrugging. "Plus, my family is huge, remember? Four sisters, one brother. And me. Our house is perfectly normal. Minus the theme park in the backyard and our private limousine, of course."

Astra elbows him. He chuckles.

"Kidding, kidding. Jeez."

The store Astra picked is cheap, but it's pretty big and the variety isn't bad. She already buys most of her sweaters here, because the fabric is soft and stretchy and doesn't make her neck itch. The mall is a tan, split-level building in the middle of a cluster of apartments and chain restaurants, and Astra and her friends are tucked into the back corner of the first floor, with clothes on one side and makeup and handbags on the other.

Astra has a crinkled hundred-dollar bill in her pocket. She swears her mom almost started crying when Astra told her she needed the money to go to the school dance with her friends.

The suits and dresses are across the aisle from each other, so at least they don't have to split up to shop. Oliver skims his hands along a row of tuxedos before grabbing one at random and disappearing into the dressing room. He's done this three times already, with incredibly mixed results.

Isla floats down the racks of dresses and pokes at a few of them. Astra doesn't really feel like trying anything on; she doesn't get why she can't just wear one of her comfortable T-shirt dresses instead, the kind with the wide necks and soft fabric. Everything here looks itchy—gemstones and sequins and stiff tulle. Her skin crawls just touching the dresses on the racks.

"This one's pretty," Isla says, pulling at the skirt of a long, silky dress with a cutout in the back and cap sleeves.

"It's purple," Astra says.

"Your bedroom is purple," Isla reminds her.

"Different shade. That one's…louder. I don't know. I just…don't like it."

She expects Isla to fight her on it, but she just drops the dress and keeps looking. Astra will never stop being surprised by Isla's easy acceptance of her quirks. That's what her mom always called them. Astra knows it's annoying sometimes—she even annoys herself—but Isla doesn't seem to mind. She never asks about it. She never treats Astra like she's different or weird.

It's so *nice* to be able to exist without having to hide a single part of herself from someone.

Oliver emerges from the dressing room with a flourish, sweeping back the tail of his tux like it's a cape. The jacket is a muddy green color and the pants are gray, and the whole thing makes him look like he's just crawled out of a swamp.

Astra gives him two thumbs up. "Very handsome. If the theme were *Creature from the Black Lagoon*, you'd fit in perfectly."

Oliver throws one hand across his stomach and bows. "Thank you. That's exactly what I was going for. Your turn."

"No, no. We're getting yours done first. I can't go. I haven't even picked out *one* yet."

"How about this one?" Isla says, holding out something blue and shiny and covered in little rhinestones. Astra wrinkles her nose at it.

"Just close your eyes and pick one," Oliver suggests. "That's what I've been doing."

"Yeah, and that's been working out *so* well for you."

"Glad you agree."

Astra sighs and closes her eyes, but she doesn't move. She feels something cold on her back, and then Isla gives her a small push toward the nearest rack. Astra reaches up and feels the fabrics, searching for something soft.

She finds one that feels okay, then opens her eyes and cringes. "Ew, no. The style is fine, but the *color*."

Isla starts laughing, full-body giggles, and shoves the dress into Astra's hands. "At least you'll match your date."

When Astra finally comes out of the dressing room, she *feels* comfortable, but she *looks* like, well—the *Creature from the Black Lagoon*. Part two.

The dress is the most awful shade of green that Astra has ever seen, like someone mashed up a bunch of moss and mixed in some dirt, then threw it all over a perfectly nice piece of fabric. She smooths out her rumpled skirt and stands awkwardly next to Oliver, who is grinning like a madman, while he takes a selfie of the two of them in their swamp outfits.

Oliver picks another tux and leaves to change while Astra rifles through another row of dresses. She can tell when Isla floats up behind her, because the back of her neck feels clammy.

"What happened here?" Isla asks, pressing one hand gently across Astra's shoulder. Astra tries not to shiver, and instead focuses on running her fingers over a sequined hem and trying to decide if the texture will bother her or not.

"What are you talking about?"

"This." Isla moves her fingers up. It tickles. "You've got bruises. On your back."

"Oh," she says, feeling stupid. "Yeah. A ghost spooked me at the hospital and I fell. I'm fine, though. Can't even feel it."

She's not looking at Isla, but she can picture her expression clear as day—her knocked-in eyebrows and her deep, dimple-less frown.

"That was probably Johnny. You shouldn't have gone there. I'm—I'm sorry."

Astra ignores her, swallowing down a lump in her throat. She doesn't need to think about the hospital right now. She doesn't want to. So, she won't.

Instead, she pulls a light pink dress off the rack and holds it out in front of Isla. The waist is cinched and the skirt is puffy and soft and speckled with little white beads.

"What about this one?" she asks. "Hold it up for a second."

She pushes the dress closer to Isla and then takes a step back. Isla holds it, looks down, and then spins the skirt a little around her legs. It almost looks like she's wearing it. And she looks—

"Beautiful," Astra says. "You're so pretty. Oh my God."

She clamps her mouth shut belatedly. Oops.

"You really think so?" Isla asks. Astra nods like an idiot. "I wish I could pick out a dress. But I'm just stuck with this."

She gestures to what she's wearing—what she's *been* wearing since Astra met her. At least it's not a hospital gown.

"I like your dress," Astra tells her. "Summer colors suit you. And I'm the only one who can see you, so my opinion is the only one that matters."

Isla smiles and twirls in a small circle, the skirt of the dress fluttering through her ankles. Astra is glad that this store is never very busy, because a floating dress in the middle of a mall would probably raise some eyebrows.

Isla clenches her hands around the fabric until her fingers start to disappear. Her smile flickers for just a moment, and she quickly hangs the dress back up on the rack and floats over to the next one.

Astra tries on a blue dress next. The color is safe, because it's nearly the exact same shade of blue as at least three of the sweaters in her closet—a light sky-blue with a skirt that hits just below her knees and puffy tulle sleeves that hang off her shoulders. It feels okay, maybe a little tight in the waist, but it probably wouldn't bother her to wear it for just a couple of hours. She looks in the mirror in the little dressing room cubicle, does a little spin, and cranes her neck to look at the back. The bruises on her shoulders are a sickly green-yellow color, and if she looks closely she can see the line where the metal bar in the elevator dug into her back.

Suddenly, the blue dress doesn't feel so okay after all. The waist is too tight. The skirt is too short, Astra's knees look like lumpy potatoes and she hasn't even shaved her legs in at least a week. The tulle sleeves are starting to itch, and there's a crisscross of ribbons on the back that she knows she isn't going to be able to tie up by herself on the night of the dance.

She quickly pulls the dress off and changes back into her soft sweater and baggy jeans and just *breathes*. Wearing her comfortable clothes feels like being wrapped up in a warm blanket on a cold winter day, and she waits for her skin to stop itching before she leaves the dressing room.

Oliver is outside already, awkwardly trying to talk to Isla. Without being able to see *or* hear her.

"Okay, so, just—blow on my hair if you like it. If you don't, then don't do anything. If you're even here right now. You could be on the other end of the store and I wouldn't know."

He shrugs and poses anyway, and from behind his back, Astra can see that the tips of his ears are red. Isla is chuckling just a couple inches away from him, hovering on her knees.

Oliver looks nice. He's wearing a suit that actually fits him well, so he doesn't look as gangly and long as usual, and the soft blue-gray of the jacket and pants actually suits him. It makes his eyes pop, and even though his posture is a little slouched, he's still holding himself with just a bit more confidence than usual.

Isla makes him sweat for a few seconds before she leans forward and blows hard into his hair.

Oliver exhales a shaky laugh. "Really? You like it?" He notices Astra standing behind him and spins around, flaring out his jacket with his hands in the pockets. "What do you think?"

"I think you're already done shopping, and I've barely even started," she says. "It looks good. Great, actually. You don't look so much like a noodle."

"A noodle?"

"Or a tree. I can't decide which kind, though."

"A juniper, probably," Isla answers with a shrug.

"Isla says juniper. She's probably right because she's a plant nerd."

Isla sticks her tongue out from over Oliver's shoulder, and Oliver gives Astra a look that tells her that she's acting too lovestruck and needs to tone it down a little before he barfs. She knocks his arm with her elbow and tries for a smile that's a little less obvious.

"You look great," she tells him. "I mean it. Buy the cheap knock-off suit, rich boy."

"You still need to find a dress."

"I have dresses at home," she says. Except that her *dresses at home* are mostly worn, baggy, and made of the same kind of stretchy material that sweatpants are made out of. "Or I can try a different store another day. It's not a big deal, I swear."

It's a really big deal, actually, because Astra has never been to a school dance before. And she's going with her friend, which is something she never thought she'd be able to say. She wants to have a good time, and show Oliver that she's not just a shut-in who hangs out with ghosts all day.

But she's also going with Isla, and that has her more stressed out than anything else. Excited, too, but mostly just nervous.

Astra isn't the kind of person that other people usually want to hang out with. And now *two* people want to go to the dance with her, and she just wants it to be *perfect*.

"There's got to be something you like," Oliver says. "Do you have a color you want? You wear blue a lot."

Astra thinks about the blue dress that she left behind in the dressing room. "Maybe not blue," she says.

"Okay. Not blue. Got it."

Oliver starts picking through the racks of shiny satin with a lot of conviction but very little actual knowledge. He keeps holding up the most gaudy, itchy-looking dresses and genuinely asking her if she likes them, and it's only endearing the first couple of times he does it. After that, it's hard to believe that he's not doing it on purpose, especially when he shoves a mustard-yellow gown into her arms and requests that she try it on.

"Absolutely not," she tells him, quickly hanging the dress back on the rack. "Your taste is literally the worst. No offense."

"I wear the same jacket every day. I think I'm past the point of being offended."

"I've got it," Isla suddenly announces from the rack two rows down. She struggles with the hanger and it takes a minute for her to get a good enough grip on the dress to bring it to Astra, but eventually she manages. She throws it at her unceremoniously. "It's perfect. Try it on."

Astra looks down at the pile of fabric in her hands. It feels... nice—soft and silky and light. The color isn't what she would have chosen, but Isla looks so excited that Astra just tucks the dress into her elbow and walks the eleven steps back to the dressing room.

The blue dress stares at her from the hook on the wall, but she ignores it. Isla's dress, though, is a little harder to ignore.

Astra looks in the mirror and barely even recognizes herself. If it weren't for her short curls and the one weird mole on the side of her neck, Astra would swear she had slipped into someone else's skin entirely.

The dress is red. Not the ketchup-red that's painted on the walls in her living room, but a dark, smooth red that doesn't give her a headache. It's long, covering the tops of her scribbled-on white sneakers, and the bottom half doesn't look much different than the other dresses she's tried on. It's the top that has her staring.

It's fitted just a little bit in the waist, but not so much that Astra feels pinched or itchy. The sleeves go halfway down her upper arms, and the neckline is almost straight across her collarbone and off both of her shoulders. She's not sure how Isla knew about her issues with the way some clothes fit, but she must have, because the dress she chose is the most comfortable thing Astra has worn all day.

The best part is the bodice, though, because every inch of fabric above the waist is covered in tiny roses, sewn in the same color as the rest of the dress. They're not gaudy, though—they're pretty. The whole dress is pretty.

And Astra feels pretty wearing it.

She tries not to trip over her own feet on her way out of the dressing room. She feels like she's wearing a fancy ball gown, and she can't help but swing the skirt a little as she walks.

She stops by the racks, doing an exaggerated curtsey, and Oliver whistles.

"You clean up pretty good," he tells her. "I still think the yellow dress would have looked better, but I guess I won't be embarrassed to be seen with you in that."

"I'll wear the yellow one if you get that swampy green suit."

"Deal. But only if I get to wear my Crocs. They're orange and I feel like it's necessary to complete the look."

"Of course," she says. She pulls up the bottom of her skirt and shows him the doodled stars on her shoes. "I've already got my footwear set too."

Oliver chuckles and pats her shoulder, then disappears back into the dressing rooms to change. Astra is about to do the same when she realizes that Isla hasn't said anything yet. Does she not like the dress? Did she get bored and leave? Or is she just floating around somewhere, waiting for them to get done?

She glances around and spots Isla, still hovering in the same spot she was in when she handed Astra the dress. The look on her face is hard to decipher. Her mouth is open just a little, and her eyes aren't as dull as usual. Is she disappointed by how Astra looks in the dress she picked out? Astra feels her confidence start to deflate. If Isla doesn't like it, then she's not going to buy it.

Isla catches her eye for a second and then blinks down at the floor. Ghosts don't need to blink, do they? They don't need to breathe either, but Isla does that a lot, too.

She must be doing it right now, because her words come out sort of breathy. "You look, um. Wow." She shakes her head like she's trying to dislodge something stuck in her brain. "You look great. Pretty. Like, *gorgeous*, actually."

Astra's rib cage feels like it's full of butterflies. "You're not serious."

"No, actually, I'm more serious than I've ever been, probably. And you know what a serious person I am."

"If you don't like it, you can just tell me. I won't be mad."

No, just heartbroken, she thinks. She swallows down a butterfly in her throat and awkwardly shuffles her feet under her skirt.

Isla looks up at her and blinks. "No way. There's *no way* you're doubting yourself in that dress. Or, like, in *anything*. You're so pretty it's unfair, and if anything, I should be thanking you, because you make that cheap knock-off dress look *way* better than I pictured when I saw it on the rack. So."

She finishes by crossing her arms and pouting, but one of her dimples gives her away. If ghosts could blush, Astra imagines that her whole face would be the same color as Astra's dress right now.

"So, you think I should put it back...?"

"God, no!" Isla hisses. "If you don't buy that dress, I'm gonna float it out the door, and then you're gonna have to explain what happened to some poor traumatized security guard."

Astra smiles, feeling pretty and lovestruck and impossibly giddy. Isla is floating around the racks, but Astra is the one who feels like she's flying. She's so happy, and prom is going to be amazing, and it's all because of Isla.

And then she changes out of the dress and notices the price tag. The crumpled bill in her pocket suddenly feels too small.

Oliver puts a hand on her shoulder and squeezes. The cut on his lip looks swollen.

"I'll pay the difference," he tells her. When she tries to protest, he holds up a hand and cuts her off. "My parents are loaded, remember? God knows I'm not using my clothing allowance on anything but new patches for my jacket. And those are, like, a buck each."

"Yeah, but still—"

"Tell you what," he says. "You can make it up to me by splitting a horrendously large order of chili cheese fries from the food court with me. They're gross and messy, but I'm *starving*, and if I have to go down then I'm taking you with me."

Astra tries not to smile, but she can't stop. Oliver is the best. So is Isla. And Astra is just so, *so* lucky.

"You've got yourself a deal."

CHAPTER EIGHTEEN

On Thursday after school, Astra finds herself standing in front of the hospital's revolving doors again. This time, though, she's come prepared.

She tugs her headphones over her ears and makes sure they're snug. She's wearing two sweaters, which probably makes her look ridiculous on such a warm spring day, but she can already feel the cold starting to seep through. The ghost that was on the bench outside is gone now, but there are two new ones in the lobby—an elderly woman with liver spots on her neck and curlers still wound into her stark-white hair, and a lady in her forties or fifties with blood all over her arms and hands but no injuries that Astra can see. The middle-aged woman stares at her when she approaches the front desk, her icy blue eyes bulging.

Neither of them bother her, though. Astra tries to remember what Ricky did when he brought her here, and she gets a visitor pass from the receptionist without any issues. She follows the dark blue tiles on the floor, counts the doors, and waits for the elevator next to a dead twenty-something man with cuts all over his face and neck.

"Hello," he says, offering her a small wave from the bench with fake plants on both sides. He's wearing a dark gray suit with a matching tie, like he died on his way to a business meeting.

There's blood on his undershirt. Astra keeps her eyes on the blinking red numbers above the elevator.

"Hi." Astra pulls her headphones down for a moment, and suddenly a hundred bees are buzzing in her ears.

"You're not dead." The man's hair is black and smooth, like it's been slicked back with gel, but there's a gash running along the right side of his face that cuts straight through it and the hair around it is sticking up at odd angles.

"No," she agrees. "I'm sorry."

The elevator dings and slides open. Astra steps inside and clamps her headphones back over her ears without waiting for a response from the ghost.

The fourth floor is just as loud and frigid as it was last time, but now that Astra knows what to expect, it isn't nearly as bad. The bruises on her back have mostly faded by now, leaving just a small, dark line where the elevator bar dug into her shoulder.

It takes her a couple of tries to get to Isla's room. She ends up getting lost, taking the long way around the second set of doors to avoid running into the ghost that went through her last time—Johnny, she thinks Isla called him—and then stopping once at a nurse's station to ask for directions. The entire floor is like a maze, with an impossible number of rooms that all look the same from the outside, and Astra swears she walks past room number 413 at least half a dozen times before she realizes that she's taken a wrong turn and goes back.

And then she's standing in front of room 421, adjusting her hold on the pot in her hands and listening for voices on the other side. It's quiet. She opens the door with her left hand and steps inside with her left foot first.

At first, everything looks the same. The same wheelchair pushed into the corner, next to the same sink and garbage can, underneath a shelf full of disposable gloves and hand sanitizer bottles. The same off-white curtain with swirls stitched all over it, pulled halfway across the middle of the room. The same speckled floor and nauseating bleach smell. The same ghost sitting on the windowsill with her legs dangling down.

Robin looks up when Astra pulls back the curtain, a small smile on her face. Her blouse is so white that the blood on the sides looks almost black. Her dark red hair isn't in its braid anymore; it's bushed out in a cluster of waves down her back and over both of her shoulders. Astra didn't know that ghosts could do that.

"You came back," Robin says, turning away from the window. It's humid outside, and the cool air Robin is giving off feels like a fan blowing on a hot summer day. Astra breathes a sigh of relief.

She pulls back the curtain and sets the pot down on a little table next to the bed. There's a vase of flowers already sitting there—sunny yellow and orange blooms with a shiny ribbon tied around the glass. Astra leans down and sniffs the bouquet, but she can't really smell anything other than bleach. She slides her small purple pot closer to the vase, which makes George the Geranium's flowers look tiny.

There are a couple of get well soon cards next to the vase, but Astra doesn't open them.

"Hi, Robin," Astra says. "How is she doing?"

"I change rooms," Robin says again. "But the doctors have been talking more. They took her out once. I don't know why. I didn't follow them."

Astra nods. Robin's arms start flickering until the gashes on them turn into bright red streaks and then disappear entirely. She cracks her knuckles without making a sound and they return to normal.

Astra pulls the wooden chair closer to the bed and sits down. The throw pillows and blankets on the mattress are the same, too, and they're rumpled and messy like they've been recently used. She ignores the pit in her stomach and turns to Isla, whose body is the only thing in the room that seems to have changed. But not for the better.

Her eyes are still closed, but they look even more sunken than usual, like large purple pits in her skull. Her hair has lost most of its curls, and it's turned into a matted, stringy mess fanned out around her face. She's so skinny that Astra can pick out each of the veins in her wrists, the muscles in her neck, her hip bones from underneath the mountain of blankets. She's so pale that she looks even more like a ghost than her *actual* ghost.

The machines around her bed are still beeping, pumping, dripping. But now instead of a tube around her nose, she's got a larger tube strapped to her mouth to keep her breathing, and Astra's heart sinks when she sees the huge monitor it's connected to, because she knows what that means. If Isla isn't breathing on her own, then her ten percent chance of waking up starts to dwindle into the single digits.

Astra watches the IV machine drip down into the tube taped to Isla's hand and counts the drops. One, two, three, four, five. The heart monitor beeps in almost the same rhythm, slow and consistent. Strong. Isla's heart is strong. If her heart still works, then maybe she'll be okay.

"She told her family about you," Robin says from her perch. "When they visited last. The parents and the brother."

Astra runs her thumb over the bandage on Isla's hand. It's clear, and she can see the paper-thin skin stretched and bruised underneath it.

"What did she tell them?"

Robin blows out an icy breath. "They couldn't hear. I could, but I'm not supposed to say."

Astra thinks about that for a minute. Maybe Isla told her parents about prom—about shopping for dresses, and helping Oliver pick out a suit, and making a mess at one of the food court benches by sneaking up behind him while he had a mouth full of fries. Maybe she told them about her bucket list, and the things she and Astra have done on it. Maybe she told them that Astra is her friend, that she actually *does* have a friend, and they couldn't hear a word.

The thought makes Astra's stomach churn, and she tries to swallow it down.

She turns Isla's hand over just enough to wrap her fingers around it, and she can feel the rough skin on her palm where she knows there are the remains of little yellow calluses. She brushes her index finger over them and feels the lines on her palm where she read Isla's fortune, what feels like a lifetime ago.

She kind of expects Isla to appear, but she doesn't. When the door opens ten minutes after Astra sits down, it's not Isla who enters.

Astra looks up and makes accidental eye contact with a woman with wild brown hair and dark freckles all along the bridge of her nose. She's wearing a simple green dress that matches her eyes, and even though she and Isla don't look very much alike in any other way, Astra would recognize those eyes anywhere.

The woman stares for a few seconds like a deer caught in a car's headlights before she shakes her head and moves across the room. Astra's not sure why, but she quickly lets go of Isla's hand and stands up.

"Oh. Hello," Isla's mom says, her dull green eyes wide. Isla has her mom's eyes and maybe her mouth, but the rest she must have gotten from her dad.

She holds out her hand and Astra gives it a small squeeze. No calluses. She steps back and clears her throat.

"I'm—I'm Astra. Vaughn. Um, I'm a friend of Isla's. I don't think she's ever mentioned me, probably. We weren't friends for very long."

Robin's static flares up and she chuckles from her window seat.

Astra wishes she could put her headphones on, but that would probably be rude, so she just fiddles with the cord around her neck and waits patiently for Isla's mom to stop staring at her.

"I'm Lydia, Isla's mother," the woman says. She moves over to the mattress and sits down, but Astra stays standing awkwardly by the bed. "Isla never told me about any friends. How did you two meet?"

Astra is caught off guard, and the loud static coming from the windowsill isn't helping. She scrambles for an answer and tries to ignore the beeping and buzzing all around her.

"Um," she starts, thinking hard. Something tells her that she can't say *at school* or *at the mall*, because from what she's learned, Isla left her house about as much as Astra leaves her apartment. So, practically never. "Online. We talked a lot online, mostly. We only met in person, like, a couple of times."

That much is true, at least. She's met Isla *in person* exactly twice now. Granted, both times have been her visiting Isla while she's in a coma in the hospital, but that still probably counts.

Isla's mom nods like Astra isn't the world's worst liar. "Well, I'm glad she has at least one friend. I worried about that when I took her out of public school. But it seemed like the best option at the time, and kids can be cruel, you know? I'd just hoped she would get out a little more, but you know Isla."

Stubborn, Astra thinks, just like when she talked to Ricky about his sister. She jerks her head in a nod and then stops halfway, blinking quickly. Her brain restarts just in time to catch a few particular words in the middle of what Isla's mom just said.

Took her out of public school and *kids can be cruel* stick out the most. Astra knows that Isla didn't go to the same school as her brother even though she's only two years older than him, but it hadn't occurred to her that it might be because Isla didn't go to school *at all*.

At least, not a public one. Maybe she was a private school kid. Maybe she was homeschooled. Maybe she was being bullied, and her parents had to take her out of school to keep her safe, because *kids can be cruel*.

Astra forces herself not to think about it. It's already bad enough seeing Isla lying in a hospital bed. Astra can't stand the thought of her being in any more pain than she's already in.

"Right," Astra agrees. She's not even sure what she's agreeing about. She shifts her weight from her left leg to her right and then back again, swaying slightly over the wooden chair. "I should probably go. I've got homework."

Astra is a terrible liar, and she doesn't have homework, because who assigns homework on prom weekend? But Isla's mom must believe her, because she nods and looks up. Her eyes are dull green, but the outsides are so, so red.

She's not crying, though, and Astra is thankful for that. She's not sure she could handle seeing Isla's mother crying over her comatose daughter right now—especially when Astra herself is trying very hard not to cry over Lydia Monroe's comatose daughter right now.

Isla's mom stands up again. "It was so nice to meet you, Astra," she says. "The doctors—they're running some more tests. I don't know when…" She pauses and sniffles, and Astra tries to take a step toward the door without making it too obvious. "Anyway, we should know more soon. I'm just glad she has people on her side. A friend. Thank you for being her friend."

"It was nice to meet you too, Mrs. Monroe."

Isla's mom makes a move toward Astra like she might want a hug, or maybe just another handshake, but Astra runs out of the room before she can get one. She hears another sniffle, then a chuckle from Robin, and then the door clicks shut behind her.

❖

Astra has one more stop to make before she goes home, and luckily she still remembers the way.

She pulls up into the gravel parking lot and walks through the patch of grass, which is now lush and green and ankle-high. It's starting to rain a little bit, and Astra holds her arms above her head and ducks underneath the awning outside the greenhouse quickly to avoid getting wet.

It feels weird coming to a greenhouse without Isla. Especially this one.

Mrs. Reeves is at the front counter when Astra walks in, pruning the dead flowers off a pot of red roses. The cloudy sky makes everything underneath the glass ceiling look hazy, and some stray rain droplets are casting shadows through the walls and onto the nearby shelves and hanging plants.

"Good afternoon." Mrs. Reeves holds up a gloved hand in a wave. "Is there anything I can help you with, my dear? How is that plant of yours doing?"

Astra is surprised that she remembers her, but it's really only been a couple of weeks since she was here last—*how has it only been that long?* she wonders—and Astra can't imagine this place being very busy. Last time, she and Isla were the only ones here; today, there's a young couple rifling through a table full of garden décor on the other end of the room, inspecting the paving stones like they're looking for buried treasure.

"It's doing great," Astra tells her. "It's probably tripled in size. I might need a new pot soon."

She remembers that she left George the Geranium at the hospital with Isla. She hopes that if—*when*—Isla wakes up and goes home, she takes the plant with her. Astra has grown a little attached to it.

"Is that what you're here for, my dear? Or are you just browsing?"

Astra shakes her head. Raindrops start to patter on the roof, making tinny echoes.

"Do you make corsages here? Like, for dances?"

Mrs. Reeves's eyes glint, and she sets down her pruning shears and takes off her gloves. "Prom, I'm guessing?"

"Yeah."

"Any particular flower you like?" Mrs. Reeves asks, stepping out from behind the counter. Astra notices a large walk-in cooler against the back wall of the room, filled with cut flowers in vases and boxes and threaded into intricate displays. There are so many colorful blooms that Astra wonders how anyone can pick just one.

She wonders if Isla has ever seen it, and she makes a mental note to bring her back sometime and show her.

Mrs. Reeves continues, making her way back to the cooler, "Or are you looking for something to match your dress?"

Astra blinks, feeling her face heat up. "It's, um, not for me. My date. She really loves flowers. Lilies are her favorite."

My date, Astra's mind plays on a loop. Technically, Oliver is her date. But Isla asked her first, and if Astra had a choice, Isla would be the one she'd choose. Every time.

The corners of Mrs. Reeves's eyes crinkle with a soft smile. Her hair is tied back in a gray-blond bun again today, but wisps of it are falling out along the back of her neck. Astra follows her to the cooler and stops by the sliding glass doors.

"Lilies are a great choice," Mrs. Reeves says. "I knew a little girl once who was obsessed with them. We have every color under the sun, my dear, if there's one in particular you were hoping for."

Astra chooses not to dwell on her comment about the little girl, but clearly she's talking about Isla. Isla in the past tense is something that Astra really doesn't want to think about right now.

Instead, she asks, "The colors have meanings, right? I was hoping that you could help me find one that fits what I want it to say."

"That's a lovely idea. Let's see." Mrs. Reeves opens the cooler doors and disappears inside. After a moment of Astra standing awkwardly outside, she beckons her in with a wave of her hand. "We've got yellow lilies. Yellow flowers in general usually represent happiness, friendship, and other cheerful things. Tiger lilies—the orange ones— mean confidence and respect. White is usually purity, but a lot of people associate it with weddings and funerals. Odd choice, if you ask me, but they'd make a lovely corsage."

Astra tries to look around without touching anything. All of the flowers are neatly arranged, pruned, and displayed so delicately that she feels out of place just standing among them. She can see why Isla loves them so much, but Astra is afraid that she'll accidentally knock over a vase or step on one of the winding trails of vines coming off the pots by the door.

She watches Mrs. Reeves rifle through them, and she gets an idea.

"Are there red lilies?" she asks. "Red is…like roses. Red means love, right?"

The florist's eyes light up and she leans forward into a cramped corner, past a rack of beautiful white roses, and when she comes back up she's holding a small bouquet in her hands.

She holds it up so Astra can see it. The flowers inside are red, dark and silky, and almost the same shade as Astra's prom dress. But they don't look like the other lilies she's seen. The flowers are smaller and curled in around themselves like little cups with spouts coming off the sides.

"Calla lilies," Mrs. Reeves says. "They're related to tulips, so maybe that's why they have a similar shape. The red ones do mean love, my dear. So if that's what you're trying to say, then I could make a lovely arrangement of these for your date."

Astra smiles so wide that it almost hurts. Even in the refrigerated room, her skin feels hot.

"It is," she says. "It really is."

They leave the cooler, and Astra follows Mrs. Reeves back to the counter.

"I can have these ready for you tomorrow, if you'd like to pick them up after school," she says, holding up the bouquet. "Your date must be a very special young lady."

Astra can't stop smiling. The young couple looking at garden décor has moved into the greenhouse, and Astra can see them poking around in the succulent section. She's thankful that they're not nearby anymore, because she's pretty sure she looks like a giddy, lovestruck idiot.

So, no different than usual.

"Yeah. She is."

"I'll see you tomorrow, then." Mrs. Reeves wraps the bouquet up and sets it behind the counter. "And tell Miss Isla hello for me, would you? Next time you see her. It's been quiet here since she stopped coming around."

It's only when she's in her car and driving away that Astra realizes how odd Mrs. Reeves's comment about Isla was. But that's a problem for another day.

Right now, she has a dance to look forward to.

Isla is in her bedroom when Astra gets home—waiting for her.

Astra's heart skips a beat and she hopes Isla can't hear it.

Isla is sitting on the edge of the mattress, scratching behind Leonard's ears and kicking her legs while her feet flicker like static. When Astra opens the door, the cat jumps down, sniffs at the leg of Astra's pants, and promptly turns up his nose and walks away.

"Geez, Leonard, I feel so loved."

"He likes being called Lenny," Isla says, patting the bed next to her. Leonard immediately jumps back up and curls into a ball, flicking his tail lazily.

Traitor, Astra thinks.

"Your cat is rude," Astra says, throwing her backpack on the floor next to her desk.

"You're just mad because he likes me more than you."

"Hmm. Maybe." She sits down next to Isla, keeping a solid foot of distance between them. The cold goes right through her layers of sweaters and prickles at her arms. "Have you been here all day?"

Isla's face brightens and she grins. "Yep. I wanna show you something."

Before Astra can ask, Isla grabs onto her wrist and hauls her backward on the bed. She's got to be using every ounce of power she has, because Astra can feel the grip around her wrist like a vise, tugging her until she's flopping onto her back and looking up at the ceiling.

Isla falls down next to her, panting icy breaths, and Astra blinks up at the dozens of little translucent stars littering her bedroom ceiling.

Glow-in-the-dark stars, she realizes, arching across the ceiling panel right above her bed like her own personal constellation.

She looks over at Isla, acutely aware that she's still got a loose grip on her wrist.

"You put all of these up? By yourself?"

Isla flickers softly like a lightbulb. "Yeah. Took me all day, too. They kept falling through my hands and I got frustrated, and then I accidentally blew a bunch of stuff off of your desk, so I had to clean *that* up too. And I had to feed Leonard because you're a terrible cat owner, so maybe he would like you more if you actually fed him like you're supposed to." Isla stops and takes a deep, lungless breath before continuing. "*And*—you're out of tape."

Astra stares at the ceiling, the shiny strips of clear tape showing on the sides of each individual star. Her walls are textured, and the tape is some off-brand that's been in her drawer for years, so there's no way these stars are going to stick to her ceiling for very long. But she doesn't tell Isla that, because it must have been a ton of work just to get them up there in the first place.

"Where did you get the stars?"

Isla shrugs. Astra feels it in the hand still draped over her wrist. "Your mom's store. I've been doing some digging—mostly at night—and you'd be surprised by some of the stuff I've found. Check underneath the shelves next time you're in there. It's like a goldmine, and I don't think your mom even knows all of what's there."

"Hmm. Okay. I suppose you didn't find any *actual* gold while you were snooping, though?"

"Unfortunately, no. But I did find a box of chocolates that expired two years ago and three bobby pins. And a full skeleton buried in the wall, which you might wanna get taken care of sooner rather than later."

"Skeletons are good for us psychics," Astra tells her. "We use the bones in our potions."

Isla chuckles like wind chimes. "That's *witches*."

"Oh." Astra tries to count the stars on her ceiling, but there are too many. It must have taken hours just for her to get a good enough grip to hold them up without dropping them. "Thanks for these, by the way. They look awesome. Way better than my nightlights."

"Well. Your nightmares—they've gotten a lot better, but I know they're not totally gone. And I get it, you know? But it's been raining a lot lately, and I don't want you falling out of the window trying to get to your little roof spot next time you need to…see the stars. Or take a nap."

The lilt in her voice makes her sound more casual than Astra knows she actually is. Her hand is flickering in and out around Astra's wrist, and Astra scoots back on the bed just enough to exchange her wrist for her own hand, holding Isla's still while she buzzes like television static.

"Plus, I realized I never actually asked you to prom. I kinda just *told* you we were going, you know? And that's not fair. And I know those promposal things are supposed to be a big deal, so I thought…"

She cuts herself off and reaches under Astra's pillow, pulling out a brown leather necklace cord wrapped and tied around the middle of the same kind of translucent star as the ones on the ceiling.

"This is gonna sound stupid, but I didn't want to steal any *actual* jewelry from your mom's store, so maybe you can wear this with your dress. That is—if you still wanna go to prom with me?"

"Of course I do." Astra takes the necklace and holds it against her collarbone. It's nice and long, and the cord doesn't feel itchy or stiff.

It kind of looks like an elementary school art project, but she also kind of loves it.

Just like she kind of loves Isla.

"That's good, because I didn't really have a plan for if you said no."

Leonard chirps and settles himself down by their heads, waving his bushy tail over the top of Astra's hair. He starts purring, and Isla reaches up to scratch at the scruff at the back of his neck.

Astra wishes she could live in this moment, looking up at the stars with Isla by her side, forever. She doesn't even mind the cold, because her heart is beating so fast that her blood feels hot and her skin feels prickly.

Isla is silent for a minute, shifting her hand and tapping her fingers restlessly. She hums, opens and closes her mouth a couple of times like she's trying to think of something to say, and phases in and out one last time before sitting up and letting go of Astra's hand.

For once, Astra misses the cold.

Isla clears her throat and breaks the peaceful silence. "Where's George the Geranium, by the way? When I was putting your stuff back on your desk, I noticed you moved him."

Astra looks over at her desk—at the lonely little wooden turtle sitting on the edge. "I took him to the hospital."

"To the—the one I'm at?"

"Yeah. Your room looked too...plain. Sterile. Plus, you said geraniums mean *good health*, right? So you need him more than I do right now."

Isla blinks at her, frowning. Astra can almost see the gears turning in her head. For all of the things she knows about Isla, all of the little habits and likes and dislikes she's discovered over the past month, she still always feels like there's something she's missing. Sometimes she catches Isla with this look on her face, like she's thinking about telling Astra what it is, but she never does.

And she doesn't today, either.

"Oh. Well, thanks. I should go water him, then. He's been growing so good, it would really suck if I let him die now."

I met your mom today, Astra thinks. *She told me you don't go to public school anymore. And that kids used to pick on you, but she didn't tell me why. I didn't ask. Maybe I should have asked.*

"Okay. I'll see you later, then."

Isla is flying out the window before Astra can even get all of the words out, and Astra feels like she's missed something important. Like she's done something wrong, or said the wrong thing, but she has no idea what it was.

Her phone buzzes from the front pocket of her backpack, and Leonard growls at her when she gets up to check it.

There's one new message, and when she reads it her heart drops.

From: Unknown Number, 4:52 p.m.
This is Ricky. They're taking Isla off life support next Friday.

CHAPTER NINETEEN

It's Saturday. Prom day. Astra is supposed to be getting ready for the best night of her life, but instead, all she can think about is how Isla is going to be dead by Friday.

She's not sure why it bothers her so much. It shouldn't. She's used to the idea of Isla being dead—she only found out that she's still alive about a week ago, and she already knew that Isla's prognosis wasn't good. She's on a ventilator. She's been in a coma for a month and a half. It's not like it's a surprise that she's dying.

But some small part of Astra had hoped that maybe she could still wake up. Astra could confess her love and kiss Isla awake like Sleeping Beauty, and they could go out in public together without people thinking Astra is talking to herself, and she could hold Isla's hand without feeling hypothermic. And Isla could *stay*. For as long as she wanted. Forever, maybe.

But not if she's a ghost. Ghosts can't stay forever. Astra has only seen a handful of them ever try to, and they all ended up like the two fuzzy lights outside her window.

"Are you ready yet, sweetheart?" her mom calls from the living room, the TV droning softly in the background.

"Almost! Just a couple more minutes."

Isla floats in through the window, and Astra immediately locks her phone and throws it down on her bed. She still hasn't answered Ricky's text. What is she supposed to say?

Isla has her hands over her eyes, and she stops with her legs inside Astra's bedside table and her back floating halfway through the wall.

"Are you decent?" she asks. She splays out two of her fingers and peeks between them, and Astra tosses a notebook through her stomach. "*Ouch*. Papercut."

"I'm dressed. But you already know that."

In truth, Astra has had her dress on for the past twenty minutes. She's spent the rest of her time rereading Ricky's message and working on giving herself a panic attack. She's probably turned her lights on and off a dozen times, and every time she paces past her closet she jiggles the doorknob loose and then has to tighten it again.

Isla's dimples pop as she scans Astra's dress, stopping on the star necklace dangling down over the patchwork of flowers on the top. Flowers and stars. If Astra thinks about it too hard, she's going to start crying.

Again.

She looks up at Isla, hoping for a distraction—from Isla. Her breath catches in her throat.

"You changed your hair."

Isla smiles and twirls around, showing off the blond French braid that goes all the way to the middle of her back. It's a little messy, but without all of the stray hairs in her face, her ears stick out just a little and her dimples are a lot more noticeable. She has a couple of scattered moles along her jaw, and her little flower earrings are on full display.

"I did. Robin lent me her hair tie. Apparently that kind of stuff is allowed in the ghost rules? I think as long as I don't drop it, I'm fine. Although I wonder what would happen if I did..."

"It looks great," Astra interrupts. "You didn't have to get all dolled up for me, though."

She means it as a joke. Probably. But Isla doesn't laugh.

"You did it for me. I mean, you're even wearing that crappy necklace I made you. I just wish I looked more..." She waves her hands down, gesturing to herself. "Presentable. Prom-ready? I'm wearing *flannel*. I'm pretty sure that's a sin in, like, the Prom Commandments. Right next to Crocs and hats and those suits with shorts instead of pants."

"Well, I got you a *proper* prom accessory, if that helps."

Astra opens the top drawer of her dresser and pulls out the corsage. It's got three dark red lilies on it, along with an assortment of decorative leaves and a silky white ribbon. It looks even better than she'd expected—it matches her dress perfectly, and she hopes Isla knows what flower colors mean. Otherwise Astra is going to just be embarrassing herself for nothing.

Isla runs her fingers over the sides of the flowers, putting just enough pressure into the touch to bend the petals.

"Calla lilies," she says. Then she frowns. "I can't wear this."

Astra shakes her head. "No, I know. But it's for you anyway. I can wear it, and since you'll be right next to me the whole time, I figured maybe you could just…pretend? I don't know. It sounds kind of stupid when I say it out loud like that. Maybe I shouldn't have bought it."

"Nope! No way. They're *beautiful*, and they're my favorite flower. I love them. Did you go back to the greenhouse without me?"

"Yeah, sorry. I wanted it to be a surprise. But we can always go back again some other time."

Astra barely catches Isla's "Yeah, maybe." But she does.

She scrambles to change the subject. Tonight is supposed to be fun. She can worry about everything else later. Tonight it's just her, Isla, and Oliver, and lots of dancing and laughing and wearing a pretty dress with a pretty girl by her side.

"I should go talk to my mom. I'm pretty sure she's more excited about me going to the dance than I am."

"Okay. Sure." Isla looks down at the flowers again, holding her hand up but not touching them. "Seriously, though. Thank you. They're perfect."

She doesn't mention the color, but Isla is a walking plant encyclopedia. If Mrs. Reeves knew what red flowers symbolize, then Isla must know, too. She knows, and she isn't saying anything.

Astra understands what that means, and it hurts to think that Isla might not return her feelings. She smiles and nods, ignoring the pit in her stomach, and leaves the safety of her bedroom to meet her mother in the living room.

Maria Vaughn is more dressed up for a dance than Astra is. She's wearing a flashy, dark blue dress that goes down past her knees and a black jacket with fringe all the way around the bottom. She's accessorized with a black belt and a shiny silver chain necklace that actually look really nice together—sort of like what someone would wear to a class reunion or to a business meeting at a fancy restaurant. But her shoes are tall purple pumps, her wrists and fingers are covered in bangles and sparkly rings, and she's got a fuzzy gray scarf wrapped around her neck. In the middle of spring. Indoors.

She looks at Astra and smiles so widely that Astra feels a little guilty. The only reason her mom is so excited about Astra going to prom is because Astra rarely leaves her room for anything, let alone an actual, *normal* high school social function. She's so proud of her daughter for finally being a normal teenager that Astra wishes she had tried harder to do it before the last couple of months of her senior year of high school.

"Honey, you look *beautiful*."

Astra does a little twirl in her dress to humor her mom, and poses awkwardly next to the couch for a couple of blurry cellphone photos. She hasn't seen her mom this happy in a long time.

"I have something for you, sweetheart," her mom says after she finally puts her phone away. "I think we're pretty close to the same size..."

Her mom digs behind the couch, underneath the window, past the sea of throw pillows that have somehow migrated to the floor. When she stands back up, she's got a pair of shoe straps hooked over her finger and she's holding them out for Astra to take.

Her strappy, red clicking heels. The ones she wears every day, even indoors, even when they don't match the rest of her outfit.

They *do* match Astra's dress, though.

She toes off her beat-up sneakers and tries the heels on. They're a little big, and her feet slip forward just a bit when she stands up straight, but she tightens the straps anyway and sways her skirt around them, watching the sides shine when they catch the light.

"Thanks, Mom. They look great."

She means it. Her mom pulls her in for a hug, another handful of poorly lit, too-close photos, and a couple more compliments about her dress, her shoes, and even the little glow star tied around her neck.

Her mom waves her off at the door with a "Have fun, be home by eleven!" And that's it. Astra is on her way to her first high school dance, and it's going to be amazing.

Hopefully.

❖

The student parking lot is almost full by the time Astra pulls up. There are students milling around all over the place, some dancing, and some swaying around like drunks, holding on to their friends for support. They're loud, and Astra left her headphones at home.

She parks in the lot on the other side of the school—the one behind the garbage bins, where the substitute teachers park and some of the older kids hide out to smoke cigarettes between classes. There are only a couple of other cars in the lot, and one of them has two flat tires and looks like it hasn't been moved all year, so Astra figures they'll be left pretty much alone back there.

Astra texts Oliver to meet them there. Isla unhooks her hand from the middle console, where she'd been holding on to avoid being thrown out of the car, and floats through the window. She makes a show of flying around to the other side and opening Astra's door for her, stepping back and bowing with one arm across her stomach.

"Ladies first," she says. Astra rolls her eyes.

"You got out first, technically."

Isla shrugs. "I meant what I said."

Astra gets out and immediately starts to wobble. Not only are her mom's shoes just a little too big, but the heels are at least three inches high, and Astra has never even walked in anything taller than a pair of sneakers with cushioned insoles. Her knees knock together and she grabs onto the side mirror for support.

"First time in heels?" Isla teases, floating with her arms crossed and a smug look on her face.

"Like you're one to talk. You're not even wearing *shoes*."

Isla looks mock-offended, throwing her hand over her chest. "I'm pretty sure it's a sin to insult the clothes someone died in."

"Good thing you're not dead, then."

Astra realizes what she's said a second too late. She clamps her mouth shut so hard that her teeth clack together, but Isla doesn't seem fazed. Astra decides that the best way to change the subject is for her to promptly attempt to walk in the shoes she can't even manage to stand up in, and she immediately trips over her own feet.

She slams into the hood of the car with a hard thud, and Isla starts cackling from behind her.

"You look like a toddler learning how to walk," she says between howls of laughter. "I wish I had a camera on me right now, oh my God."

"Yeah, yeah. You've had your laugh. Now help me up."

Isla grabs onto one of Astra's upper arms and tugs until she's upright. She doesn't let go right away, and Astra can feel small tingles of electricity on her skin from the pressure. She takes a step forward, with Isla floating along next to her and keeping her from tipping over, and she's mostly gotten her balance under control when a car pulls up right next to hers and Oliver gets out.

"Do I wanna know why you picked such a sketchy place to park?"

"It's quieter," Astra tells him. "Plus, one of my dates is invisible, and I didn't want to look like I was talking to myself in the middle of the school parking lot."

"Good point," Oliver says, joining them next to Astra's car. "Hey, Spooks."

He waves at a random point on the pavement, several feet to the left of where Isla's actually standing. She chuckles.

Astra had half expected to see Oliver wearing his patchy brown jacket on top of his suit, but he actually looks like he put some effort into his appearance. His suit looks like it's been ironed, and he's got a little white rose pinned to the front of the jacket. Instead of his threatened Crocs, he's wearing shiny black dress shoes, and his hair is tied back into a little bun. He's got flashy diamond earrings in both ears, and with his hair back, there's nothing to hide them behind.

The split on his lip has healed into a thin scab, leaving polka dots of purple bruises in one corner of his mouth. Astra doesn't know what Isla did, but the track guys have left Oliver alone since that day in the locker room.

"We're hair twins!" Isla announces, floating closer to him and blowing on the back of his neck. He jumps and throws his hand over his neck like he's been shocked. "I love it. Astra, tell him how much I love it. And his earrings. What a *look*."

Astra chuckles and tells Oliver, "Isla says she likes your hair and your earrings. She's got a braid in right now. She borrowed a hair tie from another ghost, because apparently there are no rules anymore, but she looks awesome. Picture dark blond hair in a French braid going down to about *here*"—she gestures to the middle of her own back with one hand—"and you've got it."

"God, we all look so gorgeous right now," Isla says. "It's almost not fair to the rest of them."

"Hmm. I'm actually inclined to agree with you, for once."

"I'm gonna be out of the loop all night, aren't I?" Oliver asks, but he's smiling.

Isla pokes at the boutonniere pinned to his suit jacket and grins. "It's real. Good job, Ollie."

Astra clears her throat. Her face feels hot. "I can't talk to both of you at the same time. Can I just—Oliver, would you mind going on ahead without us? I just need a few minutes. I'm not ready to go in yet."

"That doesn't really make me feel less like a third wheel, but sure. I'll see you guys inside." He takes a step back and then pauses. "Or, one of you. Sorry, Spooks."

Oliver leaves, and suddenly Astra and Isla are alone again. But something feels…different.

Astra coughs, but the lump in her throat stays put. It feels like it's got its own heartbeat.

"So," Isla asks after a few seconds of silence, "is there any particular reason why we're just standing out here in an empty parking lot?"

Astra ignores the chorus of voices in her head telling her to just *go inside, go hang out with Oliver. You have friends for the first time since you were in elementary school, don't do anything that could mess that up.* Instead, she climbs back into the driver's side of her car, turns the key, and waits for the radio to turn on. She fiddles with the knobs until she finds a station she likes, playing some soft, classic rock song that she vaguely recognizes. She turns the volume up just enough to hear it outside the car.

She stands back up but keeps the door open. Isla has that odd look on her face again—like she's trying to come up with something funny to say, but she can't think of anything. Her face is pinched and her eyebrows are knocked together, and Astra feels like if she could just figure out what that look means, she could use it to unlock all the secrets of the universe.

"Um. Are we not going inside?"

Astra clears her throat again around the lump. "Not yet," she tells her. "We're supposed to be dancing. But I can't dance with you in there, so…"

Isla catches on, and Astra watches her smile bloom like a flower. She floats over quickly and holds out her hands.

"Well, in that case. May I have this dance, milady?"

Astra nearly rolls her ankle trying to stand up straight, but she grabs both of Isla's hands and steadies herself. Cold seeps into her palms, but she pulls Isla closer and moves her hands to her waist, barely making contact. She can feel Isla focusing on the places she's touching, working hard to keep them solid while the rest of her stays incorporeal.

The song on the radio changes to something upbeat, with a guitar solo and a snare drum vibrating through the car's speakers. Isla looks down at her feet, hovering above the pavement and flickering in and out almost in time with the song. She holds her hands up and gestures with one of them toward Astra's shoulders.

"Can I...?"

Astra nods, chuckling softly. "Of course."

Isla wraps her arms around Astra's neck, and Astra fights to keep from shivering. She's pretty sure her whole body is covered in goose bumps by now, but she's also probably sweating. The hot and cold mixed together are creating a tingle, a buzz running through her skin like electricity. It's not unpleasant.

She sways along to the beat of the song. She's not sure what to do with her feet, so she mostly just shuffles around on the pavement and tries very hard not to trip over her mom's heels. They click loudly when she steps down, and her skirt catches on the toe of one of them and nearly sends her toppling into the car's hood again. Isla laughs and lets go of her neck to do a spin, her dress twirling around her knees and briefly showing off her birthmark.

She spins a second time and ends up with half of her torso inside the car's side mirror. She unsticks herself and kicks her flickering leg back into place.

"This might be a bad time to tell you that I was lying about being a good dancer," she says. "I mean, natural talent aside, I don't think I've danced since I was, like, four."

"We're on a level playing field, then."

A new song plays, faster than the other two. Isla takes both of Astra's hands in hers and spins her around, then pulls her back and waves their joined arms back and forth. Her feet tap and flicker, and Astra takes tiny steps sideways in her too-tall heels. Her dress sways around her ankles, and she notices that as it starts to get darker outside, the star on her necklace begins to glow.

Astra can hear noise coming from inside the school—loud music, laughter, and the sound of a hundred people dancing all at once. She wonders how long they've been out here. They probably don't have a lot of time before Oliver comes back out to check on them.

She wants to ask if Isla knows what red lilies mean. She wants to tell her that *she* knows what they mean—that she didn't just pick them out because they match her dress. The song changes again, and Isla lets go of her hands to perform an impromptu tap dance without her feet ever actually touching the ground. Astra swings her dress and clicks her heels and laughs so hard that her stomach hurts.

It occurs to Astra, watching Isla fumbling to keep her feet from flickering and pulling her elbow out of the car's doorframe, that she loves this girl. And not in the teasing way that Oliver always says it. She genuinely, truly *loves* Isla. Even if she disappeared right now and Astra never saw her again, she would still love her.

Even when she was just a ghost haunting Astra's bedroom, she loved her.

She wants to say it. She *needs* to say it. The music changes again, this time to something slow with a pretty piano tune in the background, and Isla puts her arms back around Astra's neck and starts pulling her along, swaying back and forth in small circles on the pavement.

And because Astra's brain never does what she tells it to, she doesn't say *I love you.*

Instead, she says, "Ricky texted me. He said they're taking you off life support next week."

Isla's face falls, but just for a moment. Like a flicker. "Oh. Yeah, I heard them talking about it yesterday."

"And you didn't tell me?"

Isla steps down, and her foot sinks through the ground. She tugs it back up again and shakes it out. "There's nothing to tell. My brain stopped responding to their tests. I mean, I knew I was kind of an idiot, but *ouch.*"

"Not funny."

The soft piano music starts to fade. A guitar riff floats through the speakers, but they keep swaying slowly, even as the bass drum kicks up and the music gets faster. A minute passes, then two. Oliver is probably wondering where they are. They should go inside.

"Have you…" Astra begins, uncertain. "Have you ever tried going back? Waking up?"

Isla's eyebrows knit together. "Of course I have. But it doesn't work that way. I can't control what my body does when I'm not in it."

"Maybe I could talk to Ricky. Or your parents. See if they can wait a little longer."

Isla shakes her head. The music gets louder. Astra wishes she had brought her headphones.

"It's already been a month and a half. They can't afford the hospital bills, and it's not like I'm getting better, anyway."

"Then I'll do some research. There's got to be *something*—"

Isla cuts her off, shaking her head. "Astra, come on. Why do you think I've been having you do all this bucket list stuff with me?" She moves back and meets Astra's eyes, keeping her arms around her neck. "I'm ready to go. I am. I *want* to."

Astra's stomach hurts, like a million tiny butterflies being crushed all at once. She stops swaying, her hands still on Isla's waist.

"But—*I* don't want you to."

Isla smiles without her dimples. "You'll be fine. Ollie's a good friend, and your mom is awesome. Plus, without me interrupting your classes all the time, you might actually have a decent chance of graduating."

"But—"

Isla holds up a hand, palm out. "No buts. We came here to have fun. Come on, dip me. I've always wanted to be dipped."

Astra doesn't move. "I can't have fun if I know you're dying."

"Then just pretend I'm already dead. Like before."

"That's—it's different."

The music changes again. A car drives past down the street with its headlights on. The school door opens up and a trio of giggling girls stumbles out, holding their dresses up and running to the parking lot across the street. A flood of music, noise, and light bursts out through the open door before it slams shut again with a metallic clang.

"How?" Isla asks. She's not dancing anymore.

Astra's throat feels dry. "I—" *I love you.* "I like you. A lot. Like, as more than a friend. I *like* you."

It doesn't feel like enough, but the lump in Astra's throat is making it hard to get any more words out. She kind of expects Isla to be upset, or disgusted, or laugh at her for catching feelings for a ghost or a girl in a coma. Or at least look shocked, surprised, startled. But she just looks sad.

"You wouldn't if you really knew me," she says.

Astra shakes her head. "No. I *do* know you."

"Really? You know that wheelchair, in my hospital room?" Astra nods slowly, vaguely remembering the black chair pushed into the corner of the room, next to the sink, underneath a shelf full of gloves and sanitizer. "Well, it doesn't belong to the hospital, if that's what you thought. It's mine. I—I can't walk. I haven't been able to walk on my own since I was eleven."

Astra isn't moving, but the ground feels like it is. She leans into the open car door for support, banging her elbow on the window and scraping her mom's heels on the pavement. Everything is tilting just a little to the right.

"An infection," Isla plows on. "The same kind I have right now. That one was in my spine, and it made my legs stop working. What do you think the one that put me in a *coma* is gonna do?"

Astra's brain starts putting things together like a puzzle, and one thing sticks out more than anything else: Isla's bucket list. Her anti-bucket list. The list of things she was determined to do before she moved on.

Climbing a tower. Going to a greenhouse that's only accessible by walking through a grassy field and over a gravel pathway. Checking out a book on the third floor of a library without an elevator. Taking a road trip in the front seat of a car. Dancing at prom.

All of them, Astra realizes, are things she couldn't have done in a wheelchair. Not without help, at the very least, and Astra knows how much Isla hates asking for help.

It makes so much sense. The way she flies around the room, kicking her legs like she's swimming. The way her legs flicker in and out sometimes, like they can't quite remember how they're supposed to move. Why she's wearing a pristine pair of socks on her feet, but no shoes. Why the palms of her hands are rough and bumpy with little half-healed calluses.

"Do you think you're still gonna like me when you find out?"

Astra searches for the right thing to say, but all that comes up is a sob, and she realizes that she's crying. How long has she been crying for?

"I thought so," Isla says. She's got that strange look on her face again, but there's hurt mixed in this time. Astra opens her mouth but nothing comes out.

The school door opens again, flooding the pavement with light. Astra looks up just in time to see Oliver walking toward them before the door slams shut.

"What's going on?" Oliver demands as he gets closer. "I've been waiting for half an hour! I drank so much punch I've had to pee three times, and—Astra? Are you okay?"

The radio is blaring a catchy pop song that couldn't feel less appropriate. Astra reaches through the door and turns the volume down to zero.

"I can't be here right now," she says, sinking into the driver's seat. "I'm sorry, Oliver. I just—I can't do this."

She doesn't wait for a response. She doesn't wait for Isla to get in the passenger seat. She just drives.

CHAPTER TWENTY

Astra doesn't go home right away. Instead, she drives the extra fifteen minutes to the hospital and runs across the parking lot in her pretty red prom dress and her mom's clicky heels. She haggles with the receptionist on the first floor for just five minutes of visitation time in room 421.

All she needs is one, though.

She's not sure why she does it. It might be a waste of time, but it feels important, somehow.

She pulls off her corsage and slips it around Isla's too-thin wrist, walks halfway to the door, then stops and turns around. She bends down and plants a kiss, feather-light, on Isla's cheek. Like Sleeping Beauty, except that Isla doesn't wake up.

Astra runs the rest of the way to her car.

❖

Her mom is waiting for her in the living room when she gets home. It's almost comical how quickly the excited smile on her mom's face melts down into pure worry when she sees Astra.

"Honey? What's—"

Astra cuts her off by throwing her arms around her mom's neck and burying her face in her shoulder. Astra's feet ache in her heels and she's not sure if she's still crying or if her face is just wet. She hiccups a sob and lets her mom lead her to the couch, where she sinks into a mountain of throw pillows and undoes the straps on her shoes with one hand.

Her mom wraps one arm around Astra's shoulders and tugs her close. "I'm guessing your dance didn't go so well."

Astra exhales a laugh that sounds more like a cry. "No. I guess not."

"Was it that boy? Oliver? Do I need to have a talk with his parents?"

"It wasn't Oliver, Mom. And it's not like that. We're just friends."

Her mom hums and uses her free hand to brush a few stray curls off Astra's forehead. She waits for her to say something. Moms always know what to say, right?

But she stays quiet, humming some tune that Astra vaguely recognizes. Like a lullaby.

Maybe it's because Astra is starting to feel tired, or maybe it's the song, or maybe it's the way her mom's hand is combing through her hair so softly that she can barely feel it—but the words just *come out*. It's like a dam bursts and everything Astra has been trying so desperately to hold back, for so many years, just comes spilling out of her mouth. She can't stop it.

She blurts out, "I can see ghosts."

The relief comes almost right away, and before the regret can start to sink in, her mom says, "I know."

She says it like it's nothing—like Astra didn't just reveal her biggest secret to the person most likely to freak out about it. Her mom even shrugs, and Astra can feel it through her own shoulders.

She sits back a little, watching her mom's face. She's staring down at a little dent in the coffee table, frowning.

"You...you *know*?"

"Sweetheart," her mom begins, gently. "I've known for years. It was just a feeling back then, like when you started wearing sweaters all year round, and the year you asked for a pair of headphones for your birthday. I didn't know for certain until recently, if it makes you feel any better."

It doesn't. "What, um...made you realize?"

"I can feel the cold, too, honey. Your bedroom is like a freezer. I've heard you talking to someone, too, and I hoped you were on the phone with a friend from school, but your friend Oliver is a boy, and the voice I heard talking back to you wasn't."

"Oh."

Astra shifts on the couch and moves a couple of pillows so that she can lean back. She tucks her legs up next to her and rearranges her skirt like a blanket, running her fingers over the soft satin and smoothing it out over her bare feet.

"I also got a call from your father a couple of weeks ago."

Astra quickly lets go of her skirt and nearly cracks her neck turning to look at her mom. There's a small, barely-there smile on her face.

"I'm not mad," her mom says. "I think it's kind of funny, actually. All these years of him not believing me—or either of us, for that matter—and now *he's* the one calling *me*, ranting and raving about ghosts in his house."

Astra swallows loudly. "Just one ghost, actually."

"Hmm. I thought so. Although I do wish you'd talked to me before driving all that way on a school night."

"The driving part—that wasn't my idea. But it was good. It helped, I think. I'm glad I went."

"That's good, sweetheart," her mom says. "From what I heard, that ghost friend of yours really gave him a good scare."

Friend, Astra thinks. Oliver is a friend. Isla is…

"Isla's not a ghost, Mom," she blurts out, her mind reeling. "She's not dead. But she…she's dying, and I don't know what to do to stop it. And I'm scared."

Astra decides to tell her mom *everything*—all of the things she never realized she needed so desperately to get out. She tells her about Isla—about meeting her at school, making friends with Oliver, and checking things off her anti-bucket list. She tells her about George and the other ghosts, the good ones and the ones that still give her nightmares. She talks about meeting Ricky, going to the hospital, and learning about Isla's sickness. Going to prom. Arguing. Leaving.

She omits bits and pieces—personal things, moments that belong to just *them*—like George the Geranium, the tulips and the red calla lilies, the glow stars on the ceiling, the fake palm reading, and kissing Isla's cheek.

And, by the end of it, the front of her shiny red dress is dark with tears and she's leaning all the way into her mom's shoulder, tucked in as small as she can get.

"I don't want her to leave," she says into her mom's upper arm. "I don't know what to do."

She feels like a little kid with a skinned knee. Everything hurts and she just wants her mom to fix it.

"Sweetheart..." Her mom sounds sad. Astra hates that she's making her mom sad. This is why she didn't want to tell her any of this. Now her mom is never going to be able to look at her without remembering all of the ways that seeing ghosts has ruined her life, and all of the ways it could ruin Astra's. "You really care about her, don't you?"

Astra sniffles and wipes her gross, runny nose on the front of her dress. The glow star around her neck is still giving off a faint green light, and she rubs on the brown leather cord with her thumb.

"I..." *I like you. A lot. Like, as more than a friend.* It's not enough. She wishes it was enough. "I love her, Mom."

Just saying it out loud feels like heaving an enormous brick off her chest. It feels freeing. It feels *easy*.

She holds her breath and waits for her mom's reaction—waits for the awkward silence, the questions, the judgment. She's not sure if her mom ever noticed that she likes girls as much as she likes boys. She's not sure if that's more of a problem than loving someone in a coma, someone who's dying, or a ghost. Which one is worse?

Instead, her mom lets out a soft laugh and says, "Well, that's pretty obvious by the way you talk about her, honey."

Astra exhales shakily. "You're not upset?"

Her mom shakes her head, her long hair bouncing around her shoulders. "Not at you, honey. I'm just upset that you have to go through all of this. And that you felt like you had to go through it alone."

"I don't—I didn't want you to worry."

Her mom gives Astra's shoulder a gentle squeeze. "I'm your mother. I'm always going to worry about you."

"If you knew this whole time, why didn't you ever say anything?"

"I wanted you to tell me yourself," her mom says. "I wanted to wait until you were ready for me to know."

Astra leans back and pushes her legs over the edge of the couch. A pillow falls to the floor, and her mom lets go of her shoulders to pick it up.

"But you already knew."

Her mom shrugs, holding the pillow in her lap and picking at a frayed corner. "Call it a mother's intuition. I *know* you. I can tell when you're keeping secrets, sweetheart." Astra opens her mouth to say something, but her mom continues, "You have *tells*. You're incredibly easy to read, dear."

"Not—not all of the time." Astra feels her face burning.

"No, maybe not. You should talk to her, tell her how you feel. You'd be surprised how much can be fixed just by talking."

It's already dark outside, and Astra glances out of the living room window like she expects to see Isla hovering on the other side, but all she sees are dark gray clouds and a pair of headlights moving down the street. She stands and shuffles around the coffee table, walks the first eight steps from the living room to her bedroom with her bare feet thudding softly on the linoleum, and then turns around.

"Thanks, Mom."

She smiles, feeling like the knot in her stomach has loosened just a little bit.

"Any time, honey. You know you can talk to me about anything, right?" Astra nods. "And one more thing, dear?"

Astra pauses with her hand on the doorknob. "Yeah?"

"You should let the cat out of your room more often. He gets lonely when you're not home, and he's very *loud*."

❖

"I thought I gave you those glow stars so you *wouldn't* have to come out here when it's raining."

Astra smiles and shuffles sideways on the damp rooftop, unsticking the back of her pajamas from the wet tiles. Isla floats closer and settles down next to her, crossing her legs at the ankles.

"It's not raining yet."

"It already did," Isla counters. "You could have slipped. I'm starting to think you're trying to summon me when you do reckless stuff like this."

"Well," Astra says, "it worked, didn't it?"

Isla hums but doesn't say anything.

The glow star around Astra's neck is giving off a hazy green light that she can see even when she's looking up at the sky.

"I'm sorry," she says after a moment. "I shouldn't have left. It wasn't because of what you said, I swear. I just got overwhelmed, and I freaked out. I should have just stayed and talked to you, but—"

Isla interrupts her loudly. "I don't wanna talk about this right now."

"Okay…"

"I'm freaking out a little bit right now, too. But I didn't come here to give you my sob story. Just—I need a distraction. Please."

Her voice breaks a little on the last word, and Astra realizes that in all of her own worrying and fear, she hasn't really paid any attention to how *Isla* must be feeling. She's the one who's dying. She's probably terrified, and all Astra has been thinking about is her own heartbreak.

She racks her brain searching for something to say, and settles on, "Did you know that tulips and lilies are related?"

"I—no way. How do you know a plant fact that I don't?"

"Mrs. Reeves told me. When I picked out the flowers for your corsage."

She winces at the memory of slipping the bracelet around Isla's thin, pale wrist, and tries not to wonder if it's still there, or if a nurse came in and took it off. Or if Isla even noticed that Astra left it there for her.

"That's not fair," Isla says. She bumps Astra's shoulder with a tiny burst of icy pressure. "It's cheating if you asked someone else."

"Does that mean you've been cheating this whole time, then? Since she's the one who taught you all of your nerdy plant facts in the first place?"

"Touché."

Astra chuckles and presses her pinkie finger against Isla's hand on the patch of rooftop between them. She can feel Isla's energy focusing, her hand flickering around Astra's until it's solid. Her skin prickles, and goose bumps burst along her arms and the back of her neck.

The sky is dark and swirling with gray storm clouds. There are only a few visible stars, tucked in between clouds and dotted around the sliver of moon peeking out from behind them, and Astra counts them in her head. When she gets to eleven, Isla's hand is laced all the way in hers.

Astra clears her throat. She counts the stars and rubs her thumb along the back of Isla's hand until it starts to sink through.

"Can I just…?" she begins, working around the lump in her

throat. "I know you said you didn't wanna talk about it, and I get that. But...I just need you to know that it doesn't matter. That you've got a wheelchair, or that you get sick a lot. It wouldn't—it doesn't change anything. About how I feel. About you."

Her face is burning. She's thankful for the chilly, overcast night and the frost that Isla is giving off. And the dark sky that's hiding the heat in her cheeks.

Isla sits up a little, leaning over in the air. "Astra, come on. Look at all of the stuff we've done together. Do you think I could have climbed a water tower with you, in my chair? I couldn't have even made it up here."

"I like spending time with you. I don't care where."

"You wouldn't say that if you had to spend time with the *real* me."

"Hmm," Astra hums. "So, lying down, holding your hand—I can't do that stuff with you in a wheelchair? I can't...pick out flowers, or try on dresses, or read books? You can't do any of that without being able to walk?"

"You don't get it."

Isla's voice has lost some of its lilt. It's low and raspy, and Astra would maybe think that her throat was sore if ghosts could actually get sore throats.

"Then tell me," Astra says. "Please."

"I don't..." Isla pauses, flickers like a lightbulb, then settles back down a couple of inches above the roof tiles. "I'm not sure if I *want* to wake up."

Astra's heart does a little sputtering thing, like it's skipped a beat and made up for it by trying to beat twice as fast on the next one. She can feel Isla's hand starting to phase out, so she squeezes it a little until Isla feels it and pushes back. It's like holding on to an ice cube and feeling it melt between her fingers.

After a few seconds of silence that Astra's heartbeat seems to be trying to fill, Isla plows on. And the more she says, the faster the words come out, like she's been holding them back.

"I get infections. Like the one I've got now, but all of the time. I was in the hospital a lot, and I couldn't keep missing school, so my mom stayed home and taught me. But now—" She breathes in and exhales slowly. Ghosts don't need to breathe. "Now she has time to do other stuff, you know? And my brother—he doesn't have to be embarrassed to invite his friends over and deal with them staring at me or asking him questions. He can just be *normal*. And my dad, he doesn't have to pick up extra shifts to pay for all of my meds and hospital stays and my chair. It's…better. It's like they're all a normal family again."

Astra tries to think of something to say, but her brain is still trying to process Isla's speech. It's like waiting for a lagging computer to finish loading a page so that she can close it out and click on something else. She tries to force it closed, but her brain gets stuck on an endless loop of *missing school* and *hospital stays* and *embarrassed* and *normal family*.

Isla lets out a dry, humorless laugh that startles Astra. She jumps and her bare feet squeak on the wet tiles.

"You know," Isla says suddenly, "I really did die. For five minutes and twenty-eight seconds. I watched them count. I guess it's better than being stuck in a hospital gown for all of eternity."

"You're—you're deflecting," Astra says.

"I am."

"And you're *wrong*."

Isla leans on her elbow and looks over at her. Astra runs her free hand over the cord around her neck, tugging on it until the glowing green star is twirling around in the air.

"I talked to your mom. And your brother. And I think it's pretty obvious that they miss you like crazy."

"They can miss me and still be better off without me."

"I don't—I don't think so." Astra frowns. Her head hurts. "I don't think you can love someone without loving *all* of them. Like, I love my mom, even after everything that happened. And I…" *I like you. Like, as more than a friend.* "I love *you*, too. Just as much now as when I thought you were just another ghost. Probably even more."

Isla blinks over at her. Astra can feel her gaze boring into her like a laser beam. Her neck feels damp, and she's not sure if it's from sweat or the leftover rain soaking through the collar of her pajama shirt.

A minute passes. Astra says, "You know, usually a confession like that warrants a response."

"Did…did you know that there's a type of orchid that looks kinda like a monkey's face?"

Astra huffs out a breath. "Did you know that I *love you*?"

"I'd, um, gathered that, yes."

"Good. Just wanted to be sure you knew."

Isla's hand twitches in hers, and it takes Astra a moment to realize that she's focusing her energy on trying to rub tiny circles with her thumb like Astra was earlier. The movement is jerky and too soft, but it makes Astra's stomach feel fluttery anyway.

She doesn't expect Isla to return her confession, so she's only a little disappointed when she doesn't.

"I haven't tried to wake up," Isla admits.

Astra nods. "I know."

"I'm not sure if I can. It's...I'm scared."

"I can be there with you. If you want."

"I don't know *what* I want." Isla exhales a shaky breath without lungs, but her chest doesn't fall. "I'm tired of being sick. And I need more time to figure out if it's—if I even want to try going back."

Astra tries to hide her disappointment. She bites down on her bottom lip and keeps her eyes on the sky. She's not sure what she expected. For Isla to return her love confession and fly down to the hospital and immediately throw herself back into her body? For her to pull a Sleeping Beauty and ask Astra to wake her up with a kiss? For her to at least *acknowledge* that Astra's feelings for her aren't one-sided?

The girl next to her right now feels so different from the one who just a couple of weeks ago was flying around the school—doing cartwheels in the gym, reciting plant facts from the greenhouse ceiling, defending Oliver from bullies, and doing the tango with George McCreary in her bedroom.

Astra doesn't like it. And she doesn't like to think that just being alive is enough to change Isla into this.

"I need more time to think," Isla admits. "About what I want. I have until Friday, right? I just need to think about it. By myself."

"Yeah," Astra says. "Okay."

Isla flickers like a glow star in the dark, and when Astra looks over again, she's gone.

Astra's hand feels colder now than it did when Isla was holding it.

CHAPTER TWENTY-ONE

O n Monday, Oliver gets to English early and passes Astra a note before he's even sat down at his desk.

I'm pretty sure ditching someone on prom night without even finishing one dance with them is some kind of cardinal sin. Was it a ghost thing, or should I assume you're breaking up with me?

There are only two other kids in the room, both sitting at desks near the front and chatting animatedly with each other, so there's really no reason for them to be passing notes instead of just talking out loud. But Astra squares off her books and sets Oliver's paper on top anyway, and scribbles out a response that's mostly crossed-out words and eraser marks.

A ghost thing. And I think I'm the one who got broken up with.

She hasn't seen Isla since Saturday night. It's been strange and a little lonely not having her around. Leonard hasn't stopped meowing, and he's got surprisingly strong lungs for such an old cat.

The door opens and four other students file in, one after the other. A boy with curly red hair and braces sits on Astra's left, and she hides the paper with her hand when Oliver passes it back.

You told her how you feel? I thought for sure that would work. For what it's worth, I think you guys would be cute together.

She's invisible to you, Astra writes back, glancing at the clock above the door. *I told her. She said she needed time to think.*

Oliver taps his foot loudly, keeping time with the ticking clock. He's got a pencil tucked behind one ear and another in his hand, and his hair is pushed back just enough for her to see his earrings. They're little toadstools today, just like one of the patches on his left sleeve, on the back of his wrist.

The tiny rainbow flag is still there, in the crook of his elbow. Seeing it floods her chest with a *fondness* for Oliver Wiley—her best friend. Who'd have ever thought that Astra Vaughn would have a best friend?

And if it wasn't for Isla, Astra would never have had the courage to do more than just joke around with him in English class.

Oliver passes the note back at the same moment Mr. Pierce walks through the door, coffee in one hand and a stack of graded assignments in the other. Oliver looks up for a moment, snatches the paper back, then scribbles something else at the bottom and slides it on top of her desk.

That's not a no, the first part reads. Then, at the bottom, *Look at his cup. I've never seen that kind before.*

Astra rolls her eyes, but she glances up at the front of the room anyway. The coffee cup perched precariously on the edge of the teacher's desk is off-white, with a swirly purple logo on the side that she doesn't recognize. Definitely not biodegradable.

You're gross, she writes back. She bumps her forearm into his elbow and smiles. The little rainbow wobbles.

Mr. Pierce's mustache looks like it's been trimmed over the weekend; it's smaller, but no less curly. It looks like it's developed a personality of its own. When the teacher looks back at them and fixes Oliver with a glare, Astra swears she sees it twitch.

Maybe you just need to give her some time, Oliver writes back. *I think she's into you. I'm totally getting a gay vibe from her.*

The chalkboard screeches as Mr. Pierce writes out the answers to their last assignment. Astra waits until his back is turned to hand Oliver their note under his desk.

You can't see or hear her. And time is kind of the problem.

Oliver blinks up at her in a silent question and passes the paper back without writing anything on it. She sighs and figures it's better just to rip off the Band-Aid now, instead of when Oliver inevitably reads Isla's obituary in the newspaper and questions her about it.

Isla is dying, she writes. *She's in a coma and they're taking her off life support on Friday. So that's about all the time she has to figure out what she wants to do.*

Oliver reads the note, looks up at Astra, then reads it again.

And then, very loudly, he shouts, "*What?*"

Mr. Pierce whips around so quickly that his mustache actually *bounces*. Astra is caught between wanting to laugh and cry, and instead she compensates by making a choked noise in her throat that's somehow *louder* than Oliver's outburst.

If Mr. Pierce had laser vision, they'd both be a gooey mess on the ceiling by now. Astra's face heats up like it's anticipating the inevitable explosion.

"Mr. Wiley," Mr. Pierce says, agonizingly slowly. His eyes narrow, like lasers focusing, right at Astra's face. "Miss Vaughn."

Astra squirms in her seat, nearly knocking her supplies to the floor, and she barely resists the urge to square them off again. Instead, she sits up straighter and takes a deep breath.

"Sir," she says to the teacher. "I, um…I was trying to ask Oliver if I could borrow a pencil, and I accidentally kicked him. My foot fell asleep. I didn't realize I'd done it so hard."

Oliver hides his lopsided grin behind his sleeve, and Astra tries to discreetly hide her pencil up her own. She inches it under her palm, maintaining eye contact with her teacher and trying very hard not to look away.

She's really bad at lying for someone who does it so often.

"Right, uh—" Oliver fumbles for the pencil behind his ear, tugging it free and quickly handing it to her. "Here you go."

She takes it. "Thanks."

Mr. Pierce's eyes narrow even more, and Astra can feel the laser beams aimed right at her forehead. His mustache perks up on one side like it's giving her the finger.

Then he looks away and turns back to the board.

"I've got my eye on you two," he says. Astra finally releases the breath she's been holding and pulls her pencil out of her sleeve.

Ow, my shin, Oliver writes back to her a minute later. *You should be a soccer player.*

He takes the paper back and adds, *What's with you and always owing me explanations?*

Astra gives him his pencil back, smiling when he tucks it behind his ear and she can see the little red toadstool again.

I'll tell you after school. At my place. Feel like finally meeting my mom?

Oliver grins. *Absolutely.*

❖

Astra doesn't see Isla on Tuesday, either.

She texts Ricky during lunch, asking how she's doing. He texts her back half an hour later, telling her that nothing has changed and that the doctors repeated their tests, just in case, and...nothing. She's still not responding to any of their treatments. Her body is basically being powered by machines, and without them she's as dead as Astra thought she was just a couple of weeks ago.

Astra skips lunch that day, and instead spends her time rearranging her locker. She spins the lock—left, right, left, right. One, two, three, four. Four is a nice, safe number.

She thinks about going to the hospital, but she promised Isla that she would give her space.

She wears her star necklace tucked underneath her fluffy blue sweater.

She hopes that Isla remembers to water George the Geranium.

❖

"Tell me again why we're running?"

"Exercise. It's good for you."

"So is kale," Astra pants from the other end of the track, "but you don't see me forcing you to eat salads, now, do you?"

Oliver grins and spins around, jogging backward slowly while he waits for her to catch up. The track is mostly empty, save for a handful of kids in the adjacent field kicking soccer balls at each other. Astra watches a boy with dark skin and a buzz cut run at the net and get intercepted by a goalie with platinum blond dreadlocks.

She doesn't understand sports. How can kicking a ball at each other's knees be *fun*?

Running isn't any better. She's got a stitch in her side and one of her legs is starting to cramp, and she's only gone halfway around the track.

"I like salad," Oliver says. He runs in place, kicking his knees up like he's trying out for the marching band. Astra slows to a fast walk while she catches her breath.

"I like watching TV on the couch and reading in bed. And doughnuts."

Oliver groans dramatically and loops his arm around her elbow, dragging her with him. He has to stoop to keep their arms together, and Astra has to lean up on her toes, and neither of them can go very fast in that position. At least it gets Astra out of sprinting for a few minutes.

"So, really," she says once she can breathe again. "How much longer before we can just leave and go get muffins at that one café on Twelfth?"

"The one with the fancy cups?"

Astra nods.

"Hmm. Pierce might be onto something. I could go for a bran muffin right about now."

"You know, I can't tell if you're being serious or not. But I wouldn't be surprised if you were."

Oliver shrugs, his lips pulled up on one side in a shark-toothed grin. "One more lap around the track and I'll buy you a latte to go with your gross poppyseed muffin."

Astra rubs at the stitch in her side and tugs her arm out of his. "Deal."

She runs ahead, but he catches up with her in exactly three long strides. It's like trying to race a giraffe. It's like a *snail* trying to race a giraffe. Oliver is all legs, and Astra is mostly torso and the two bean burritos she had for lunch.

"I need the practice, anyway," he tells her when they're halfway through their second loop.

"Practice for what? Running from kidnappers? Chasing down mountain lions?"

He falls back to run next to her. "Nope. I still have no idea what Spooks did to the guys that day, but Jake got kicked off the team when Coach Simmons found out. I think the other guys sold him out, because they've all been really nice to me since then. Too nice. It's actually a little creepy."

"So…?"

"So, I'm back on the team. But I've gotta build my muscle back up before the next meet if I wanna qualify for regionals."

Astra smiles, abandoning her running in favor of a nice, leisurely walk. She steps over the painted white lines on the track, and Oliver jogs circles around her with all of the energy of a toddler eating sugar straight out of the bag.

"Yeah, you've clearly lost all of your strength."

Oliver ignores her. "Plus, you wanna be in good shape for your girlfriend when she comes home, don't you?"

"Oliver Wiley!" she hisses.

He sticks his tongue out at her—*toddler*, she thinks—and runs away. She tries to catch up with him, but he ends up cheering her on at the finish line a full five minutes before she finally makes it there.

He tugs his jacket on, bumping her elbow with his hip. There's a new patch there—right over the pocket, in between a lemon and a fuzzy cartoon spider: a sunny yellow flower.

"So," he says, "what kind of coffee d'you think Pierce drinks?"

Astra gets the text message on Thursday afternoon. She's in the middle of her history class. There are only twenty-three more minutes before the final bell rings, and she can feel her phone vibrating through the pocket of her jeans.

She pulls it out under her desk, angling it so that no one else can see.

From: Ricky, 3:07 p.m.
She's awake.

Astra bolts upright in her seat so quickly that she slams her knee on the metal bar on the side. It makes a tinny thudding sound, and suddenly everyone's eyes are on her.

But, for the first time, she doesn't care. She barely even notices. She's probably going to have a huge bruise on her knee later, but right now she couldn't care less. She can't even feel it.

Miss Foley stops her lecture midsentence, her index finger hovering over a page in the textbook she's holding.

This is the second time in a week that Astra has gotten in trouble with a teacher. She's never been in trouble before. She's never even been *grounded*. Her new friends must be really bad influences.

"Is everything all right, Astra?" Miss Foley asks. She's a young teacher—maybe in her mid-thirties—with dark hair that curls in at her shoulders and big, round glasses that make her look like she's constantly surprised. She wears pencil skirts and fluttery blouses every day, and she's so short that she actually makes Astra feel tall.

Astra likes her. It's a shame that she hates history class, though.

Astra glances at the clock again. Nineteen more minutes. She could just wait. It's not that much time.

Instead, she starts shoving her books into her backpack and throws her pencil on top.

"It's a family emergency, miss. Can I be excused, please?"

She's so, *so* lucky that Miss Foley is one of her favorite teachers. She's pretty sure that if she tried this in English class, Mr. Pierce would karate-chop her desk or use his mustache handles to give her a stern double-frown.

"We'll discuss this tomorrow, Astra. Read chapter twenty-six for homework. You're free to go."

"Thank you, miss."

Astra is actually kind of thankful that Oliver has been dragging her along on his runs, because she's not quite as out of breath as usual when she skids to a halt outside his sixth period biology classroom.

She throws open the door without thinking. The whole room smells like burnt cheese, for some reason, and Oliver is sitting at the second lab table from the door, wearing dorky goggles that are too big for his face and a pair of wrinkly plastic gloves.

His hair is tied back, which makes sense, because he's holding a beaker full of some kind of off-white chemical. He's been wearing his hair back more often lately. Maybe it's just because it's getting warmer outside, but it looks nice. It shows off his little dangly pom-pom earrings really well.

"Oliver!" she nearly shouts when she sees him. He looks up, and the liquid in the beaker sloshes around dangerously close to the top. "Your mom called! It's a family emergency."

Oliver has a different biology teacher than Astra does—because he's a genius taking college credits and she's, well, *not*—so Astra has no idea how the older man with curly gray hair will react. But all he does is shrug and tell Oliver to remember to study for the quiz, and Oliver is out of his lab gear and through the door before he's even got all of the words out.

Once they're in the hallway, Oliver tugs his backpack on and blinks down at Astra.

"Why would my mom call *you*? She has my number."

"Oliver," Astra says. "I don't even *know* your mom. She didn't call me."

"Then why did you say…?"

Astra grins. She can't hold it in. "Ricky texted me. Isla's awake."

The running practice really comes in handy on the way to the hospital. Oliver takes off down the hallway, his sneakers slamming loudly on the linoleum, and Astra manages to keep up with him and even overtakes him when they get to the parking lot.

"Run!" he goads from behind her. "Use those muscles I gave you and go get your girl! But also, wait for me, because I need a ride."

Astra's heart is in her throat the whole way to the hospital, which leaves plenty of room in her chest for a cluster of butterflies to fly around. They swoop in her stomach too, and she feels floaty and a little dizzy, and the drive ends up taking three minutes less than usual because she keeps anxiously plowing through yellow lights.

She wonders if she should stop somewhere and buy flowers, or a card. Balloons, maybe? But that would take even more time, and the twelve minutes that it takes for her to drive from the school to the hospital is already too long.

Astra remembers the path to Isla's room like she's walked it a hundred times instead of just three. Revolving doors, twelve steps to the front desk. The receptionist is the same woman as the first time she was here, but there's a new ghost hanging out next to the counter. The middle-aged man with an obvious head injury tries to talk to her, but she ignores him. Her skin feels clammy, but Oliver mostly manages to distract her from the loud static by shuffling his feet on the tiles and making teasing comments about Isla.

She doesn't mind, because Isla *chose* to wake up. That has to mean something, right?

She counts twenty-seven steps to the elevator. They go up three floors, past two nurses' stations, two sets of bathrooms, and four square blocks of identical doors. She spots Johnny out of the corner of her eye, flickering back and forth between open doors, and she changes directions to avoid running into him. Or *him* running into *her*.

Five more steps and she's there. Four, three, two, one. The door is ajar, and Astra can hear voices coming from inside. She thinks about knocking, but the door pushes open before she gets the chance to.

"Isla's friend." Ricky greets her with a nod. He glances over Astra's shoulder at Oliver, who waves. "Another friend?"

"Oliver," Astra tells him. She's out of breath and her words come out in huffs. "Is it okay if we come in?"

"I wouldn't have texted you if it wasn't."

He steps aside and Astra follows, left foot first. Five more steps before she's in the middle of the room. The curtain is pulled back, and there are three people standing around the bed. Astra recognizes Isla's mom, and the man next to her looks like an older version of Ricky, so she assumes that's their dad. A second man is standing next to the tall, beeping machine, wearing a white coat and holding a clipboard in one hand and a pen in the other. He's got fuzzy gray hair and wire-rimmed glasses, and he keeps tapping his pen on the top of the clipboard while he talks.

"She can't see me anymore," Robin whines from the window, kicking out her legs. Astra ignores her.

The doctor stops talking when he notices Astra and Oliver, and Astra feels like she's intruding on something private. Something just for family. She almost wishes she had waited the extra nineteen minutes to come, but then she sees Isla.

And if the heart rate monitor was pinned to *her* finger, everyone in the room would be able to see all of the beats her heart is skipping right now.

The first thing she notices is that Isla is sitting up. Not all the way, and not on her own, but the back of the bed has been propped up just enough to let her look around. Her eyes—her dull, mesmerizing green eyes—are open, and her complexion is more white than purple now. Her lips look a little chapped, but the tube in her throat is gone. The little nubs in her nose are back, but that just means that she's breathing on her own now. She's still hooked up to machines and wires and tubes, and covered in tape and bandages and little red needle marks, but she's awake. She's *alive*.

George the Geranium is still sitting where Astra left him, but he looks healthy and bushy and nearly too big for his pot now. There's a fresh vase of flowers next to him, where the orange and yellow bouquet used to be. The new flowers are fluffy blue and silky white blooms in a sky-blue vase, with a few petals falling off onto the table. Whoever's been taking care of George obviously hasn't been quite as diligent with the other plants.

"Astra, dear," Isla's mom says, waving her closer. "We're so glad you could make it."

Oliver introduces himself, and Astra tries not to stare at the red around Lydia Monroe's eyes. She wonders how different this scene would be if it was taking place tomorrow instead.

She does stare at Isla, though—at her pink cheeks, her messy hair, and the way her eyebrows are pushed together like she's thinking really hard. She's staring back, but she's not smiling.

Astra doesn't know what to say. What's the protocol for a situation like this?

Hey, Isla, it's nice to see you alive for literally the first time since I've known you. I'm glad you decided not to let yourself die, because I was losing my mind worrying that you might. Also, the last time I saw you I confessed my love to you, and I was just wondering if you've had the chance to think about whether you feel the same way or hate my guts now?

Oliver hangs back by the curtain, chatting animatedly with Mrs. Monroe. The doctor excuses himself, and Mr. Monroe mutters something about getting coffee and leaves a minute later, and Ricky sticks to his mom's side like glue, and Astra can't think of what to say.

It turns out that she doesn't need to, though, because Isla does instead. Her voice is raspy and lower than Astra is used to, but that's not what makes Astra's heart feel like it's stopped.

Isla narrows her dull green eyes and asks, "Who are you?"

From the window, Robin scoffs. "Huh. It looks like she can't see *you*, either."

CHAPTER TWENTY-TWO

"Help me move this table into the corner. Over there by the bookshelf with the kitchen stuff on it."

Oliver rolls up his sleeves for the fifth time in an hour and pushes a stray lock of hair behind his ear.

"We literally just moved it *here*. And now we're moving it again?"

"It's a square," Astra says. "It'll fit better in a corner. The round ones have to stay in the middle. Everything else can get pushed back against the walls."

Oliver groans and throws his hands up with enough drama to slide his sleeves back down. He tugs off his jacket—which is more patches than actual jacket material by now—and drapes it over the back of a nearby chair. His arms are as noodle-y as his legs, and he's wearing a striped rainbow T-shirt with *Sounds Gay, I'm In* written on the front.

Astra is *so* glad that Oliver Wiley is her best friend.

"Fine. But you're paying me overtime for this."

"*I'm* not even getting paid for this," Astra reminds him. The shop closed two hours ago, but the last customer came in at noon.

They haul the heavy stone-topped table into the corner by the front counter and push it all the way back against the wall. Astra props up a few ceramic plates and painted water pitchers on top of it and stands back to admire her work.

"One down, ten to go."

Her phone beeps in her back pocket, and she pulls it out so quickly that she nearly drops it.

From: Ricky, 5:07 p.m.
They got her in her chair today. Took her for a ride down the hall. Made it two minutes before she got tired. Starting PT on Tuesday.

Astra smiles sadly at the screen and types out a quick reply—*Thanks for the update.* It's generic, just like her last five responses have been.

She's glad that Ricky keeps her updated—she really is. And she's glad that Isla is off the machines and moving around on her own. She's so glad about it that it actually *hurts*.

But none of Ricky's texts have said what she wants to hear. Because Isla still doesn't remember her.

"Any news on Sleeping Beauty?" Oliver asks from over her shoulder.

Her face heats up and she locks her phone and shoves it back in her pocket. "I should never have told you about that."

"Hey, I'm just saying. If you can wake her up with a kiss, who knows what else you can do?"

Astra doesn't say anything. She shuffles a few items around on the countertop, sliding a jewelry display to one end and spinning it around so that the chain necklaces and chunky bangles are in the front. Oliver's shoes squeak on the floor as he comes to stand next to her.

He bumps his elbow against hers and holds it there. "Hey. She'll remember you. She has to. You guys have, like, an insanely strong connection. I bet she can feel it, even if she doesn't know what it is yet."

Astra sucks in a breath and lets it out slowly. "Yeah. Maybe."

"Not *maybe*. For sure. And if she doesn't, then I'll just have to drag you back there and make you guys fall in love all over again. You can listen to smooth jazz and eat crappy hospital food. I'll even bring some mood lighting. My little sister collects lava lamps."

Astra sniffles and laughs at the same time. "Molly?"

"No, Molly's the one with the turtles. Mia's the one with the lava lamps. And hedgehogs. Not real ones, though—just stuffed animals and those posters with inspirational stuff on them. Like, *Hang In There.* But with hedgehogs."

"And lava lamps."

"Yeah. It's like the seventies exploded all over her bedroom."

Astra's head hurts just thinking about it. She wonders what it would be like to have siblings. Getting photos of her half brother once a month in the mail doesn't feel quite the same, but at least her dad is trying.

"I'd like to meet them all sometime," she says. "Your family."

She winces, thinking that maybe she's overstepped. It's one thing for Oliver to meet her mom—which went about as well as she'd expected, and ended in Astra's mom complimenting Oliver's style and making him promise to visit more often—but it's another for her to meet his huge, chaotic family. Astra barely even has to take one step to make room for him in her small, simple life.

Oliver smiles and bumps her shoulder. "Think you can take some time off from your renovation tomorrow?"

"I don't know, I'm kind of busy..."

He rolls his eyes and pushes off of her. The closest table is round with a glass top covered in bowls of fake fruit and painted ceramic animals. Oliver carefully gathers up an armful of statues and starts carrying them over to a tall purple shelf on the other side of the room.

He glances back at her and grins. "Well? We've got a lot more to get done tonight if you wanna have time to meet my weird family tomorrow."

Astra smiles back and rushes to catch up.

❖

Three days later, she gets another update: a photo, taken from a few feet away, of Isla. Her arms are up and her hands are curled tightly around a metal bar on either side of her. Her hair is messy and falling over her eyes, and her face is sweaty and as red as a tomato.

And Astra's heart aches.

❖

The next update comes on a Thursday. Astra is sitting at her desk, doing homework while Leonard paces over her papers and rains wispy orange hairs over everything. She reaches up to scratch behind his ears and he doesn't hiss, but he doesn't purr either. He bumps his squished nose into her hand and then jumps off the desk and trots out of her bedroom.

She sets her phone on top of her notebook and taps on the screen.

From: Ricky, 4:15 p.m.
Her last course of antibiotics is done. The doctors think they've been giving her weird dreams. She said she dreams about flying.

Astra pulls her hand back, her heart thudding into her rib cage like a battering ram. If she remembers flying, then…what else does she remember?

Ricky never mentions how strange it is that all of Isla's memories have returned *except* for the ones about Astra and Oliver. At first, the doctors threw around terms like *brain damage* and *amnesia*. But, by some miracle, she's gone from zero percent brain activity to ninety-nine.

That last one percent, though—that's where Astra is. Still. Weeks later.

She should be glad that Isla doesn't remember being dead. If she doesn't remember all of the good parts about being a ghost, then she won't regret her decision to leave them all behind. Astra doesn't regret it.

Even if Isla never remembers her, at least she's alive.

Astra tells herself that's enough. She tells herself so many times that she almost starts to believe it.

❖

Ricky's next text comes four days later. Astra is in the living room, squished in the sunken middle couch cushion, with a mountain of throw pillows on either side of her. Her homework is spread out on the coffee table, between a stack of expired coupon books and a handful of pocket change that appeared one afternoon and has since doubled.

The television is on, playing some game show that's mostly background noise, and Astra's mom is in the kitchen sorting through the spice containers. For the second time this week.

Astra blindly grabs for her phone and knocks a few coins onto the floor. She bends down to pick them up, bangs her elbow on the corner of the table on her way back up, and curses under her breath while she unlocks her phone.

From: Ricky, 6:42 p.m.
Today was good. I think she's getting bored though. She's driving the nurses mad. She told me she dreamed about an orange cat. Any idea what that's about, or has she finally lost her marbles?

Attached is another photo of Isla. This one wasn't taken during her physical therapy sessions like the last one. She's in her hospital room this time, sitting in her wheelchair next to the window. She looks like she's been caught off-guard, because she's got a devilish grin on her face and she's reaching for the camera, her messy curls spilling over her shoulders as she leans forward. Her dimples are deep and her eyes are bright.

Astra stares at the photo for a moment and then saves it to her phone.

An orange cat. She should probably be offended that Isla remembers Leonard but not Astra. Instead, she chuckles and shakes her head at the ball of fluff curled up on the arm of the couch.

To: Ricky, 6:46 p.m.
That's my cat. Tell Isla that Leonard says hello.

She snaps a quick picture of the sleeping cat and sends it to Ricky.

She sets her phone in her lap and tries to focus on her homework, but the shuffling and clicking coming from the kitchen are too distracting. She sighs, closes her notebook, and squares it off before joining her mom at the counter.

"Hey, Mom." There are three jars of cinnamon in a row in front of her mom, and all of them have been opened. Astra's not sure if they've ever actually been used, though, because she's never seen her mom bake anything.

"Hi, honey. How's your friend doing?"

She gestures to the phone in Astra's hand. Astra shakes her head. "It wasn't Oliver. It was Isla's brother."

Her mom hums and swaps two jars around, pauses, and then switches them back. "How is Isla doing?"

Maria Vaughn has been surprisingly cool about her daughter admitting to falling in love with a girl—who also happened to be a ghost and a coma patient, and is now an amnesiac in a wheelchair. She doesn't even pester Astra about it. She just talks when Astra wants to talk, and leaves her alone when she doesn't.

Her mom is pretty much the coolest person ever, and Astra truly hates that it's taken her seventeen years to figure that out.

"She's getting better. She remembers Leonard. And Ricky sent me a picture."

She opens up the newest photo and shows it to her mom. She smiles and her hands pause above a jar of cloves and a small tin of cracked black pepper.

"She's beautiful, sweetheart. I can't wait to meet her."

Astra doesn't say what she's thinking—*If you meet her. If she ever remembers me.*

Instead, she locks her phone and shoves it in her back pocket, and reaches for a container of mustard seeds.

"Here, let me help you with that."

❖

Six days later, another text comes. Astra expects to see Ricky's name, but instead she sees a phone number she doesn't recognize.

From: Unknown number, 11:52 a.m.
I remember you.

Astra rushes to the hospital, but the nurse tells her that Isla was discharged early that morning. She texts the unknown number back—one, two, three, four times—but doesn't get a response. She doesn't know where Isla lives. She doesn't know what Isla remembers, or how she feels about it. How she feels about Astra.

So she goes home. And she waits.

❖

"Honey, I'm having kind of an off day. Are you all right to watch the shop for a little bit so I can lie down?"

Her mom is standing in her bedroom doorway, looking a little frazzled, and Astra sighs and closes her notebook. She'll be lucky if she graduates, at this point.

"Sure, Mom."

The first thing that clues her in to something being wrong is her mom watching her leave from the hallway. When her mom is having an unraveling day, she nearly runs to get to her own bedroom and sleep it off. She's usually so exhausted that she can barely stand, and she *definitely* doesn't follow Astra down the stairs.

Her mom probably thinks she's being discreet, but the creaky steps and her noisy heels give her away. A chirp from behind her tells Astra that Leonard is tailing her too, and she's tempted to sneak a peek just to see how ridiculous the two of them look.

The second clue is the sign in the shop window being flipped around, so that it reads *Closed* from the outside. It's barely even noon on a Saturday. And why would her mom ask her to watch the shop if it's closed?

The third clue is the biggest one, though. And the best. Because it's Isla Monroe, sitting in her wheelchair, right in the middle of the store.

She's so glad that she asked Oliver to help her move things around. Now that the tables and shelves are all pushed back and everything is neatly organized, there's plenty of space on the floor for a wheelchair to move through the room. She wasn't even sure if she would ever see Isla again, but she still wanted the shop to be accessible. For *anybody* who might come through the door.

But she's so, *so* glad that it's Isla.

Isla's mom is with her, standing by the door. They both look up when Astra opens the side door, and Isla smiles so wide that her dimples look endless.

Her hair is combed, and thick, shiny curls are falling over both of her shoulders. She's wearing another dress—light pink with white lace along the hem—with a knit gray cardigan on top. Astra has never seen her in anything other than hospital clothes and her yellow sundress.

She was right, when she held up the prom dress in front of Isla so many weeks ago. Pink really *does* suit her.

Her birthmark is just barely showing—a jagged purple spot on the inside of her leg—and all of the needle marks on her skin have faded into smooth white scars. She looks healthier, more alive. The most *alive* Astra has ever seen her.

Leonard meows loudly and bounds across the room faster than Astra has ever seen him move before. He leaps onto Isla's lap and starts purring and nuzzling and throwing wisps of hair all over her dress. Astra would be insulted if she wasn't too stunned to move.

She probably stands there gaping in the middle of the doorway for a second too long, because Isla clears her throat loudly.

"Hey," Isla says. Her voice has a lilt to it, like a bell. The raspiness from the tubes is long gone.

Her voice wakes Astra up and gets her moving. Oliver's track practice has her across the room in seconds, not even bothering to count her steps or look at her feet. She only hesitates for a moment, just long enough to look at Isla's face close-up—her dimples and her shiny green eyes, and the little freckle smiley-face in the corner of her mouth.

Astra throws her arms around Isla and relishes the feeling of solid, warm skin—the puffs of air on her neck, the hands that reach up and grab at the back of her sweater and pull. It feels like a dream. Leonard squeaks in protest and jumps down, hissing at the back of Astra's legs.

She doesn't want to let go, so she waits until Isla drops her hands before she stands and takes a small step back.

"I dreamed about you," Isla says in a whisper. "Not in a creepy way, but...I didn't think it was real. I hoped it was, though."

"I thought you'd never remember me. I thought maybe you'd be better off if you didn't."

Astra's mom's heels click on the floor as she makes her way across the room. Astra can hear talking, and more footsteps, and then suddenly Maria Vaughn and Lydia Monroe are walking through the door. And Astra and Isla are alone.

Isla frowns for a moment, her dimples disappearing. "Can I tell you something stupid?"

"If it's another flower fact, I'm pretty sure I know them all by now. I've read all of those books, front to back. I might even be a bigger plant nerd than you at this point."

Isla's grin returns. "I doubt that," she says. "But that's not what I was gonna say. You know my bucket list?"

Astra nods. "Anti-bucket list. Technically."

"Well, I was never actually *dead*, so…" She shrugs. Astra is just short enough that she only has to bend a little bit to be at eye level with Isla, but her knees are starting to ache, so she pulls a stool out from a shelf near the counter and sits right on top of the *Sale* sticker. "Anyway, the bucket list wasn't real."

Astra stares and blinks slowly. She scoots the stool closer so that her knee is bumping into the wheel of Isla's chair.

"I don't understand."

"There was never a bucket list," Isla continues. "I'd been, um, watching you. I went to school to check on Ricky, and I saw *you*, and I knew you'd be able to see me too, but I chickened out. And I saw you and Oliver, and that's how I knew you guys never hung out besides in school. And I guess—I saw you, and I liked you, and I just wanted an excuse to hang out with you. So I made up a bunch of stuff that I only kinda wanted to do, just to get you to spend time with me."

Astra's brain short-circuits. It gets stuck on an endless loop, like a broken record, and she spits out the first thing it actually manages to process.

"You…liked me?"

Isla's ears are poking out from under her curls, and they're the same color as her dress. "I thought that was obvious? I mean, why else would I ask you to tag along with me when I could have just done all of that stuff on my own?"

"I don't know. Vengeful spirit?"

"How was I being *vengeful*?"

"Fine. Annoying spirit, then. I just figured you were bored and wanted someone to talk to. And that you liked trying to get me to crack up in public."

"Okay." Isla grins, all teeth and dimples. "You got me. That one's true. In my defense, though, I figured you would never like me back if you saw what I was like without all of the cool ghost stuff. I'm still not totally sure, but…"

Astra blinks. "I told you I loved you."

"Yeah. Red calla lilies. I wasn't sure you knew what they meant."

"I'm a plant nerd now too, remember?"

Isla chuckles. It sounds like a wind chime. In a moment of bravery, Astra reaches over the arm of the chair and grabs Isla's hand. Astra can feel the familiar calluses on her palm. Her skin is warm and soft, and Astra's heartbeat is loud.

"I can't believe I made you climb that rusty old water tower," Isla says. "And the track team—did I really…?"

Astra holds up her free hand. "I have no idea what you did, and I really don't wanna know."

"Yeah, no. You don't."

Astra laughs, and Isla joins her, leaning forward against Astra's shoulder with her hair falling in waves over her face. Astra reaches up and pushes some of it behind her ear. She's still wearing her little flower earrings.

"I missed you," Astra says.

"Yeah. Me too."

It hits her, in that moment, just how much Isla has changed her life. She's not a shut-in anymore. She's not afraid of ghosts anymore. She gets along better with her mom, she's made her peace with what happened with her dad, and she's got friends. Real, living friends. Places to go on the weekends besides her bedroom.

She went to prom. She got a cat. She faced her fears. She fell in love.

And now, she's kissing the girl of her dreams. She's not sure who leaned in first, but it doesn't really matter. What matters is that Isla is real, and she's alive, and her lips are soft and a little chapped and they fit against Astra's like they were made for each other. Astra cups her hands around Isla's face, feeling the edges of her dimples and the soft waves of hair falling over her ears.

She's wanted this for so long, and now that it's finally happening, it's better than she could ever have imagined. When she finally pulls back, she's smiling so widely that her jaw aches.

Isla's cheeks are bright red and she's still got her hands on Astra's shoulders. When did she put them there?

"Wow," Isla says. "I guess it's too late to ask if you still like me, huh?"

Astra pulls her hands down and laces their fingers together. "Well, now that you mention it, I kind of have a thing for translucent girls. So this whole *being solid* thing probably isn't gonna work for me."

"Hmm. That's a shame. Guess I did all that PT for nothing."

Isla's hands are smooth and soft. Astra rubs her thumb over the back of one of them, and even though Isla isn't a ghost anymore, Astra's skin still tingles from touching her.

"Can I ask…what made you decide to come back? I wasn't sure you were going to."

"I didn't know, either, to be honest. I spent a lot of time looking at those red lilies you left and wondering if you really meant it."

"What convinced you? That I do?"

Isla glances up at the door for a moment, where her mom and Astra's are standing on the sidewalk, facing away from the window. Lydia Monroe laughs, full-bodied, and throws her hand out onto Maria Vaughn's shoulder, and Astra wonders if she's not the only one who's made a new friend.

"Your mom came to the hospital," Isla says. "After prom. She told me what you said, and I guess…I realized you were telling the truth."

"My mom is terrified of hospitals."

Isla smiles. "She must be very brave, then."

Astra looks out the window again, and watches her mom smile and smooth down her skirt with an arm covered in shiny, jingly bangles.

"Yeah. She is."

"Keep your eyes closed. I'll be able to tell if you're peeking."

"You literally won't, though. You can't even see me back here."

"I'm psychic. I'll know."

Isla chuckles, but she covers her eyes with her hands anyway. There's an attachment in the back seat of the Monroe family's van that Isla's wheelchair clips into, but it's so far back that Astra can only see her if she turns all the way around in the driver's seat. Which is probably not a good idea on the highway.

She's thankful that Mrs. Monroe let her borrow the car for the day, but it's huge and kind of hard to drive, and Astra is *nervous*. Not just about the driving part, though. Her hands are sweating so badly that she can barely keep a good grip on the steering wheel.

Isla hums. "What number am I thinking of?"

"Um. Seven?"

"One hundred and eighty-two. You're a terrible psychic."

Astra chuckles. "Yeah. I know."

"You're a pretty decent girlfriend, though."

Astra's stomach floods with butterflies. She's not sure if she's ever going to get used to this. She kind of doesn't want to.

"Hmm. I'd reserve my judgment on that one, if I were you. You still don't know where I'm taking you."

"Okay, axe murderer. Just remember—if you kill me, I *will* come back to haunt you. And you *know* how annoying that's gonna be."

They speed closer to their destination, and Astra switches lanes and takes a left turn onto a stretch of gravel. She drives until she reaches a patch of thick, green grass and she puts the car in park and pulls out the keys.

"Okay, change of plans," she says, turning around in her seat. Isla still has her hands over her eyes. "Since I can't murder you, we're gonna have to do something else instead."

The grass rustles under her feet as Astra makes her way around the car. She slides the back door open and unlocks Isla's wheelchair, pulling out a ramp on the side of the van for her to get out.

She swallows down her nerves and says, "Okay. You can open your eyes now."

Isla drops her hands and glances around. She looks up at the greenhouse, down at the grass, and follows the path between them with her eyes before looking back up at Astra. She opens her mouth and closes it again twice before she finally says something.

"You…you did this? For me?"

Astra nods and takes a step back—onto the wooden path that runs from the gravel parking lot all the way to the front door of the greenhouse. It's just wide enough to fit a wheelchair, and she made sure it was sturdy by having Oliver run laps across it with his loud, heavy sneakers on.

"It's not the best. Maybe we can get it paved someday. But I just didn't want you to regret not being able to come back here again."

Isla sniffles and reaches out to tug on the collar of Astra's shirt, pulling her close and pecking a quick kiss on her lips.

"I love it. God, this is *so much* better than being axe murdered."

She chuckles, wipes her eyes off on the sleeve of her sweater, and then slides her wheelchair down the car's ramp and onto the wooden pathway. Astra walks next to her while she wheels herself along, moving with just as much grace and fluidity as she did when she could fly.

The sun hits her curls and makes her eyes shine, and it's worth every penny Astra had to raise and every splinter she had to pick from her fingers just to get here.

It's worth all of the tears, too. The fear. Going to the hospital, missing prom, and getting soaked in the rain on the roof of her mom's store. Getting overdue library fines, and buying more tape, and crying to her mom and Oliver and even Leonard.

When they reach the greenhouse, there's a large sign tacked to the top of the doorframe: *Welcome Home, Isla!* It sways in the breeze, painted in a rainbow of Oliver's neat handwriting. Inside, there are balloons, streamers, bouquets of pretty flowers, and tables loaded with food and drinks and gifts. And Oliver, Ricky, Isla's parents, Astra's mom, Mrs. Reeves—everyone who's worked so hard to get Isla here is waiting inside to greet her.

She looks up at Astra and smiles in the sunlight. "Thank you."

"You don't have to thank me. Just get in there. Before the ice cream melts or Ollie breaks something."

Astra holds the door open and watches Isla enter. A chorus of shouts from their friends and families kicks up, and she listens for a moment before she follows, right foot first.

About the Author

Abigail Collins is a caregiver and single mother from eastern North Dakota. She began writing while attending college as a mathematics major and has gone on to write multiple Young Adult novels. In her spare time, she enjoys crocheting and volunteering at her local animal shelter. She identifies as proudly queer and aims to create the kind of stories that teens of all identities can relate to.

Books Available From Bold Strokes Books

Flowers for Dead Girls by Abigail Collins. Isla might be just the right kind of girl to bring Astra out of her shell—and maybe more. The only problem? She's dead. (978-1-63679-584-3)

Good Christian Girls by Elizabeth Bradshaw. In this heartfelt coming of age lesbian romance, Lacey and Jo help each other untangle who they are from who everyone says they're supposed to be. (978-1-63679-555-3)

Not Just Friends by Jordan Meadows. A tragedy leaves Jen struggling to figure out who she is and what is important to her. (978-1-63679-517-1)

Proximity by Jordan Meadows. Joan really likes Ellie, but being alone with her could turn deadly unless she can keep her dangerous powers under control. (978-1-63679-476-1)

A Talent Within by Suzanne Lenoir. Evelyne, born into nobility, and Annika, a peasant girl with a deadly secret, struggle to change their destinies in Valmora, a medieval world controlled by religion, magic, and men. (978-1-63679-423-5)

Take Her Down by Lauren Emily Whalen. Stakes are cutthroat, scheming is creative, and loyalty is ever-changing in this queer, female-driven YA retelling of Shakespeare's *Julius Caesar*. (978-1-63679-089-3)

Two Winters by Lauren Emily Whalen. A modern YA retelling of Shakespeare's *The Winter's Tale* about birth, death, Catholic school, improv comedy, and the healing nature of time. (978-1-63679-019-0)

Boy at the Window by Lauren Melissa Ellzey. Daniel Kim struggles to hold onto reality while haunted by both his very-present past and his never-present parents. Jiwon Yoon may be the only one who can break Daniel free. (978-1-63679-092-3)

Three Left Turns to Nowhere by Jeffrey Ricker, J. Marshall Freeman & 'Nathan Burgoine. Three strangers heading to a convention in Toronto are stranded in rural Ontario, where a small town with a subtle kind of magic leads each to discover what he's been searching for. (978-1-63679-050-3)

#shedeservedit by Greg Herren. When his gay best friend, and high school football star, is murdered, Alex Wheeler is a suspect and must find the truth to clear himself. (978-1-63555-996-5)

The Infinite Summer by Morgan Lee Miller. While spending the summer with her dad in a small beach town, Remi Brenner falls for Harper Hebert and accidentally finds herself tangled up in an intense restaurant rivalry between her famous stepmom and her first love. (978-1-63555-969-9)

Bury Me in Shadows by Greg Herren. College student Jake Chapman is forced to spend the summer at his dying grandmother's home and soon finds danger from long-buried family secrets. (978-1-63555-993-4)

I Am Chris by R Kent. There's one saving grace to losing everything and moving away. Nobody knows her as Chrissy Taylor. Now Chris can live who he truly is. (978-1-63555-904-0)

The Dubious Gift of Dragon Blood by J. Marshall Freeman. One day Crispin is a lonely high school student—the next he is fighting a war in a land ruled by dragons, his otherworldly boyfriend at his side. (978-1-63555-725-1)

Jellicle Girl by Stevie Mikayne. One dark summer night, Beth and Jackie go out to the canoe dock. Two years later, Beth is still carrying the weight of what happened to Jackie. (978-1-63555-691-9)

All the Worlds Between Us by Morgan Lee Miller. High school senior Quinn Hughes discovers that a broken friendship is actually a door propped open for an unexpected romance. (978-1-63555-457-1)

Exit Plans for Teenage Freaks by 'Nathan Burgoine. Cole always has a plan—especially for escaping his small-town reputation as "that kid who was kidnapped when he was four"—but when he teleports to a museum, it's time to face facts: it's possible he's a total freak after all. (978-1-163555-098-6)

Rocks and Stars by Sam Ledel. Kyle's struggle to own who she is and what she really wants may end up landing her on the bench and without the woman of her dreams. (978-1-63555-156-3)